THE MISSION

MAUREEN EUSTIS

The Mission by Maureen Eustis

For Billy, Maddie and Jack

PROLOGUE

READING, MA, 1978

The thirty-two-year-old mother thumped her head hard
against the closed door in the dark bedroom and ran a
hand over her face as if trying to rearrange its features. Muffled
voices below were proof that the other hostages hadn't realized
she was missing yet.

They were all being held captive by the storm; the woman and
so many children.

The white stuff just kept coming down. The weatherman was
predicting a dozen more inches before nightfall. For days and
days the tiny flakes had blanketed New England as if on a
mission to suffocate everyone in slow motion and then erase all
traces of color just for the hell of it.

It was a sick game to the snowplow driver, too. Every time he
made another pass around the cul-de-sac in front of the house,
the pile doubled in size. Today the snowbank was easily ten feet
tall; so tall that the young mother could no longer see the street
when she watched the children from her dining room window.

Her husband was snowed in at Grand Central Station while
their house became its namesake. A dozen neighborhood kids
had returned for the fifth day in a row to play in the fort they'd

1

all helped carve out of the icy plow-mountain, taking regular trips inside the house to break something or build a fort with furniture cushions while blood crept back into their frozen toes and fingertips.

Her brain understood this storm was temporary, but her gut worried that it was the harbinger of a second Ice Age. She'd run out of hot chocolate two days ago, and the hall was a crime scene of wet mittens and caked snow. While some people learned their limit for alcohol after one too many, she now knew that four days was her limit for house arrest.

Minutes earlier, she'd walked into the dining room to find her two middle girls having a tea party with three friends and her set of sixty-year-old, paper-thin Royal Dalton china. She'd sent them away and put every piece back in its place one at a time. Before she closed the cabinet doors, her gaze fell on her old hiding spot in the form of a covered serving dish. She checked over her shoulder and then reached in, lifted the lid, and picked up a small blue box the size of a cigarette pack. Then she replaced the lid and elbowed the door closed. She slipped down the hall, careful not to be seen, and sprang up the stairs soundlessly as if on cat's paws. Once inside her bedroom, she opened the box. The tiny arthritic hinges groaned. For the first time in a dozen years, since before her first daughter was born, she stared at the sparkling pin nestled within a bed of yellowing satin.

The pin brought her no real joy except that she admired its luster. She wasn't the type to wear expensive jewelry and this little adornment, which could likely feed her town for a year, would eventually find a new home once she had time to sit down and think about where it could do the most good. Though with four kids under the age of twelve, she barely had time to brush her teeth, never mind to vet charities. She was sure that sooner or later the pin would make someone's day. Just not hers. And not today.

She snapped the box shut as her gaze swept the room,

searching for a new hiding spot before landing on the big desk between the windows, the one she'd bought at a yard sale the summer before.

Her husband, Jim, though not one prone to complaining, couldn't help himself the day she had brought the desk home. As they struggled to force it up the staircase to the second floor, he'd said, "Hey Sweets, remember when we took the girls to Plymouth to see all that Pilgrim stuff during the heat wave last summer?"

She'd stopped pushing to wipe her forehead with her arm. "Yeah, why? Because it was this hot?"

"Nope," he grunted as he slid his end onto the hardwood landing. "Because this desk smells like the *Mayflower*."

As they had leveled the desk off, and paused to catch their breath, she'd also caught a whiff of the musty wood. It had smelled different outside when she bought it, but she didn't want to bring it back down the stairs.

"Antiques are supposed to smell," she said.

He laughed. "I'll remind you when I'm eighty."

Now she decided the desk was the best place to hide the bauble before it ended up pinned to a stuffed animal or covered in dirt at the playground, to be discovered by some weekend treasure hunter's metal detector. She slid open the small hidden panel the yard-sale lady had shown her in the back, placed the box inside, and closed the panel again just as a bang, a pause, and then her youngest screaming as if her fingernails were being peeled back signaled the end of her respite.

"Let's see how long it'll take one of them to find it," the tired mom said to the empty room.

It would take thirty-nine years.

NORTH KINGSTOWN, RI, 2017

"**G**oddammit!" she yelled at the top of her lungs. Silently, though, just to herself, because she never swore out loud.

No one swore in her family while she was growing up. Instead of saying "shit" her mom would say "sugar," and her dad didn't even drop the f-bomb the day he cut off his fingertip with a saw. Even her three sisters lacked the talent for it. Her friends swore all the time, but like a late-blooming ballerina, because she had waited too long to start, at forty-eight, she couldn't pull it off. If she slipped once in a while, people who knew her would nearly die laughing, as if the foul words were coming straight out of Snoopy's mouth. Years ago, she'd made a mental note to tell her future grandchildren to get started early with the art of swearing or they'd never be taken seriously.

She turned her attention back to the laptop screen in front of her and tried to make some sense of the document's multilevel numbering. She was in the middle of a job interview and in over her head farther than the swimmer in the old *Jaws* movie poster.

Minutes earlier, her potential new boss—a professionally dressed bald man in his early sixties—had asked her to show him what she knew about MS Word by "cleaning up this SOP." She didn't know what an SOP was, and certainly didn't know how to clean it. She was starting to rethink the decision to lie about her prior software experience. Claiming to be an expert in all things Microsoft Office was a bluff and her interviewer had just tossed a poker chip on the table and said, "Call." Panic was making her hands sweat, and when she wiped them on her dark jeans, the blue dye transferred to her palms. Looking down at them, she felt like the victim of a botched double hand transplant.

The space heater on the floor exhaling dry air in a continuous breath didn't help her perspiration situation. Above the window a wooden plaque caught her eye. "Chemistry is FUN" it read, with the last word spelled out with elements from the periodic table: fluorine, uranium, and nitrogen. Stealing a glance over the laptop she was supposed to be using, she studied the man across the table. She thought he looked like a thumb with glasses. His attention was glued to whatever was showing on his laptop and his face was aglow with the reflection of the computer screen; glasses sliding down his nose, lips parted, eyes darting back and forth horizontally. Either his aftershave or his breath smelled of green apples and it reminded her of her seventh-grade math teacher who named his worksheets after a professional golfer. *What did he call them?* she thought. *The Tom...what was it...Tom...Tom Watson Worksheet!*

Focus! she told herself for the third time in ten minutes.

As The Thumb stared at his screen, he fanned a small pad of sticky notes repeatedly. *Ticka-ticka-ticka-ticka-ticka.* The sound made her suicidal, homicidal, and jealous that she wasn't closer to its breeze.

"Excuse me? May I use your restroom?"

Without taking his eyes off his PC, he stretched the hand that wasn't busy with the sticky notes and pointed in the direction where she had entered twenty minutes earlier. She slid back her chair on the flat carpet and rose silently to her feet. The so-called lobby was a tiny space with upper and lower cabinets sporting a

1980s notched wooden border where a handle should be. There was also a mini fridge and a fake granite countertop crowded with a microwave, a tiny sink, and a coffee machine. Opposite the kitchenette was the bathroom.

Once locked inside, she switched on the light that activated the overhead fan. Leaning her back against the door, she fished her phone from the pocket of her blazer with one blue hand, pushed the Home button, and whispered into its bottom edge, "Siri, what the heck is an S-O-P?"

Instantly, a cheerful male voice with an Australian accent responded. "Uck-ay. I found this for 'What the heck is an SOP'" and a list appeared on the screen. But while she was comforted by his familiar company in the strange space, she was pretty sure the SOP definition she needed wasn't a piece of bread dipped in gravy or a Philippine TV series, so she switched to Google. For a split second she thought of her kids making fun of her for always "googling" Google to open the search engine, but she did it anyway because she was nervous. The first result explained that SOP meant "standard operating procedure." So naturally she googled that too, and learned that it was "a set of step-by-step instructions compiled by an organization to help workers carry out routine operations." She dropped her phone into her pocket and then quickly pulled it out again and considered Google-googling "escape from a windowless bathroom."

Forgetting to wash the blue dye off her hands, she returned to the conference room long enough to grab her coat and purse, tipping her chair over backward as her purse strap caught on the arm. She picked up the piece of furniture and offered The Thumb a lame excuse about food poisoning. He first turned his head in her direction and then dragged his eyes slowly away from his computer screen as if a magnet were fighting to keep the two connected. His sticky notes, motionless in mid-fan, suggested he'd forgotten she was still there. As he opened his mouth to speak, she bolted like an untrained dog out the door and down the stairs.

The bitter cold hit her like a frying pan in the face. Running in her high-heeled boots across the salt-covered pavement, she tucked her chin and mouth into the turtleneck of her sweater until she reached her white Jeep Wrangler waiting patiently for its harried driver. She ran to it so fast that she had to stop herself with her hands to prevent a collision. Then the tears she'd been holding back spilled over hot and wet down her face as she let herself in.

"What the hell, Coco?" she sobbed out loud, holding a balled-up fist against a vent that was unready or unwilling to blow warm air onto her blue hand. This was her fifth fruitless interview in fewer than two weeks.

Coco's given name was Gabrielle. Thirty or so years ago, her college roommate was studying fashion design and had taken to calling her Coco after the Chanel founder whose real name was also Gabrielle. The nickname stuck and her mother couldn't stand it. "Gabrielle is a beautiful name. Why would you want to change it?" her mom would say. "Coco sounds like a dog's name."

Thanks, Mom.

Coco had started strong out of the gate a few weeks ago when she went on an interview for an archiving job advertised on the town hall website. She was called in the next day for Interview #1. But then her sly interviewer, a dowager who stroked her wiry gray braid like a ferret, tried to trick her into taking a job no one wanted—catching residents who were pulling off the crime of the century by not registering their dogs for $8.

Then, she'd answered an online ad from a health-care provider in a loft building downtown who was looking for a "friendly office assistant." It seemed like a slam dunk until Interview #2 went down the toilet after she answered a question about the software programs she was proficient in.

"None, unless you count PowerPoint, circa 1992," she'd

admitted with a snort. The interviewer's mouth had remained open in an O while his eyes continued to blink for a full fifteen seconds.

Last week she'd met with two different managers. The one in the real estate office required three references. *Hahahahaha.* The one in the retail store wanted her to work evenings and most weekends. *Whoa, whoa, whoa.* R.I.P. Interviews #3 and #4.

Then she'd gotten the call from Boss Contestant #5: The Thumb. He'd seen her résumé on Craigslist and explained during the phone interview that he needed a "girl who's not afraid of chemicals."

So this is what's it's come to? said the devil on her shoulder when she didn't immediately hang up.

"Gabrielle?" he'd asked on the call. "They probably call you Gabby? I hope that doesn't mean you're a talker," he said. Even over the phone she could tell he wasn't smiling.

"No, not at all," she lied. "But, don't worry, *they* actually call me—"

"Good."

He gave her a little background on his business, and she learned that his one-man firm sold chemicals and laboratory supplies and was located in the next town to hers—only five traffic lights away. The position was part time with the potential to become full-time. Unlike him and his business, she and he had no chemistry. But she hoped it would be better in person, so she ignored her intuition and agreed to meet with him. For the next two days before the interview, she worked hard to memorize the periodic table.

Now, three weeks after her job search had begun, it appeared to be over. In her Jeep, Coco was fleeing Interview #5 with The Thumb, 118 elements, and her self-esteem in its rearview mirror.

This was a new low. The interview "process" had only shown her what she didn't want to do. She didn't want to chase down dog owners, she didn't want to work nights or weekends, and now she definitely didn't want to clean up SOPs. Who the hell did she think she was, Mariah Carey?

I've waited too long to go back to work and this is what happens, she thought as she drove the salty streets. *The list of things I'm willing and qualified to do keeps shrinking, and soon I'm going be sitting in my special chair reading AARP newsletters and thinking I'd better get a reverse mortgage before they're all gone.*

She didn't even need a job. But she was slowly realizing that she wanted a job really bad.

The last time she'd held a paycheck with her name on it, President Bill Clinton was saying "How you doin'?" to interns and The Spice Girls were at the top of the pop chart. She had chosen to quit her desktop publishing job in a large Boston law office when she got pregnant with their daughter eighteen years ago. Then their son had come along a little over a year later. She'd always planned to be a stay-at-home mother like her own, and she loved it. But now, with Charlotte finishing her junior year of high school and James a self-sufficient sophomore, she was getting phased out and looking for a way to feel useful. Her husband, Rex, was a partner at a private equity firm so she didn't feel the pressure to pitch in financially, but she was finding it challenging to identify new ways to feel fulfilled. Maybe *fulfilled* wasn't even the right word, but she'd be damned if she knew what was.

Now, post–Botched Interview #5, she drove aimlessly around her town of East Greenwich; her sad face streaked with mascara liquefied by the H_2O and $NaCl$ from her eyes. The State of Rhode Island, just thirty-seven miles wide, was outlined by a whopping four hundred miles of coastline. Within it sat the town of East Greenwich, the so-called birthplace of the U.S. Navy; a picturesque bedroom community incorporated in 1677 and situated on one of the state's many coves. Downtown EG, as it was affectionately called, was bisected horizontally by Main Street.

The Hill section sat to the west and The Harbor section to the east.

The Hill reached upward with its historic homes, impossibly narrow side streets, steepled churches, and quaint shops. The Harbor stretched downward from Main Street toward the cozy marina and housed more historic homes, the old jailhouse, restaurants, a small yacht club, and tracks for trains that no longer stopped there on their accelerated trips between Boston and New York City. The rest of EG was mostly subdivisions built on land that had once been farms or pastures. It was common to hear about a contractor who'd unearthed the remains of a large farm animal while digging yet another foundation or in-ground pool.

She drove aimlessly along the oak-lined streets feeling like a failure.

As she passed the frozen Little League fields where her son James's teams had clashed with other grade schoolers in their oversized batting helmets, she was filled with nostalgia for all the buggy nights sitting on blankets and cheering on both teams between her shifts at the snack bar. Today, that shack was boarded up tight. She continued past the pool club where Charlotte's basketball coach passed out awards at the end of every season during the team's potluck dinner. Coco smiled at the memory of last year's dinner, when her daughter was recognized for both her rebounding talent and for having the worst singing voice on the bus. She continued past the lower elementary school her children had attended and mused that she'd put in almost as many hours there as they had.

Next, she drove past their church, where James had been confirmed the previous year. Alongside the church was a cemetery he had called "the graveyard" after watching a Scooby-Doo marathon. How many times had she said, "It's called a cemetery and no, James, we're not walking through it at night"? He would always stare at her in the rearview mirror from his car seat, shrug his rounded shoulders, and look out his window, unfazed.

Watching the cemetery go by, she thought about how much she missed her early days of motherhood when she was the boss and the kids were in bed by eight. Now, starving for attention, she tossed a few Jeep Waves at oncoming traffic.

At the Jeep dealership a few years back, she and Rex had settled into the two chairs across the desk from the plump sales guy whose middle name, according to the nameplate on his desk in quotes, was Chubby. She of all people was not one to thumb her nose at nicknames, but that one disappointed her. While Rex signed the sales contract, Chubby had made it a point to say, "Folks, you know about the Jeep Wave, right?" They actually didn't, and he was so excited to explain it. All Jeep Wrangler owners were encouraged to wave during the day when they passed each other on the road. Not like one was trying to signal a search plane, but just a slight lifting of a few fingers off the top of the steering wheel as the two long-lost brothers from other assembly lines passed. Most days Coco enjoyed this secret handshake, but today she wasn't doing it justice and felt bad about it.

Reliving Interview #5 as she drove, she recalled the tiny smirk on The Thumb's face when he got to the part of her short résumé that listed her volunteer work in her kids' schools. She was proud of her efforts over the years in their classrooms and at their sporting events and resented this guy for finding it amusing. She had included it to justify the major gap in her employment timeline, but also because she thought it would imply that she was an organized team player.

Besides making sure the class assholes were given the worst pinecones for their Thanksgiving decorations, the best part of volunteering in the schools was feeling like she was part of something bigger than herself. She knew she and her fellow parent volunteers weren't changing the world for these upper-middle-class kids, but it was fun to feel like she belonged to a group. Of course, there was the odd mom who was just there to gain favor with the teacher because her kid was the asshole with the deformed pinecone, but most of the parents were there for the right reasons.

Driving along now smiling at the memory, she wished she was volunteering instead of looking for a job.

Holy shit! she thought, running a stop sign and braking so hard that the rogue pomegranate, which had escaped from a shopping bag almost a month ago, rolled around on the back floor again. She made another mental note to fish that stupid thing out when she got home.

Stopped in the middle of the road, a smile spread across her tear-stained face as it had the first time she'd jumped her car battery by herself. "I'll just start volunteering!" The friendly toot of a car horn encouraged her to continue the celebration elsewhere, so she made a sharp right and headed for home.

"Why didn't you think of this sooner, dummy?" she said, pounding her forehead with her fist as she traveled along the maze of side streets. Forget finding a career; her new mission was to find a place where she could force herself on people for free. Volunteering would check all her boxes. It would be a job, it would give her something of her own to be proud of, and it would help her satisfy her New Year's resolution.

Now, rushing to get home and tell her family, she navigated the twists and turns of her development like a race-car driver until finally turning right onto Goose Lane and left into her driveway. Her enthusiasm fizzled when she saw that the driveway was empty and the house windows were dark. No one was home to hear her late-breaking news. And her excitement felt like a balloon she didn't want to land and pop.

Sitting quietly for a minute in her idling car, hands still poised at ten and two o'clock, Coco admired her home from the driveway. Twenty-two Goose Lane was a beautiful Craftsman-style structure with exposed architectural details and a covered front

porch held up by columns of stonework. The white trim comple-
mented the gray of the shingles, and a weathered copper whale,
pointing east toward the ocean, sat atop the lighted cupola on the
garage roof. It definitely wasn't the largest house on a street full
of large houses, but it was the perfect size for their family of four.
The frozen lawn was the color of a dirty tennis ball and rolled in
a gentle slope down to the street. The circular drive looped
through it like an upside-down smile face. Or a frown, if you
were a pessimist.

She pulled into the middle bay of the three-car garage around
the right side of the house and clicked the visor button to close
the overhead door. Gathering her purse and phone, she stepped
down from the Jeep. On her way to the door that led to the
kitchen, she was careful to avoid her son's guitars and amplifiers,
which were set up on a big black rubber mat in the first bay of
the garage. He had taken to practicing there because he liked the
way the sound echoed off the bare walls and concrete floor. His
sheet music and picks sat in a box on top of an old oak desk from
her parents' house which never made it into the house because it
smelled not-quite-right. Coco let herself through the unlocked
door at the back of the garage and into the dark kitchen.

She inhaled the scent of lilac from the candle that had been
burning earlier that afternoon. Now everything had changed and
she drew another deep breath with her eyes closed and tried to
stay positive. After a moment, she opened them, switched on
some lights, and took in her favorite room. It had an open layout
full of white walls, trim, and subway tiles. Marble countertops
divided the white upper cabinets and espresso-colored lower
cabinets. Dark hardwoods covered the floor and the center island
was large enough for four stools, which were covered in a drag-
onfly pattern of turquoise and browns and surrounded with
silver nail-head trim. The back wall of the kitchen was covered
entirely in French doors that opened out to a deck and in-ground
pool.

Rex was still at work, and she checked her phone for a clue about where her kids might be. A text from Charlotte explained that she was headed to the pharmacy and then to pick up her brother at his friend Liam's house, where they were working on a project for school.

For Charlotte's seventeenth birthday, she had been given a gray 2000-model Lincoln Town Car that had belonged to her grandfather. Coco's three sisters all had children younger than James, so the Lincoln had found its logical home on Goose Lane when her beloved dad passed away. Apparently the big sled was so retro it was cool now, but it was impossibly long and wide. Charlotte was uncomfortable pulling it into the garage so she preferred to park it out front. The fact that Charlotte drove was a big help, but it still made Coco a nervous wreck when both kids went out in the car together—especially that car, since it was the same age its current driver.

Coco didn't see herself as a helicopter mom, but something smaller. A drone? Now that the kids were older, though, she was finding fewer occasions to fly it. By the time Charlotte turned four, Coco had appropriated her own mother's sayings, which now played on a loop: "It's not you, it's the other guy I worry about"; "Turn off the water"; "Close the door so we're not paying to heat the closet"; "Put it in the dishwasher"; and "Wait until your father gets home"—which was hilarious because Rex was not the disciplinarian and neither was her own father, but it took the kids a few years to figure that out. Moms said these things because they were supposed to, and the kids moaned and rolled their eyes because *they* were supposed to. In addition to getting a jump on their swearing, Coco would have to remember to tell her grandchildren she'd give them a dollar each time they rolled their eyes at their parents.

In the first floor master bedroom located down a hall off the kitchen, she changed out of her interview clothes and went into the bathroom to wash up.

"You look like a zombie movie extra," she said to her reflection as she scrubbed the dried mascara from her cheeks and the blue dye from her palms.

Houdini, her old white Persian mix, jumped up on a cushioned stool and then onto the vanity between the two sinks. He purred and walked under her chin as she patted her face dry and leaned in to take a closer look at her clean reflection in the mirror. For a forty-eight-year-old unemployed mother of two, she wasn't that bad-looking, she decided. Her thick dark-brown hair that she'd straightened for the interview reached past her shoulders and her chocolaty eyes stood out against her pale winter skin. Sure, she could stand to lose five pounds, but with many months to go before the pool cover came off, it was far down the to-do list after finding a job and that damn pomegranate. She tilted her chin up to make sure that one dumb hair hadn't started to grow back yet as Houdini reversed direction and dragged his fat tail against her face.

"I know. I'm going."

After throwing on some old jeans and a soft black sweater, she headed back to the kitchen barefoot. Using the stool again, Houdini jumped off the bathroom counter with a geriatric squeak and followed. She tossed a handful of food in the cat's metal bowl then turned on some music and started making dinner.

Thirty minutes later, the two kids walked in the front door at the same time that Rex's garage door went up. Charlotte and James walked single file from the front of the house to the back, where lemon chicken and Coco's off-key voice filled the air. Peeling potatoes, she swayed back and forth in front of the sink and sang along with Adele. "Send your love to me in a le-e-ter."

"Mooommm-uh," Charlotte groaned in that Kardashian sister way with the extra syllables as she put her plastic bag down on the island.

Her mother turned at the waist, dropping the slippery spud

into the sink. "Hi! What?" Lowering the volume of her phone on the counter, she grabbed a dish towel to wipe her hands.

"Mom," Charlotte said again, with the thinning patience of a kindergarten teacher late in the school year, "I told you, it's 'send my love to your new lover.'" She spoke the lyrics instead of singing them. "Double-google it."

James snorted his appreciation of his sister's joke as he dropped his heavy backpack on the floor by the table.

"You're funny," Coco said. "My lyrics are better. Who would send their love to their ex's *girlfriend*?"

"Adele," Charlotte deadpanned.

Rex came in through the garage.

"Hey, Dad."

"Hi," he said to the room as he touched his hand to Coco's waist, kissed her cheek, and pulled some grapes from the bowl on the counter. Handsome Rex's six-foot-four-inch frame made him almost a full head taller than his wife. He still had all of his brown hair. That he only had a few grays on each side of his head defied the fact that he, like his wife of twenty-four years, was fewer than seven hundred days away from turning fifty. He wore a dark-blue pinstripe suit that matched his eyes, a white dress shirt, and shiny black dress shoes.

"Hi, honey," Coco said. "Listen, I'm glad you're all here."

"Did you get the job?" Rex's question wrinkled his forehead as he fished his phone out of his chest pocket and plugged it into a charger on the built-in desk.

"What job?" James asked. Poor James, thought Coco. Their tall, slim, and handsome son never came to the family meetings because, when he wasn't in school, he was in one of three places: a friend's house, his room playing Xbox, or the garage playing guitar. He never knew what was going on in his family and that fact didn't seem to bother him at all. He lacked the same desire to keep his finger on the pulse of his friends and classmates. Sweet

James had his mom's eyes, his dad's height, and, much to his sister's horror, no social media accounts.

"Mom got a job," Charlotte said to her brother. "She's going back to work so you are on your own now, little buddy." The old term of endearment still stuck even though James stood nearly six inches taller than Charlotte now.

"Cool," her sibling replied, avoiding her passing hip check. "Do we have any poster board?"

"No, no, no." Coco shook her head.

"No?"

"No. Yes. I mean, I don't know. I didn't get the job."

"Sorry, Mom."

"No. Don't be sorry. I didn't *want* the job. Blech." She shuddered. "But this is even better." She held her palms out, facing each other, and her whole family watched her like she was a jack-in-the-box on its last note.

"Wait for it." Charlotte tried to play along, with one eye on her cell phone and the other on the cat who followed her to a stool. She'd stiffened her foot to give him a place to scratch his back.

"I'm going to volunteer instead!" Coco said with a clap of her hands.

The room was silent except for the sound of the oven's convection fan. After a few seconds, James played the cricket ring tone on his phone and then looked around, feigning ignorance. His sister laughed, stole another glance at her phone, and made a few quick maneuvers to text or tweet or snap something. Coco marveled at the fact that her son could pull a sound effect out of thin air but couldn't master the geometry of the lower dishwasher rack.

"Volunteer? Great," said Rex cautiously with the frozen smile of an anchorman.

"Where?" Charlotte asked.

"I don't know yet."

"Cool, Mom," James said, grabbing a water bottle from the

pantry and heading up the back staircase. "I have to work on the project."

"Don't go far. Dinner's almost ready."

"Aw-right," he said, just before disappearing out of earshot.

"I want to hear all about it, babe, but I have to get out of this suit. Smells good, by the way." With that, Rex loosened his tie and headed toward their bedroom.

God love my husband, she thought. He was a solid ten when it came to supporting her ideas. Last spring, when he'd pulled into the driveway, she'd hollered down to him from the sunroom roof as she used a leaf blower to clean out the gutter. He looked up and waved but didn't stop her. When he noticed her draining twenty thousand gallons out of the pool to repair a light on the wall underneath the diving board, he gave her a thumbs-up. And a few days ago, when he came home to find her replacing the taut cable that lifts the garage door, he patted her on the shoulder as he passed by. *Is he supportive or does he want me dead?* she wondered just now.

Turning to her daughter, she watched the teen place her beloved phone on the counter and remove a few toiletries from a plastic shopping bag. She wore a maroon varsity basketball jacket over black leggings, and her long, straight brown hair was tied in a loose knot with the careless perfection that only girls her age could pull off. Charlotte was the lone green-eyed person Coco knew in EG and, mysteriously, also in the family tree. She often noticed how her daughter's tightly proportioned five-foot-eight-inch body turned heads on the street when they walked together. Coco remembered back when she had been the one to turn heads on the street. But those heads also had been covered in mullets and Walkman headphones.

"What do you think, Charlotte?"

"I think it's great, Mom," she said from her stool as she picked up her phone again and scrolled through tweets on her feed. Her kids couldn't keep their hands off their phones longer than they could hold their breath. Charlotte looked up when she felt her mother's stare. "What?"

"But what?"

Charlotte stopped what she was doing and looked up with an expression that Coco used to wear when she looked over the kids' elementary school homework: *Is this really your best effort?*

"But Mom, you could get any job you wanted."

I really can't. Coco felt a pang of shame, as if she'd given up and now she was letting her daughter down. Or maybe Charlotte secretly wanted her to take the retail job for the employee discount. It was hard to say. The teen leaned her elbows on the cold marble counter and crumpled the plastic bag into the size of an egg.

"Didn't you say you wanted to try something new?" She walked over to the recycle bin to drop it in. "You've done a ton of volunteering already. Won't you get bored? Why volunteer *again*?"

That last one was a great question. The honest answers were: *Because I'm qualified for nothing; I can't seem to buy a job; and I feel like a loser every time I walk through that door after an interview. And, P.S., if I volunteer, they can't reject me.* The confidence Charlotte showed in her mother was heartwarming, but terrifying. Charlotte had a way like no one else in the family of holding a mirror up to Coco. Ever since she was a little girl, her candid and confrontational manner had kept her mother a little off balance. Coco didn't want to admit the truth to the young woman; that her own lack of confidence was the motivation behind her new decision. What kind of terrible example was that to set for a girl who was on the edge of entering the real world?

Coco moved to the sink to push the potato peels into the disposal with unnecessary force.

"Mom! You should go to work downtown at that new store, Chic Freak. Or, oh"—she snapped her fingers and pointed —"what about that graphic design place on the Hill? In that loft building with the giant windows? You could get sick Insta pics there."

"You know me so well, Charlotte."

"You know what I'm saying, Mom. I mean, why do you want to work for nothing?"

Nothing.

For whatever reason, Coco put her left foot in a figurative stirrup, mounted her high horse, and, with her back to the room, exhaled softly. "I don't know, Charlotte. I guess I think there are a lot of people out there who could use my help." *Fake news.* She looked sideways without turning her head. Then she carried the potatoes to the cooktop, and the running water from the pot filler filled the silence and the pot at the same time.

Charlotte might have considered a follow-up question to continue the discussion, but instead, the self-assured seventeen-year-old said, "Aw-right," with a smile. "Wherever you end up, they'll be lucky to have you. As long as it doesn't involve singing."

Coco shut off the water and turned with a grateful smile. "You should talk."

The teen winked with her mouth open in an exaggerated way and started up the back staircase that connected the kitchen to the kids' bedrooms. As she did, she reached down with both hands and scooped up Houdini, who had been observing the riveting discourse from the fourth step.

With the cat held up in front of her face, she turned back to her mother and made his front paws move as she said, in a low slow British accent, "You make a living by what you get. You make a life by what you give."

Coco stared at her. "What?"

"I'm researching Churchill for APUSH. That dude was a boss!"

"Churchill never said that," James called from the upstairs hall. "Commonly misattributed quotation."

"Shut up James. Get a life," Charlotte hollered. Then to her mother she said, "Hey, maybe Dad can lock down a volunteer job for you like he did for me."

"Maybe. Don't go far. Dinner's almost ready."

She watched the girl and her cat go upstairs and thought of when Charlotte had blazed a volunteer trail of her own a few years back.

To say her daughter liked animals would be like saying the Pope liked people; a colossal understatement. When Charlotte was twelve, Rex used a connection he had with a guy—who happened to be a huge donor to the animal shelter in town—to get her a volunteer position there. She was six years under the minimum age limit to volunteer, and the staff was openly miffed about having her there, but they allowed her to empty litter boxes and play with the kittens anyway because they had to. They probably figured she'd lose interest and move on to another hobby like gymnastics, but she didn't. And for the next two years, because she was so young and an insurance liability, Charlotte had to be driven and supervised by her mother each week at the shelter until she became a trusted member of the group and was allowed to be dropped off and picked up when she was through. In only a few years' time, though, she had earned their trust to such a degree that she was bathing hundred-pound Rottweilers and interviewing the families who were interested in adopting them. And changing litter boxes, still, but never the one at home. God forbid.

Her own family's nineteen-year-old litter box soiler was the litmus test that newlyweds Coco and Rex had used to determine if they would be good parent material. Shortly after they married, Rex had been leaving the gym one Saturday when he was approached by a woman with a box full of kittens. He ended up taking one home and surprising his wife, who was thrilled because, when she married him, she'd left behind a house full of pets and people. Their first apartment in South Boston had seemed so empty when she would return home from work, night after night, hours before Rex did. The arrival of the little cat changed everything.

During the first few days after Rex brought him home, the kitten they had named Big Tuna after the New England Patriots head coach at the time, had spent so much time disappearing into strange hiding spots—inside the back covering of the couch, the soffit above the kitchen cabinets, or the space between the shower curtain and its liner—they'd changed his name to Houdini. The snow-white cat had moved with them over the years from apartment to house to bigger house.

Last year, true to his name and up to his old tricks, Houdini had disappeared. An exhaustive search took place for the deaf, elderly, indoor cat. After several days of turning the house upside down, they came to the conclusion that Houdini had done what old cats often do: found a dark, quiet place somewhere in the bowels of their house to die. Coco and Charlotte were devastated. Rex felt bad. James didn't know about it for a few days because he'd missed another family meeting.

After a week had passed, Charlotte went off to summer basketball camp in Massachusetts, the litter box was thrown away, and leftover cans of cat food were given to a neighbor. Upon returning from the weeklong camp, a sullen Charlotte headed back to the shelter to help out as usual. After hosing down the dog kennels that morning, she was introduced to some new animals who'd arrived while she was away, including an esti-mated nine-year-old stray cat they'd named Julian, curled up in a ball asleep in the back of a lower cage. When Charlotte sat on the floor, opened the cage, and gently reached inside to touch the sleeping feline, it swung its head around suddenly and lo and behold, it was a skinnier, but still deaf, Houdini. Ta da!

Coco had struggled to understand her hysterical daughter when she'd called from the shelter that day to tell her Houdini was alive. Apparently he had escaped from the house two weeks earlier, unbeknownst to everyone. He was eventually trapped by

Animal Control (no collar), held for the requisite seven days, and then put up for adoption. Since they didn't know Houdini had gotten out, they hadn't thought to contact the shelter. And since the shelter didn't know what Charlotte's cat looked like, they hadn't called her.

When they got Houdini back home that day, they bought him a big can of tuna fish and a new litter box. The local paper got wind of the story and interviewed Charlotte. It was all a happy to-do.

But the animal shelter was Charlotte's thing, and Coco needed to find her own thing.

2

A month earlier, late on New Year's Eve, Coco's drunken declaration had opened the can of worms that was her current job search. As usual, Rex and Coco had hosted a party on the last night of the year. Over the course of five hours, a few dozen neighbors and friends had come over to share in the food and festivities.

Midway through the night, Coco had settled onto a kitchen stool to listen to some of her neighborhood girlfriends share their work-related anecdotes. She racked her brain for a way to jump in but had no work stories to share. Oftentimes she grew bored of the constant shop talk, and tonight was no different. After topping off everyone's glasses, Coco sat with an elbow on the counter and her chin in her hand and listened to her neighbors Ava, Marybeth, Piper, and Sophie one-upping one another with client stories. Since she was the only one who wasn't talking, she drank wine instead.

Ava Logan, the haughty neighborhood ringleader, was a tall, stunning redhead. As if that weren't enough, she was also CEO of the foremost public relations firm in Providence. Normally a ball-buster at work and book club, she seemed to Coco uncharacteristically subdued on New Year's, like a big dog who'd eaten a sock.

"So I said to the douche, 'If your ass isn't in my office at eight a.m. sharp on Monday,'" Ava said dryly, "'this time next year your bank balance will be somewhere between your IQ and your current blood alcohol level.'"

"Whoa," said Coco as she and the other women, with the exception of Piper, marveled at the story.

"C'mon, tell us who it is," Sophie pleaded.

"I can't."

"C'mon. Please?"

"No. But let's just say the Boston Garden won't be raising his number to the rafters someday if he doesn't take my advice next week."

The women all looked at one another, trying to figure out which Celtics player she was talking about.

In addition to professional athletes, Ava's clients included actors, international pageant queens, reality-show stars, and Grammy-winning singers. If Coco hadn't heard about Ava's successes through third parties, she'd find her stories about celebrities to be completely farfetched. But the framed photos in Ava's home showing her with a multitude of celebrities were solid proof that the woman led an exciting life. Coco would never admit that she was jealous, but a part of her had always envied Ava's glamour, confidence, and career.

For all the years Coco had known her, Ava had always hated stay-at-home moms. Not really. But Coco felt inferior around her because of the knack Ava had for showing with a simple look that she ranked above you on the social, economic, and professional ladders in your book club, your neighborhood, and womankind.

Ava and her husband, Johan, an entertainment lawyer, had no kids. They raked in money hand over fist, traveled the world, and drove fancy cars instead. If there was a poster for child-free living, these were the poster children. But the flu doesn't care how much money you have, and Ava had already told the group that Johan was under the weather and had to stay home.

Piper, Coco's best friend and next-door neighbor, had even less patience for Ava's superiority complex. And it seemed that her level of animosity toward her successful neighbor had intensified over the last dozen months. Piper hadn't been to book club in almost a year, and Coco suspected it was because she'd had enough of Ava's haughty attitude. When she asked her friend about it, Piper simply said she no longer had time to read the books because she was too busy. *Sounds fake, but okay,* Coco had thought at the time, because they had a month to read each selection and Piper only had one kid. But she had also gone from a stay-at-home mom to a successful caterer almost overnight, so Coco accepted her excuse. Maybe it was a case of the irresistible force and the immovable object, but at any rate, it was a rare occurrence to see both Piper and Ava in the same place at the same time anymore.

Coco knew, though, that neither neighbor would skip the party. Ava wouldn't because it was an opportunity to talk to minions, and Piper wouldn't because she was Coco's closest friend.

"Can I get one of your pomegranate martinis?" Piper asked the hostess, changing the subject and redirecting the attention away from Ava.

"Sorry, sweetie. I can't find the stupid pomegranate I bought for you. I think the kid at the store yesterday forgot to put it in my bag. How about some more wine?"

"Any more stories, Ava?" Marybeth asked.

"What are you, a fucking groupie?" Piper snapped.

"Calm yourself down, woman," Marybeth said playfully. "I'm just interested, that's all. All my clients are sad or dead."

Marybeth was a mother of twin fifteen-year-old boys and a four-year-old surprise named Maeve. She was in her mid-forties, short and fleshy, with a sparkling sense of fun completely in line with her former job as a first-grade teacher but somewhat mismatched with her current profession. She and her husband, Oliver, were funeral party planners. When they started the venture five or six years ago, Oliver wanted to call the company Stiff Drinks, but Marybeth persuaded him that they should call it A Greater Plan. They worked with funeral homes in the area to connect with families who wanted help coordinating the after-party for a deceased loved one. When they were hired to plan the event in a home, Marybeth and Oliver subcontracted to Piper to cater the food, drinks, and servers while they handled keepsakes for the guests, photo collages to display, and last-minute house-cleaning services. When the event was taking place outside of a home, the couple worked with the family to choose the best loca-tion suited to their budget and the personality, ethnicity, or wishes of the deceased loved one. Then they coordinated with the venue to take care of every detail before, during, and after the event. In a town like EG, concierge services were expected, and Marybeth and Oliver made a healthy living because people were always dying.

"Don't be such a crybaby, Marybeth," Sophie said. "Speaking of which, where's Charlotte, Coco? I was bummed that I couldn't get her tonight." Sophie had tried to get Charlotte to babysit her five-month-old, Ruby, but Charlotte had plans so Piper's daugh-ter, Katie, took the job instead. "She's the only sitter who can get my little crybaby down."

"Great," Piper said under her breath, picturing her own daughter walking around with a screaming baby on her shoulder for four hours.

"No, no, Piper. I'm sure Katie is doing just great with the baby." Sophie took a swig from her glass and turned away to hide her flaring eyes.

Sophie was a tall, broad-shouldered woman in her early forties with a short brunette bob. She used to live on Goose Lane, but recently had moved to a little bungalow a mile away after she and her girlfriend, Brenda, broke up when the latter couldn't come to terms with the fact that the former was hell-bent on having a baby. Little Ruby had arrived last August. Sophie was the only one in the neighborhood who had actually grown up in East Greenwich and was also somewhat of a local celebrity. After graduation from EG high school back in 1991, Sophie had gone on to win an Olympic gold medal in the four-hundred-meter individual medley in Barcelona. After the Olympics, she became a swim coach at a private school across the bay in Portsmouth, but quit when she moved back to EG to start her line of small structured evening bags shaped like classic novels. Pocket Books by Sophie quickly became a staple at all the boutiques on Main Street and in nearby Newport.

It seemed to Coco that all her friends continued to reinvent themselves, and she admired that about them.

"Charlotte's at Zoë's," Coco replied. "They're havin' their own pah-ty, but Zoë's parents said they'd be home awwl night." Coco was mildly aware that her Boston accent was creeping out as it always did when she drank too much. "Who ah you textin', Ava? Ya werse than tha kids."

"Yeah. Who are you texting, Ava?" Piper turned half around on her stool and addressed the men in the room. "Husbands, check your phones," she hollered.

"Fuck off, Piper," Ava said under her breath without looking up from her phone.

The other women were taken aback, and Coco said to her drunk self, *Rememba to ask Pipa about this tomorra.* And then she clapped her hands like a toy monkey. "Lez head inta the otha room, ladies." As the women decoded her sentence and then heeded her suggestion, Rex and the other men ambled in the opposite direction to the family room where the pool table was.

Sophie and Piper carried a few plates of appetizers into the living room and set them on the large glass coffee table. A gas fire roared in the fireplace, and the flat clock above it warned that it was thirty minutes to midnight. The ladies seated themselves and Houdini wound in and out between their ankles while the individual conversations morphed back from smaller ones into one big one. Talk of work turned to ski vacations, and then, finally, to the dreaded topic of New Year's resolutions.

"The new trend is missions, not resolutions," Ava said, lifting her wineglass to the light in order to hunt down and remove a tiny piece of floating cork, real or imagined. "Resolutions always fail because they're passive. You have to be more aggressive. Go on a mission for what you want and take it."

"Pathetic cougar," Piper muttered into her wineglass, sounding like the speaker at a fast food drive-through.

Coco, who sat beside her, slapped Piper's leg hard and said, "Mean."

Piper shrugged and fluffed the back of her hair with her free hand.

"Now," Coco continued, "does anyone have a resolution or a *mission?*" she said seriously and slowly as if talking to non-English speakers.

Sophie sat on the floor in front of the coffee table and used a tortilla chip to scoop a chunk of guacamole from the bowl. She raised her other hand and announced that she was going to get into her pre-baby jeans by June.

"To be clear, though, I'm not working on that until both of that clock's hands are straight up. In the meantime, my mission is to finish this guacamole. By myself." She licked her chip and double dipped.

Marybeth said her mission was to stop texting her twins while they were in the house with her.

"I text them all the time."

"About what?" Sophie asked.

"Everything." She held up her hand to count on her fingers. "To tell them to do their homework, or that dinner's ready, or to ask them where the fucking Scotch tape is. It's moronic, but I can't help it. It's just easier. But now I'm fighting back."

"Why not just call them on their phones?" Sophie said, as only a brand-new mother would.

"Oh god, no!" Piper gasped. The two other moms were shaking their heads in unison as if Sophie had just asked them if they watch barnyard porn.

Sophie looked around like they were playing a joke on her. "Why the hell not?"

"These kids don't use their phones like *phones!*" Piper said.

"Why not?"

"Because," Coco announced holding an index finger up and taking a breath as if she had a long explanation. Then she exhaled and took a sip of her wine.

Piper glanced sideways at Coco and smiled.

"Because why?" Sophie prodded.

"Because they don't want to *talk to anybody*." Marybeth laughed.

"They don't use doorbells anymore, either. Those will be gadgets in a sad museum soon enough."

"Kids these days are fucked up," Ava said sourly, as if the sock was still working its way through the maze of her intestines, like the big dog who had eaten one.

"Millennials." Coco rolled her eyes. "Am I right?"

"Technically your kids are Generation Z or iGeneration, not Millennials," Ava informed them.

"Of course they are." Piper shook her head, aggravated.

"Cha-lotte says callin' someone on their phone is supah aggressive," said Coco in a low, serious voice, chin down.

"Mmmhmm," other moms agreed.

"So how are you going to get them to come downstairs if you aren't going to text them and you can't call them?" asked Sophie.

"Um, hashtag UnplugTheRouter," said Piper.

"Genius!" shouted Marybeth too loudly. "That'll bring them like flies to meat."

"Flies whining. 'Moooooooom!'" Piper mocked kids and then laughed. "And Katie told me when I use punctuation in my texts I seem angry. I can't use periods and question marks? What the fuck? Why does that make me angry?"

"What doesn't make you angry?" Ava said under her breath. Piper didn't hear it but Coco did and she squinted at Ava and tilted her head like a little bird.

Ava had an air of boredom about her which was accentuated when she repeatedly checked her phone during the conversation. *Rude*, Coco thought, but then realized that Ava probably knew nothing about kids and social media habits personally. The only involvement she had was neutralizing a problem when teen clients did something stupid with their accounts. She had nothing to say about normal children and their cell phones.

"I keep thicking." Coco said and laughed. "I mean, I keep thicking. No." She wet her lips because that was obviously the impediment to clear speech. "I keep wondering," she said, "what would my mom have said about this."

"Mine hates technology. She calls a computer a machine." Marybeth laughed. "Can you imagine our parents texting us to come downstairs?"

"We didn't even have a microwave when I was a kid. So, no," Piper said with a straight face. "No lie. My mother thought we'd get cancer. Said we were lucky to have a toaster. Even if there were cell phones when I was a kid, I swear she would have given me a walkie-talkie."

"Well, it *is* the toaster of cell phones," Sophie said.

The women laughed. Coco was enjoying the conversation despite the effects of four hours of too much alcohol and not enough food. "Okay, back to business." She turned to Piper. "What ah you gonna mission to do, Pi-pah?"

"Well, I think we should stop texting altogether, as a matter of fact," she said, trying to catch Ava's eye.

"Good luck with that," Ava said, watching the fire but not seeing it.

Piper made a juvenile face and mimicked her under her breath.

"Good fa you," Coco said, slapping her best friend on the leg.

"Ow, Gab." Piper leaned her shoulder into her friend. "You're really moving the needle on that Boston accent. Red zone, babe. It's time to switch to soda."

"No," Coco whispered. "Soda's bad for ya teeth."

"So is falling on your face," Piper said, and they both giggled.

"What about you, Ava?" Marybeth asked. "Do you have a resolution? Or a mission?" She used air quotes for the last part.

"Oh." Caught off guard for some reason, Ava looked up at a point on the ceiling as she thought and rocked her head from side to side a few times like a metronome. "Nothing, really." She shrugged. "Unless my mission can be not to change a thing." She shrugged in mock apology. "Sorry." *Not sorry.*

"Oh c'mon. Everyone has something they want to change," Sophie said.

Ava crossed her long legs and her silky green dress rode up her endless thigh. "I'm sorry I don't have a phone-addicted child. Or a muffin top." She looked pointedly down at Sophie, who was halfway to her mouth with another guacamole-covered chip. She put it down in a napkin on the coffee table and licked the corner of her mouth.

"What a bitch," Piper said into Coco's ear.

Coco looked at her friend with exaggerated shock and pinched her leg.

"Ahhhhh! I'll drink to that! To muffin tops!" Piper raised her glass and squealed from the pain in her leg. She covered her drunk friend's hand with her other hand.

There was a lull because Ava had ruined the silly mood. Then

Piper turned to Coco and said, "How about you, my drunk friend?"

Coco looked surprised, like she's been selected out of an audience of thousands. She was too tipsy to say something witty and she hadn't made a New Year's resolution since 2008, when she committed to stop watching reality TV. Nine years later, she was up to seven unscripted shows a week clogging up the DVR so that hadn't worked out well. In fact, on a regular basis Rex would call out to her from the other room in a frenzy because he tried to change the channel and the warning came up on the screen asking which recording he wanted to cancel as the timer ticked down to make his decision. Ten-nine-eight. It virtually paralyzed him. Seven-six-five. She would always know what the problem was when she heard him yell, "Co-Cooooooooo!" from another room. The man closed million-dollar deals on a regular basis, but the remote might as well be the control panel of a fighter jet.

Coco moved to the edge of her seat with the help of Piper's hand on her back. She was definitely over the legal limit to drive and walking wasn't a given, either. After a brief struggle with the sofa cushion, she cleared her throat.

"Ahem, ladies and genel-men?" She drew out the last three words like an announcer at a prize fight.

"There's not one guy in here." Piper gestured around the room with her hand.

Coco hesitated. She wanted to say something important, but had nothing to say. Literally nothing. But with a compulsion to impress Ava and the other women, she blurted out the first thing that came into her head.

"I've decided ma mission"—she winked at Piper—"is ta find a werhk!" The last word was higher pitched than the others in her sentence. Her mouth and eyes opened wide as if she had just yelled, "Surprise!"

The women's faces made the announcement worth it and delivered instant satisfaction to Coco. It didn't occur to her that they were more amazed by her syntax and blood alcohol level than by her announcement.

"Boom!" she said, pointing at Ava, who looked at Marybeth, rolled her eyes, and mouthed, *Wow*.

Piper stared up at her friend with raised eyebrows, waiting for the punchline. "You mean a job?"

"Thatz-right."

Piper was puzzled, because it was the first she was hearing of this from a woman she spoke to every day. She lifted up Coco's half-empty glass and moved it to the end table on the other side.

"I'm gonna make work." Coco pointed at each woman, starting and ending with Ava. "Like you, and you, and you, and you, and you."

"We get it," Ava said.

"Well, that's news!" said Marybeth. "What work are you . . . making—"

"Up-bup-bup." Coco raised her finger in front of her own face as the universal symbol for *hold that thought* and then she managed to say, "I'ma gonna get us some champagne first. S'amost midnight."

"Need help?" someone asked.

"Nope. You bettah stay. B'right back."

Discouraging questions to which she had no answers, she made a beeline for the kitchen. That is, if bees tripped over shoes and grabbed for doorways.

Nine years of book club had improved her vocabulary but not her tolerance for alcohol. Once she reached the empty kitchen, she threw her back against the refrigerator and looked from side to side while humming the theme from *Mission: Impossible*. She pretended to draw her gun, hold it alongside her ear with both hands, and slide along the wall.

Realizing no one but that cat had followed her, she exhaled an exaggerated sigh of relief and then giggled. She walked over to the junk drawer and rummaged through it for a pencil, then scribbled her resolution on a sticky note and stuck it to Houdini's head. When the kids were little, they'd loved watching the cat look in all directions trying to figure out what was different as a sticky note sat on his head like a graduation cap. At the age of forty-eight—and drunk—Coco found this hilarious.

Forgetting her promise to fetch champagne, she checked her hair in the reflection of the microwave and went to shoot pool with the guys until next year.

3

That next year arrived painfully for Coco Easton.

At noon, she crept down the hall, squinting in agony as the sun's reflection off the snow whited-out her kitchen like an atomic blast. She felt like she had just climbed out of an over-turned car that had rolled six times. *Jesus Christ, why did we buy a house with windows?* Houdini sat beside his empty food bowl with his white tail curled around his front paws, its tip quivering like a rattlesnake's as he stared at her. She made a kissy sound and bent to pat him, but he scampered past her up the steps in a hurry. The blood rushed to her head and intensified the pounding.

"Ugh. Cats."

Her only objective, if she couldn't find a loaded revolver, was to find a bottle of Advil and a Diet Coke. Rex had straightened up the other rooms before heading off to Oliver and Marybeth's house to watch football, but he'd apparently saved the kitchen for her. First she laid her eyes on the sink full of dirty dishes, then on the counter full of empty wineglasses ringed with different shades of lipstick, and then on the neon-orange, fur-covered sticky note on the floor reminding her of her public announce-ment. Because bending over again was out of the question, she used her bare toes to grab the tiny square and transfer it to her hand. Then she read it. *No*, she thought as the words came into focus and the memory came bubbling up like a clogged toilet that's flushed again.

Three Advils, two Diet Cokes, and one hour later, she managed to put the kitchen back together, but she still felt like a raccoon had shit in her mouth. Just as she took a seat at the center island, she heard Charlotte breeze in the front door calling out to her mother in song as if she were Snow White at the beginning of the movie before the witch poisoned her.

"Hello. Mooommm? Hell-lloooo?"

"In here," Coco said weakly.

Charlotte walked down the hall and into the kitchen.

"Hi, Mom. Why didn't you answer me? Happy New Year!" she sang out with a smile, her arms held theatrically wide. The she banged cabinet doors open and closed looking for a snack. Charlotte was showered, made up, and dressed in her beautiful oyster-colored quilted jacket and matching leggings with knee high-boots in caramel brown.

Oh my god, has she been drinking? Coco projected, covering her ears with her hands.

"Why are you so cheery?" she asked her daughter, squinting with one eye shut to block out the glare more than to express suspicion.

"I'm glad you asked. I stopped at the ATM on my way home to deposit the checks from waitressing and babysitting. Guess whose bank balance now has a comma in it?" She pointed to herself with a thumb. "Yup. That's whaz-up." She reached for a double high-five from her mother, who didn't move.

Charlotte definitely had not been drinking, but right now Coco was beginning to side with the witch in the story.

"That's great, kiddo," she managed.

"Are you okay, Mom? Didn't you have fun last night? Or —*oh* . . . right . . . *too* much fun." She nodded and raised her eyebrows with a comical look of someone who had just solved a complex mystery in front of a room full of guests.

Duh, thought Coco. "Yuh. We're too old for these parties." She covered her ears again to stop the sound of her own voice from getting into them and whispered, "How was . . . ?"

"Zoë's?" Charlotte filled in the blank, a smile creeping up her face.

"Uh-huh."

"Fun. Well"—she grabbed a water bottle from the pantry —"until her cousins lit fireworks in the backyard and set the pool cover on fire."

"What? Oh my god." Coco momentarily forgot that her head was an anvil.

"No, it was fine. It put itself out when the cover burned away," Charlotte said, distracted. Then she put the water bottle on the island and bent down, disappearing out of view.

"Did they have to call the fire department?"

"Nope." Charlotte straightened back up holding the furry note from last night. "What the heck?" She raised it up as if she was a referee penalizing a soccer player.

"Oh god." Coco lowered her forehead to the cold granite countertop. She didn't hate the sensation. *Didn't I throw that out?* she wondered pointlessly.

"Are you going back to work, Mom? Seriously?"

"I think. Maybe. Meh. I don't know." Her forehead remained fused to the island.

"Mom!"

"What?" She turned her head, resting her cheek on the cold surface.

"This is a *great* idea! Oh my god. What do you wanna do?"

"I wanna go back to bed."

4

Three days after New Year's Eve, the tide of Coco's hangover had finally receded and taken all the seaweed of self-doubt with it. Returning to her old optimistic self, she warmed to the idea of her new mission to get a job. While she knew she could back out of it by claiming atomic intoxication, she was beginning to recognize a need that she'd been ignoring for some time now.

When she came into the kitchen dressed for her daily power walk, she found Rex and Charlotte at the table. They were each deeply focused on their phones; Rex analyzing NASDAQ futures and Charlotte trying to determine which one of her thousand damned Instagram followers had unfollowed her overnight, and why.

"Hi, babe." Her husband poured more coffee into his cup. "Charlotte told me your big news. When did this happen?"

"Sorry, Mom, was it a secret?"

"No, of course not," Coco lied. "Just something I've been thinking about." She queued up a podcast for her walk.

"Until liquid courage made her own it."

"Charlotte!" Coco slapped her hands on the counter and looked at her daughter in shock.

"Chill, Mom. I'm almost eighteen. It's fine." She went back to her detective work on the phone.

"Jeeze," she said in her daughter's direction. "It's not a big deal, Rex. I'm going to find something to do to keep busy, that's all." She plugged her earbuds into the bottom of her phone.

"I think it's great." He shrugged and got up from the table to kiss his wife on the top of her head on his way to the sink.

"Me too. This is big news, Mom. You haven't worked my whole life."

Coco turned to her daughter and tipped her head in disbelief. "Really?"

"You know what I mean."

"Have a good day, ladies. Babe, you should get your résumé together," Captain Obvious said as he put his coffee mug in the sink and walked through the door to the garage.

"Dishwasher. And duh," Coco said. "Why does no one understand how this appliance works?" She dropped open the door and put the mug onto the upper rack. "It doesn't *fetch* stuff." She lifted the door with her foot and pushed it closed.

"Yo! James! *Let's goooo!*"

Coco levitated when her daughter yelled up the stairs.

"Was that really necessary?"

Charlotte licked her spoon and made a show out of putting it, and her cereal bowl, into the dishwasher.

A minute later, James came bounding down the stairs, propelled by his absurdly heavy backpack. For reasons Coco could not fathom, he and his sister never used their lockers at school. James didn't even know where his locker *was*, never mind the combination. They carried everything with them, including their school-issued laptops, and wore their packs absurdly low because properly adjusted bags were social suicide. Charlotte had coached her brother on the do's and don'ts when he'd transitioned from middle school to the Big Show a year and a half ago. Consequently, he would have her to thank for his chronic back problems in thirty years.

"Mom, the faucet upstairs keeps dripping," James said, pulling on his sneakers without untying them.

"And my room is freezing again. Nothing's coming out of the thingy on the floor," Charlotte added.

"Same," James said.

Honest to God, they think I'm the super. Coco let out a sound she used to make to herself when one of the kids would demand she read another bedtime book. *Please let me go*, the sound would beg. *I just want to go downstairs and be alone.* But she'd be the first to admit that she did this to herself. Her parents had taught her how to do a lot of chores and repairs, especially her father. There was always something that needed to be done. Growing up, her family of six did all the mowing, shoveling, firewood stacking, vacuuming, et cetera. And her parents were of the generation that repaired instead of replaced when something was broken. Whether it was a can opener or an entire home, you took the time to understand how it worked, figured out what the problem was, and then fixed it. Also, she was cheap. When the kids were young, she got into the habit of fixing things herself because they couldn't afford the unpredictable cost of repairmen. Now that they could, the practical side of Coco often refused to pay to fix something she could learn how to fix on her own. She kept reminding herself to show the kids how do to small repairs before those two knuckleheads ran off into the real world helpless and unhandy. Add it to the list: find a job, find the pomegranate, lose five pounds, and google-Google *Household Repairs for Teens.*

"Be careful and have a good day. Text me if you're not coming straight home."

"Yah-yah. C'mon, James. You take longer than I do."

"Bye, Mom."

After the front door closed, Coco scratched out the day's list with a pencil on a skinny pad of paper someone had put in her stocking. It was white with blue stripes and had an owl on the top. Her list was simple: "(1) walk, (2) fix faucet, (3) fix thermostat, (4) get a job."

She decided to postpone the walk and the repairs and jumped down to number four on her list. Taking a seat at the built-in desk area, she pried open her sleeping laptop. The Craigslist tab was still on the screen from the night before with its blinking cursor mocking her in the blank Search Jobs box. *Loser. Loser. Loser.*

Forget Craigslist. Back to the résumé, she said to herself. She knew she had to create one, but the problem was that she didn't feel qualified to do anything anymore. The PowerPoint presentations she was wowing her boss with twenty years ago were something kids now mastered in second grade. She considered looking into a job at a hardware store or even a big box store because she fancied herself to be pretty handy, but the thought of Ava catching wind of that gave her hives. She pictured herself in an office job, but the night before she'd spent almost an hour contemplating what to type into the white 'job search' box. Dozens of teachers and hundreds of children could attest to the fact that she could organize a great Reading Week or Ice Cream Social, but she didn't know a spreadsheet from a bedsheet.

Thinking a résumé would be easier, she opened a blank page in Word and typed her name and contact information at the top. Then she centered it and concentrated on choosing a font as if the security of the nation depended upon it. She ended up with CG Omega, which was the default font she'd started with. Finally, she faced the brutal fact that she needed to write the objective.

After a five-minute staring contest with the blinking cursor, she slapped her computer closed and exhaled. Houdini jumped up on the desk and plunked himself down on the side of the PC where its fan blew out a tiny stream of warm air. Serving cold

MAUREEN EUSTIS

revenge for the sticky note incident, and with the limited
resources of a cat, he took on the role of the blinking cursor;
rhythmically and silently curling and uncurling his fat tail on the
desk while staring at her. *Loser. Loser. Loser.*

"What are you looking at, old man?" Her eyes narrowed. She
rubbed her face hard with both hands, opened the PC again,
and typed.

"OBJECTIVE: To find a position of responsibility in a fast-
paced environment which optimizes my creativity and organiza-
tional skills."

Backspaaaaaaaaaaaaaaaace.

"OBJECTIVE: To find a position which capitalizes on my
volunteering experience."

Backspaaaaaaaaaaaaaaaace.

"OBJECTIVE: To find a position."

Backspaaaaaaaaaaaaaaaace.

"OBJECTIVE: To drive around aimlessly five days a week for
the next ten years so my family thinks I'm at work, but I'm really
just waving to Jeeps and lip-synching to Imagine Dragons."

She slapped the computer closed. Even alone here with the
cat she felt judged. She pushed back her chair and tucked
Houdini under her arm.

"Bath time, traitor."

After washing the repentant cat with a warm wet cloth and
brushing his long coat, she replaced the washers on both faucets
in the kids' bathroom, reset the circuit breaker for the upstairs
thermostat, and took a long walk to clear her head. Only then did
she manage to sit down and create a one-page résumé with
generous margins.

On that cold day three-and-a-half weeks ago, she'd thought
that creating the résumé would be the worst part. But interviewing was far worse, and, after all the searches and rejections,
she had made zero progress. Even when she decided to forgo a
salary, the volunteer job search wasn't as easy as she thought it

would be, either. Originally, it seemed to her that the possibilities were endless because she could make her own hours and leave the job anytime she wanted to. But she came to realize that, if job hunting was hard, unpaid job hunting was wicked hard. She had a few good leads online, but none of them jumped out at her.

Rex knew a lot of people through his position on the EG's finance committee, but Coco's pride prevented her from asking him for help. She had to do this on her own.

Tomorrow.

5

Tomorrow turned into another week, and life got in the way of her search. This was reaching the point of embarrassment. Not only would she not have a job before the next book club rolled around, but she might not even have a *volunteer* job. Scandalous.

Ten days after her interview with The Thumb, she decided to invest some time in cleaning out a few of the black holes known as her closets. She figured having something to show for her efforts at the end of the day would boost her morale. Her goal today was to dig out enough blankets and sheets to fill at least three giant trash bags for the animal shelter.

When she and Rex bought their house ten years ago, they never thought they'd fill every closet, cabinet, and built-in, because the starter home from which they moved was exactly the size of their current garage. But fill every space they did. Over the years, she had acquired the bad habit of hanging on to something just because she had a place to stuff it.

Now she was spending a few days every few months cleaning out closets and making piles for donating. No bedding, board games, or bathing suits were safe when she went on decluttering benders. *That could have been your resolution, moron*, she thought as she opened the first closet. The deep space was overflowing with a large selection of sheets and other bedding and towels she had brought home from her parents' house a few months earlier. She and her three sisters had recently lost their father after a long battle with a degenerative muscle disease. Their mother had preceded him by fourteen years, shortly after suffering a stroke. After their father's death, Coco and her sisters were tasked with emptying out the family home of forty-four years and putting it up for sale. It was a sad, emotional, and colossal project, which took the four of them and their families a full nine months to complete.

In their parents' will, each daughter had been bequeathed something of substantial value. Jan was given an acre of land their parents had purchased in New Hampshire and never built on; Donna was given their mom's wedding ring set; Carolyn was given Apple stock; and Gabrielle was left a pin belonging to a deceased relative. Unfortunately, no one knew where the pin was. The will said it was in the china cabinet, but it wasn't. When their dad passed away last year, Gabrielle had politely declined her sisters' offers to share in their inherited items. She had no attachment to a pin she'd never seen, from a great-aunt she'd never met.

In the process of dividing, donating, and dumping the contents of two stories, a basement, a shed, a patio, a garage, and an overstuffed attic, she and her sisters hadn't found the pin, but they had come across more than a few items they considered "hot potatoes." These were things that were too embedded in the history of the family to throw away or donate, but far too unappealing to keep. Among these were religious-themed decorations, a full-size ceramic Dalmatian who'd stood sentry beside the fireplace for thirty years, and a huge and musty roll top desk that had been a fixture in their parents' bedroom for as long as any of them could remember.

But the mack-daddy of hot potatoes was a piece of framed art. For nearly forty years, a pastel portrait of Coco's oldest and youngest sisters had hung over the sofa in the living room. In the piece, the two girls were seated in an orange velour chair, as Jan (the oldest) read a story to Carolyn (the youngest). They were both staring out as if the viewer has just interrupted the fable about the fox. Their mother Mary had hired a local artist with the intention of having a similar painting done of Coco and her Irish twin Donna when the first painting was finished. Unfortunately, while the first work was being framed, the artist and her husband had been killed in a car accident while on vacation in Seattle.

During the process of cleaning out the house, that portrait became a hot potato. Not because it wasn't well done or because of the tragedy associated with it. Not even because they wore bathrobes and center-parted 1970s hairstyles. But because it was enormous. Five feet wide by three feet tall. Couldn't throw it out. Couldn't keep it. Couldn't hang it up. It was a hot potato.

In the end, the two stars of the painting had no choice but to "share" it. When Jan's paper covered Carolyn's rock, the little sister was the first to have physical custody; so it was driven to her storage unit with the understanding that someday it would be driven to Jan's storage unit. Or, if Jan was lucky, Carolyn would forget about it.

The whole experience of cleaning out the home she'd grown up in made Coco think about tackling her own clutter on a regular basis, but it also made her wonder what she might have in her house that could one day become the hot potato for her own children. The front-runner right now was the glass chicken on a swing that Rex bought last year at the Wickford Art Festival. But since he would miss that, she instead got rid of two Chinese-inspired lamps, a clock she made in junior high woodshop, and Rex's prom tuxedo (the last tangible reminder of his gorgeous high school girlfriend). But for all she knew, Coco didn't even own the biggest hot potato yet, and that was disconcerting.

Once she had filled not three but five heavy-duty trash bags with linens, she enlisted James to help get them to the car. As she rolled the heavy bags down the stairs, he stood at the bottom to keep them from knocking anything off the wall. One at a time, together they carried each bag out the front door to the Jeep. In the driveway, as she and James hauled the last one up and into the Jeep's back deck, she heard Piper hollering from her yard next door.

"Need help hiding Rex's body?"

Just the sound of that voice always made Coco smile. She turned and watched as her friend sauntered across the lawn with her old chocolate Lab ambling by her side.

Piper had been the first person she'd met when they moved into the house a decade ago. The moving truck hadn't even arrived yet when Piper had come hobbling on crutches across the yard between their homes to say hello. Charlotte, who had just turned seven, stood by Coco's side in their new driveway.

"Hi! Welcome to Real Housewives of Goose Lane! I'm Piper Harper," she had said as she limped her way across the strip of lawn between them that July morning. The first thing Coco remembered thinking was that it was going to be a tough name to say without her Boston accent rearing its ugly head. Piper was a beautiful little thing. She had a pretty, heart-shaped face with dirty-blond hair that sat pertly on her shoulders. That day she'd worn a teal T-shirt and khaki shorts showing off tanned legs down to her cast. Her good foot was bare and her nose and forehead were sunburned. A young girl walked alongside her carrying a stuffed rabbit.

"This is my daughter Katie."

Katie strongly resembled her mother with a smattering of freckles across her cheeks and nose. She was also petite with blond hair and wore a navy-blue sundress, the hem ringed with white and yellow daisies.

Coco regretted throwing on the only clothes she hadn't packed that morning: cutoff shorts with loose threads hanging down, a faded blue Red Sox T-shirt, and, sadly, Crocs.

"Hi. I'm Coco Easton." She reached her hand out to her new neighbor.

"Ha-ha!" Piper and Katie laughed and then the little girl covered her mouth with her rabbit and looked up at her mother.

"What?" Coco said with a fake smile, all the while thinking she was now stuck living next to these lunatics.

"Sorry. Coco's our dog's name. Chocolate Lab. Original, I know," Piper said, smiling.

Well, touché, Mom, Coco said to herself.

After Coco explained how she'd gotten the nickname, Piper said that it was probably best for everyone if she called her Gabby. "At least until the dog kicks the bucket."

"Momma!" Katie said in shock, elbowing her leg.

"Kidding. I'm kidding." She looked down at Katie and then flared her eyes at Coco and mouthed, *No, I'm not.*

"You can definitely call me Gabby. My parents would be happy. What happened to your foot?"

Piper said she'd broken her ankle two weeks earlier when the aforementioned Coco pulled the leash—and Piper—off the front steps and into the bushes while bolting after a squirrel in their front yard. The squirrel got away, as they always did, and Piper needed five hours of surgery, a metal rod, and thirty-eight stitches on both sides of her ankle. She leaned with her crutches tucked in her armpits and her bad foot suspended behind her as she told the story about how her husband Brian had to stop to pump gas into the car on the way to the hospital that day and she'd kept laying on the horn at the gas station to get him to hurry up. She admitted to being a bit of a drama queen, and to the fact that the car was on gas fumes that fateful day only because she never kept the tank full, even though Brian always nagged her to. Her descriptions were so comical that Charlotte and Coco laughed the whole way through the story. The two women hit it off, and for the next twenty minutes they discovered they were both addicted to Tom Brady, DIY projects, and Diet Coke.

As the huge moving truck pulled past the driveway and slowly began backing in, Piper said, "We'll let you go. Good luck and come get us if you need anything."

"Thank you. When we get settled, we'll have you all over for a swim."

"Yay!" Katie jumped up and down.

"The last owner never invited us to use the pool," Piper explained while smoothing Katie's hair and untucking it from behind her ears.

"What? That's bananas!"

Katie and Charlotte laughed.

"That nonsense stops this summer," Coco said, bending down with her hands on her knees. "What good's a pool if kids can't swim in it?"

Katie looked up at Coco with a wide, toothless grin, and asked if "Car Lot" could come play on her swing set. The women laughed and off Charlotte and Katie ran to the backyard next door.

"I'm glad you finally got here, Gabby."

"Me too." Coco smiled.

Piper was the fastest friend Coco had ever made. All these years later, and with so many inside jokes between them, they all still laughed about Car Lot, four-legged Coco, and the broken ankle.

Last year, Piper had started a catering business out of her home, and she and Coco spoke every day. They would talk about everything and nothing over the phone while Piper was at her house making sauces for a wedding or mini quiches for a bar mitzvah, and Coco was at her own house on speaker phone as she paid bills, painted a bedroom, or folded a basket of laundry. The pair was notorious in town, over the past decade, for their tandem volunteer work in the school system. It usually began with Piper's lack of impulse control, which led to all of her hand-raising at the parent group meetings. But Coco was always willing to be her wingman because Piper was entertaining to be around and had a fun attitude.

Today, in the cold driveway, Piper asked James how his guitar lessons were going and teased him about his beautiful new science teacher. Piper knew Coco's children almost as well as her own child because she cultivated her relationships with them individually. She had regularly played board games with James when he was little and, in fact, she had been the one who eventually took him to visit the "graveyard" one night when he was five. Charlotte and Katie were the sisters each one never got and they couldn't remember a time when they didn't know the other. Lately, Piper had been paying the two girls under the table to pass hors d'oeuvres at some of her local catered events, a contributing factor to the comma in Charlotte's bank account.

"Are you looking for a girlfriend?" Piper asked, bending to try to establish eye contact with James when he went down on one knee to scratch the dog's ears. "I can help you, big guy. Katie has friends on the volleyball team who like tall boys. And that new girl from Tennessee's pretty, right?"

"No. I'm good, thanks," James replied. His cheeks reddened as he stood up. "I gotta go practice. See ya, Mrs. Harper. Bye, Mom." Then he scurried back into the warm house to play guitar before the matchmaking got real.

Coco slowly closed the heavy tailgate. "Watch your fingers."

"I love that kid." Piper stepped back as the door closed. "What are you up to today, Gab? How's the faux job hunt going? Did you *find werhk yet?*" she said in a drunken Boston accent and tucked her hands in her armpits.

"Shut up. And I'm not hunting for a *faux* job. For your information, I'm hunting for a *free* one."

"I beg your pardon, your highness. How is the *free* job hunt going?"

"Meh. Long story. I'll tell you tomorrow. I have to get these blankets and sheets to the animal shelter and then get stuff ready for Charlotte's pasta dinner tonight. They're all at practice right now. Big game against Barrington Monday."

"Barrington *sucks*." Piper annunciated the second word with precision of an anchorwoman. "Such a bunch of assholes up there. Remember Cake-gate?"

"I do. R.I.P. Marilyn." Coco bowed her head out of respect.

If towns could have arch enemies, then Barrington was East Greenwich's. Incorporated a full forty years after EG, Barrington was the younger sibling in a never-ending competition. The two affluent towns had battled it out on the playing fields and in the world of academia year after year for as long as anyone in the Ocean State could remember. The other thirty-seven towns in Rhode Island had to settle for rankings of third or worse, while EG and Barrington toggled between first and second place for Rhode Island's superlatives (best restaurants, best public schools, best high school sports teams) like two brothers arm wrestling in the back seat of the car. Forever.

Over dinner a few months ago, the kids had told Coco and Rex that their principal had called for an assembly in the auditorium that morning for the sole purpose of announcing to the entire student body and staff that the U.S. Department of Education had released its local annual rankings of public high schools, and EG had retaken the number-one slot, while Barrington dropped way back down to number two. The auditorium had erupted into a standing ovation for themselves, with kids and teachers high-fiving one another. And when the EG boys baseball team had beaten Barrington in twenty innings last year to snag the state title back, the school held a raucous pep rally in the gym to celebrate the team as if they were triumphant warriors returning from battle. Conversely, when the lacrosse team, debate team, and finance club had fallen victim to the town whose name started with the letter *B*, no mention was made of it, in or out of school.

The rivalry also existed on a micro level. Case in point: Last year, Piper had been hired to cater a sweet-sixteen party for the daughter of a pair of wealthy Barrington lawyers. When she'd inquired about a budget, the smug parents informed her that there was none. But a party without a limit was a Trojan horse; a disaster disguised as a gift.

The party was to be a poolside, Hollywood-themed event with everything from searchlights to a red carpet with fake paparazzi. For six months leading up to the event, Piper had been in daily contact with the parents and the guest of honor, a terrorist named Courtney. The poor caterer had been verbally abused by the teen, suffered through two panic attacks, and lost eleven pounds leading up to the event.

Four days before the party, Coco was called next door by Katie to comfort her mother, who was in the throes of a melt-down. After screaming expletives and emphasizing them with thrown utensils, the caterer had sobbed into her best friend's shoulder, claiming that the pressure from the obnoxious parents was killing her.

"Why is that little runt such a bitch?" Piper had cried.

"I have no idea, honey," Coco said, patting her friend's hair. "Maybe she wears her thongs on backward?"

"Oh my god!" Piper pushed away, grabbed Coco by both arms and shook her back and forth. "Are you *ever* going to let me live that down?"

"Why would I?" Coco laughed as she got shaken.

"One time. I did that one fucking time!"

"Two times."

"Okay. Two fucking times!" Piper laughed.

Coco's laughter came out in snorts, which made Piper snort, too. The madness escalated until Coco was doubled over with hiccups and Piper had thrown her torso onto the counter with the good kind of tears running down her face. After they pulled it together, they worked late into the night rolling out homemade fondant for the cake.

Piper poured her heart into all the food for the party, but it was the cake of which she was most proud: a beautiful five-foot-tall, life-size likeness of the birthday terrorist in a red gown clutching a golden Oscar. She'd even named the cake Marilyn. On the morning of the event, Coco had helped her deliver the cake, slowly and carefully, in the back of Piper's minivan.

The night of the party, the one-of-a-kind creation stole the show as guests marveled at Marilyn sitting high atop a poolside table surveying her fans. The dreaded cake-cutting was to be the final scene in this movie-themed horror show, and Piper had gotten choked up just thinking about it. Many of the guests waited in line to take selfies with it while Piper hovered close by to ensure that no one touched it. It didn't escape her attention that more people wanted a photo with the cake than they did with the actual overdressed birthday girl. In hindsight, Coco surmised that Marilyn stealing the spotlight may have ignited Courtney's fuse.

According to Piper, an hour into the celebration, everything was moving right on schedule. But when the excited parents quieted the crowd of over a hundred kids and adults to present Courtney with her brand-new, bow-draped Mercedes coupe, all hell broke loose.

It turned out that Courtney hadn't wanted to be publicly gifted with the car until her frenemy Maddison arrived at the party, but she wasn't there yet. And she had wanted the color to be Diamond Silver Metallic, certainly not Iridium Silver Metallic. Hysterical Courtney was so enraged that she screamed like the victim in the scary movie who sees the murderer in her bathroom mirror. Then she threw the key fob back at her parents, stormed over to the nearby cake, and pushed it right off the table onto the pool deck.

The guests were frozen in shock as poor Marilyn's body lay in an elongated heap; a ten-million-calorie skid mark. Marilyn's head had rolled over the side of the pool and sank to the bottom. The family's two giant black Newfoundlands padded over to the victim, who'd been murdered in the second degree, and started devouring her like hungry bears.

Poor Piper couldn't believe that the cake she had created, talked to, and come to love had been reduced to a pile of crumbs, folded fondant, and worse. With uncontrolled rage, she stalked over to Courtney in four strides and pushed her hard backward into the swimming pool.

And that's when Maddison walked in.

Recalling the story in her mind now, Coco felt a surge of love for her friend all over again.

"I should have taken a bat to that fucking car, too. Bitch killed my cake. That was messed-up what she did," Piper said with her trademark straight face.

Coco nodded in solemn agreement with lips pursed to keep from smiling. Obviously Piper didn't consider naming a dessert, talking to it, then seeking retribution for its passing messed-up at all.

"*And* they still haven't paid me."

"They haven't?" Coco said and scratched the top of her head. "Hmm. And it's been, what now?"

"Like a year. But I keep sending that invoice every month." Now they were both smiling.

Word had spread like wildfire around EG at the time, and Piper ended up getting a lot of business as a result. This rivalry was epically immature.

"Hey, I just thought of something," Piper said through the

turtleneck she'd pulled up over her mouth. "I was over by Char-lotte's animal shelter this morning, and they're closed."

"Wait. What? Why?" Coco tugged the sleeves of her sweater over her cold hands and tucked them into opposite armpits.

"They moved?"

"Why do you think that?"

"Because they had a sign that said, 'We Moved.'"

"Ugh. That's right. Charlotte told me. What am I going to do with all this stuff?" She turned toward the Jeep while blowing a lock of hair out of her eye. "The team's going to be here in three hours expecting pasta. I haven't even showered or started the stupid food." Then Coco looked back at her friend and said in her sweetest voice, "Hey pretty, would you happen to know anyone willing to cook for twenty smelly girls on short notice for free?"

"Yeah, I'm gonna take a hard pass on that. Besides, you're the only one who works for free around here."

"Bite me."

"Seriously, though, I've got to do a birthday dinner tonight in Narragansett for that handsy ninety-year-old I told you about. He's only four feet tall, but what a fucking pervert."

"Did you make a cake of him?"

"No. I couldn't figure out how to make the fondant all saggy."

"Gross." Coco shivered. "Fine. I'll do the stupid pasta myself—"

"You literally just have to boil water."

"Some friend you are." She turned to go back to her house.

"Oh hey, Gabby—wait." Piper snapped her fingers and pointed at her friend.

"What? I'm freezing." She hopped up and down, her breath hanging visibly in front of her face.

"*What? I'm freezing*," Piper mocked and looked down at the dog. "Lady Coco is such a pussy." Then, to her friend, "You're such a pussy."

"Spit it out, you foul-mouthed woman!" Coco shivered and walked back over to Piper.

"There's a sign inside the bank about a linen drive. New and used. They had a big donation box in the lobby. That might be a way to get that stuff out of your car today. Fuck the animals."

Coco reached to cover the dog's ears and shook her head at Piper.

Language, she mouthed. Then, fishing her phone out of her back pocket, she glanced at the screen. "Is the bank even open? It's Saturday and already two."

"Two? Shit!" Piper hissed. "I gotta go!"

"Who is it for?" asked Coco. "The linen drive? Maybe I'll just go straight there." The tiniest fall of snow started to appear out of nowhere; little flakes in no particular hurry to land.

"Oh. Um . . ." Piper rolled her eyes skyward and put a fist to her forehead trying to pull the name out of her mental file cabinet. "The Mission of Charity, or Hope, or Hope and Faith—"

"That was a sitcom."

"I don't know." Piper shrugged and walked backward in the direction of her house. The dog shook his body from head to tail to remove the tickling flakes. "It's that place off of 117 in Dover that gives old stuff to good people, or the other way around. Marybeth went to their yard sale last year. Ask her."

"Thanks. Hey, you sure you don't want to come back to book club? Next month's mine and I could pick that first bondage book from the trilogy." Coco said the last part in her singsong voice.

"Nah," Piper yelled with her back to Coco. "Already read all three." Only Piper. "I'm all set. Go inside, you big baby!"

"*Go inside, you big baby*," she mimicked her friend to the dog. "Your mother's so bossy!"

Canine Coco followed along behind Piper, tail wagging, and stuffing his big nose in small chipmunk holes as she went.

6

Coco emerged from the house less than a minute later wearing her white winter coat and jumped into the Jeep. With the radio on, she backed down the driveway and out of Goose Lane on her way to Dover. The weekend traffic was light and she rolled along the back roads enjoying the dry snow that swirled all around her but didn't stick to the road. Twenty One Pilots' "Stressed Out" played through the speakers so she turned the volume up and sang along.

She liked to think she was a closet pop music fan. But it was a walk-in closet because everybody knew about it. She had loved Top 40 music since she was a child and had listened to Casey Kasem's weekly countdown religiously. Rex was an '80s and alternative-rock fan and, though Charlotte's taste was mostly current, she also loved the "vintage" '80s music like her dad.

"Remember when '80s music was just called 'music'?" he would say to Coco.

James only listened to dead rockers. In fact, Rex had trouble finding a concert to take him to since their son didn't like any musicians who were still alive and refused to see "lame" cover bands. On top of everything, Amy, Coco's best friend in college, was a big radio DJ in Boston who was constantly rubbing shoulders with famous bands and musicians. But Coco resisted all their attempts to make her appreciate cool music and only sang louder to artists like Taylor Swift, Charlie Puth, and Pink.

In the car, she belted out songs like a rock star at Coachella, but in slow traffic she was careful to sing like a ventriloquist in case some kid was capturing it on video and posting it to social media. It had happened once before and the kid had been her own. ("No Charlotte, it's not funny and I don't care how many views you got.")

As she drove through the streets of EG and crossed over into West Warwick and then Dover, Coco wondered what the future had in store for her.

Last night, she'd searched the Internet once again for volunteer opportunities within a twenty-mile radius. After all these years of living in Rhode Island, she'd become brainwashed by the belief held by most Ocean Staters that a destination greater than twenty miles away was something to be avoided. Nowadays, she was accustomed to staying within the boundaries of the towns that surrounded East Greenwich because that's where most of her family's errands and activities took place. Recently, her excursions to Massachusetts had ceased when she and her sisters had sold their childhood home in the Boston suburb of Reading, MA. There was no reason left to go back to her hometown, and the new owners might not appreciate it if she used the key she still kept on her keychain to let herself in the old green colonial, which she'd dreamed about doing more than once.

As she meandered through Dover along Route 117, her thoughts drifted back to that beloved old house and she almost missed the turn for Somerville Road. The panicked orders of her Aussie navigator brought her back to the present.

"Calm down," she said to the disembodied voice. She pictured him as the confident type and he disappointed her when he lost his cool. Cutting the wheel sharply to the right, she turned onto

Somerville with tires squealing. The mechanic who had recently replaced her front brakes called her an aggressive driver, which she thought made sense because her hygienist had called her an aggressive brusher. She cringed when the car horn behind her blared and then trailed off as the driver passed. "Sorry, sorry," she said into her rearview mirror. *Thud* went the pomegranate, but Coco ignored it because she was concentrating. Slowing to a crawl, she hunched forward over the steering wheel and squinted left and right for a building resembling a charity.

The narrow road was mostly one of open lots and potholes. Lots of potholes. So deep were they that Coco put the Jeep into four-wheel drive to crawl through and around them. The lots on each side of the road were rocky beds of dead weeds. A few small houses dotted the landscape, with chain-link fences dividing the properties. Rusty "Beware of Dog" signs hung from each boundary marker, but the condition of the signs made Coco think that the dogs they warned about were long gone. Finally, at the very end of the street, she spotted what she was looking for.

Facing her, as she rolled slowly forward, was a multilevel red-brick structure with a few windows in the front and a yellow door in the center. Behind the one-story portion, a metal roof rose up to what looked like a warehouse of some sort. An over-sized plastic owl decoy sat perched on its roofline to scare away real birds.

She smiled when she thought of owls, and had ever since Rex sent a group text to the family with a link to an article from the satirical website *The Onion* entitled, "Owls Are Assholes." It had become a part of the Easton Family Humor Hall of Fame along with the latest entries: Charlotte's "Buddy the Elf, what's your favorite color?"—which was how a man had answered the phone when, out on a Christmas-morning coffee run, Charlotte called to tell him she'd caught the runaway dog he hadn't realized was missing yet; and "Roll Tide!"—which Coco yelled while watching college football with her family and mistakenly thought Alabama had scored the winning touchdown when the other team had. Now that was what they yelled in jest whenever Coco messed up. *Roll Tide!*

To the left of the building sat an unmarked white box truck with a matching white cab. To the right were a few parked cars and a dumpster. The small wooden sign affixed over the door read, "The Mission of Hope." *Well, Piper was close*, she thought.

After rolling to a stop, she shifted the Jeep into Park and turned it off. As she stepped out into the snow flurries, she was immediately ambushed by an enormous gray dog with a long curved tail that wagged like the feathered fan of a Vegas showgirl. His fur was overgrown everywhere and nearly covered his eyes. The only parts of him that weren't gray were the white patch on his chest and his pink tongue.

"Hey there, big fella," she said, extending her open hand so he could smell it.

The big goofy mutt approached her. She smiled at the snowflakes clinging to his long eyelashes. His nose was in high gear as he picked up the scent of Piper's dog. He entered her personal space without permission or apology; and, before she understood what was happening, he rose up on his hind legs and put his front paws on her shoulders, sniffing her hair and panting loudly into her ear.

"Oh! Okay," she said with surprise while a glob of saliva drip from his panting tongue and landed between her coat collar and her bare neck.

"Oh. Oh no," she said as the warm bead of spit dribble down her chest.

Although her current pet was a cat, she loved dogs. She and Rex had talked about getting a dog on and off for a few years now. Rex had had a Chihuahua when he was a kid and he talked about wanting an actual dog someday. Charlotte was constantly suggesting they adopt her favorite dog du jour at the shelter. But, time after time, Coco and Rex would come up with an excuse to delay the decision. In dramatic fashion, Charlotte would always complain that they were torturing her with their empty promises. Now that Coco was considering spending her days outside the house, it seemed there would never be a good time to get a dog. And maybe that was okay, because right now she had paw prints on her white wool coat, saliva between her breasts, and dirt on her jeans from the undercarriage of this supersized canine. She also had mud on her mouth, and now her earring was caught in his fur.

"Wait. Jeeze." She had her left hand on the dog's right forearm as she tried to hold him close until her other hand could free his beard from her earring. His hairy chin was resting on the top of her head and they looked like a young couple at a '50s dance.

A loud whistle got the dog's attention.

"Oooohh!" she squealed as she unhooked the fur just in time.

The dog used Coco's chest to push off as he spun to see who had signaled for him and then galloped toward the building with his big tail waving her a cavalier goodbye. With one hand making sure her earlobe was still attached and the other trying in vain to wipe the dirt off her coat, she looked up to see a giant in the doorway of the building leaning down to pat the dog's head. He was a massive black man, about six and a half feet tall and probably four hundred pounds. All she could think of to compare him to was a New England Patriots' defensive lineman. He had on faded blue jeans and a black long-sleeved turtleneck sweater. His leather work boots were massive and they flared at the top because he hadn't—or couldn't—tie them.

Jeeze, she thought. *What the hell's in the water in this town?*

He started walking toward her with the ridiculous dog close by his side.

"Hi." She smiled bravely and tried to seem nonchalant. "I, uh, I have some things here I thought you might need. Blankets and sheets and towels. And blankets." She walked toward him as she gestured with her thumb to the back of the Jeep. "My friend thought—"

"I got it," the man said as he lumbered around the opposite side of her car with the dog in tow. "You can go inside and get a receipt."

She offered to help, but he waved her away and opened the heavy tailgate, with its attached spare tire, as if it was merely a flap on a cereal box.

With a shrug, she walked quickly to the yellow door before the dog could remember she was there. A bell attached to the top tinkled happily to announce her arrival. Once inside, she pushed it closed tightly behind her and wiped her muddy mouth with the back of her hand. Warmth and the smells of sawdust, coffee, and laundry detergent embraced her and, almost immediately, the voice of an older man who was seated about a dozen feet away drew her attention. He offered her a kind smile as he rose to his feet and walked, gingerly at first, around the desk like his feet weren't on board with the sudden activity.

"Hello there, young lady," he said.

"Good afternoon." She smiled back and closed the distance between them. "My name's Coco. I brought some linens for you. My friend said there was a sign somewhere that you were collecting them."

"Yes. Yes. Thank you." He offered his outstretched hand. "I'm Ernie. Welcome to The Mission of Hope." Ernie was a round-faced, gray-haired man in his seventies with kind blue eyes and a pink complexion. He wore a primary-colored plaid shirt, khaki pants with a brown leather belt and brand-new white sneakers. He reminded her of her dad and she liked him instantly.

"Have we met? You look very familiar."

"Hi, Ernie. I don't think so. This is my first time here." She smiled and reached for his extended hand. He covered it with both of his. With her free hand she gestured behind her. "The other man is getting the bags out of my car, but he probably needs—"

Suddenly she was cut off by the sound of the metal door swinging inward and banging against the stopper attached to the wall behind it as the little bell trembled out of fear. She and Ernie both turned as the linebacker she had just seen in front of the building burst through the entryway, blocking out the daylight, with all five bags piled high in his arms. He carried them into the room and she could hear the sound of air escaping the plastic in relief as he dropped them on the sofa against the wall. Then, without a word, he turned around and went back outside.

"Never mind," she said to Ernie.

"I see you've met Bull."

There has never been a more aptly named person or thing on the face of the earth, she thought. *Well, maybe "fireplace."*

"Not really. But I did get a heck of a greeting from your dog." She looked down at her marred clothing and held her hands up.

"Oh. Sorry about that," he said with a sheepish grin. "Chewy loves people, but he doesn't know his size."

"Chewy?"

"Yeah. He's Chew-Barker."

"Cute." She smiled. She wasn't a *Star Wars* fan, but she didn't live under a rock.

"I just made that name up. He's not actually our dog. He's a friendly son of a gun, though. Came around about a month ago and never left. No tags, no chip. We feed him. I let him sleep here in the office at night and he wanders around the place during the day. Not much trouble, except"—he gestured to her clothing—"I guess no one trained him. I talked to Animal Control and the police, but no one's missing him. Hard to believe, huh?" Ernie laughed and a smile spread up his Irish face, his cheeks rising like they were being pushed up from underneath by invisible hands. He had a special glint in his eye that mesmerized her. *When Irish eyes are smiling . . . run like hell,* her dad used to say.

She smiled back. "My daughter volunteers at the shelter over in EG. I'll ask her to find out if anyone is missing a . . . uh, what is he? A werewolf?"

"Ha!" Ernie chuckled. "I wouldn't doubt it, but probably a wolfhound."

"If you say so." She glanced around at the doors dotting the hallway off the main entry area. "This is quite an operation you have here."

"It is. Come out back. I'll get you a cup of coffee and show you around."

"I'd love to," she said, glancing up at the wall clock. "But I have to get going. Maybe another time?"

"Of course. Let me grab you a receipt." He walked back to his desk, scribbled on a form he pulled from a pile, and handed it to her. "You can fill in the rest if you want."

"Thank you. It was nice meeting you, Ernie." She reached out her hand and they shook.

"Likewise, Coco. Sorry about Chewy. Want me to make sure he doesn't follow you to the car?"

"That's okay," Coco said with a smile. "I needed a good reason to go coat shopping, anyway."

"I like your attitude, young lady." He winked. "Find the shine!" he said, smiling, as she left and closed the yellow door behind her.

7

L ater that night Coco surveyed the aftermath of the natural disaster that was the East Greenwich High School Lady Avengers basketball team. Charlotte had gone upstairs to take a shower and Coco let her because she stank.

This was the third pasta dinner Coco hosted. The point was to have a team-building meal to cement the cohesive spirit before the next big game. Sounded sweet on paper. As usual, the players came to the dinner straight from practice, reeking and raucous. The volume grew so loud so fast that Rex, James, and the cat hid out in the basement, as far away as possible from the deafening voices and hip-hop music pulsing from the kitchen. The dinner was a hit and run. The players were in and out in less than an hour. After they stuffed their faces with ziti, salad, rolls, and cookies, they took selfies, listened to a quick pep talk from their coach, and then left like those flocks of black birds that appeared in the yard without warning then all flew away together.

And no one helped clean up.

Coco was used to it by now, but she thought someone ought to write a pamphlet to prepare future sports moms for this. Or maybe she'd just figured out why they didn't do that.

As she started to clean up, she played her own song list. The Chainsmokers were singing about Paris as Coco dropped dirty plastic plates and utensils into the trash, using an occasional serving spoon as a microphone. As she wiped down the countertops with a wad of wet paper towels, her mind wandered back to her visit to The Mission of Hope earlier that day. She couldn't help thinking how much that man Ernie reminded her of her father; all kindness, positivity, and plaid.

The grandkids had called her dad "Papa Jim" to distinguish him from Rex's dad, whom they simply called "Papa". Sixteen years ago, when they found out she was carrying a boy, Rex had lobbied to continue the family tradition and name their son Theodore Rexford III; but two T. Rexes in the family was enough, and, as much as she loved her father-in-law, she'd put her foot down and they agreed to name their son after her dad.

Papa Jim was a smart and modest man. Compassionate, humble, generous, and full of humor. And romantic. Coco had clear memories of her parents dancing in the kitchen on a night no more special than a Tuesday, or sitting in the screened porch on a summer evening listening to their Irish music compete with the crickets while they discussed whatever was on their minds. Often as a child she remembered them coming home from their date nights and, realizing she and her sister Donna were still awake but pretending to sleep, her dad would stand in the doorway of their bedroom, backlit by the hall light, and marvel. "Look at the little angels," he would say with an exaggerated sigh of pride. They dissolved into giggles every time, and he loved it.

Her parents had been married over forty years when her mother Mary suddenly passed away at the age of sixty-five. She had been a kind and sensitive woman who'd handled the highs, lows, and surprises of raising four girls like a superhero getting attacked by a room full of ninjas. Her dad was the first to say that their mother had done all the hard work, but to the girls, their dad was as strong a force in their lives, especially as they grew older and his retirement provided him with abundant free time to spend with them and their children.

When they were kids, they'd been trained to make choices that would not disappoint their parents. Not in an "I'm-an-engineer-and-you're-going-to-be-one-too" way but in a "we've-taught-you-right-from-wrong-and-given-you-every-advantage-now-all-we ask-is-don't-let-us-down" way. Whenever one of them screwed up and had to walk the Heavy Hallway, as their dad referred to the area leading to the den where he and Mary watched TV at night, she always walked away with the heavy heart of someone who had broken a trust and would have to work extra hard to earn it back. Earning back trust was akin to smoothing out wrinkles in linen, it could be done, but it took hard work. She figured that's why he called it the Heavy Hallway, and assumed every kid had one in their house.

She realized another reason Ernie reminded her of her dad. Papa Jim had dedicated many, many hours to volunteer work before his failing legs kept him from the charities he loved. He had worked at soup kitchens, driven sick children and their parents from Logan Airport to the local hospitals for treatment, and donated lots of money to any charity that caught his eye or heart. Money wasn't special to him, but time was; and, after Mary passed away, he'd spent all of it with his daughters, sons-in-law, grandchildren, and people he enjoyed from church. He used to say the best things to share were time, talent, and treasure. And that's just what he did.

He'd been gone over a year now and Coco missed him every single day. But she smiled now, remembering his roguish grin and playful wink. She and her sisters couldn't bear to part with his old plaid shirts so they'd each kept a few. Ernie's similar disposition and fashion sense caused her dad to be in her thoughts all through the hectic dinner that night. His kind face kept popping into her mind and gave her the feeling that she'd just seen her dad that very day. It felt like a hug.

With the Lady Avengers now gone, the guys cautiously found their way upstairs. First Houdini, then James, and finally Rex, each looking side to side before ascending the top step into the kitchen.

"What are you smiling about?" her husband asked while his gaze darted around to make sure they were all gone.

"You look like Iowans coming up from the root cellar," she said, reaching for her phone to turn the music off.

"Jesus. A tornado is what it sounded like from down there."

"Tornadoes are over quicker and cause less destruction. Here, come get it while it's still hot."

As they feasted on leftovers, Rex asked his wife about her progress cleaning the closets earlier that day.

"I got a lot of stuff cleaned out. Mostly linens from Reading." She stared wistfully at the countertop in front of her. "It was kind of sad giving them away. I remember using some of those sheets and towels when I was a kid."

"Whoa. Those are some old towels," Rex joked.

"Watch it." She brandished a serving spoon. "James helped me with the bags. Right, big guy?"

"Yeah. They felt like they were full of rocks," James said with his mouth full.

"Nice." Rex shook his head at his son's poor table manners.

James shrugged and swallowed his food the way frogs do, with a long blink. "C'mon," he pleaded, "we were trapped in that basement for an hour. I'm starving." He guzzled a glass of water but suppressed his burp when he saw his dad's face. "I would have helped you, Mom. I didn't know you left. Was the shelter psyched to get all of your forty-year-old towels?" He smiled at his mother but prepared to run.

"I ended up taking them to Dover, wise guy."

"Why?" asked Rex. "Was someone in Dover looking for circa 1970 towels?" The Easton men laughed in solidarity.

"No, but you guys should write for Conan." She closed the

dishwasher door and pushed the Start button. "The shelter was closed and Piper told me about this charity that needs linens. They collect them and hand them out to the needy, I suppose."

"They'd have to be pretty needy to want those, Mom."

"You're funny. Did I mention I haven't bought any of your birthday gifts yet?" Coco said, leaning with her forearms on the island, while James focused on his pasta with great interest. "The owner over there reminded me a lot of my dad."

"Papa Jim," James said with a thoughtful grin. "I miss him."

"Me too." She smiled at her father's namesake. "The guy who runs the place is the spitting image of him. Same roguish ways, too."

"Really?" said Rex as he mopped up the sauce with a piece of bread.

"Yup." She smiled, ran the faucet, and flicked the switch on the disposal. After ten seconds, she turned it off.

"What else do they do over there?" Rex asked.

"I'm not sure. It's called The Mission of Hope. He wanted to give me a tour, but I had to get back and cook for the team."

Rex got up to pour himself a glass of ginger ale. "You could go online and find out—"

"Mission of Hope," James said in a formal voice as he read aloud from his phone. "'A place where people not only receive new beds and donated household essentials free of charge, but also are treated with kindness, respect, and compassion.'"

"Huh," Coco said. "Thanks, James. You're birthday gifts are back in play."

"Cool."

James went back to his ziti and whatever memes he'd been perusing while his mother uncorked a half-full bottle of red wine, poured a glass, and leaned with her back against the counter to survey her clean kitchen.

"Why don't you go back over there sometime and see if they

could use you. You're great at organizing and fixing stuff," Rex said.

She walked over to her husband, took a cherry tomato off his plate, and popped it in her mouth. She knew Rex appreciated the things she did, but hearing the words just now meant more than she thought they would. Maybe she was feeling sappy thinking about her dad, but she set her wineglass on the countertop and said, "Thanks, handsome. I think I will."

After wiping his mouth with a napkin, he reached out with one arm to grab his wife around her waist. She squealed and he pulled her into him as they exchanged a quick kiss.

"Oh gross," Charlotte said, coming down the stairs.

"You know what's gross?" Rex dipped his wife low, planted a loud kiss on her neck, and then looked at his daughter. "That towel on your head is forty years old."

8

O n Monday, Coco decided to bypass the telephone and drive straight to The Mission and ask if they could squeeze in one more volunteer. She was surprised by how much she hoped they could. After turning down Somerville Road, she parked her car next to the others along the side of the building. This time she looked around warily for the creature before getting out of her car. The coast was clear and she sprinted to the yellow door.

The bell again announced her arrival, but this time the office was empty. She was greeted only by the familiar smell of sawdust and detergent. No Ernie. No linebacker. No werewolf.

She walked slowly around the room as a local radio station played oldies on a transistor radio from a crowded shelf behind the desk, its antenna fully extended at a ninety-degree angle. On the floor by the couch were a few brown paper bags filled with bedsheets. Beside them were several small appliances, a few in their original boxes; a one-cup coffeemaker; and two electric can openers. A brown bulletin board above them held a flyer about the linen drive, which had brought her here two days ago, and a sign-in sheet for volunteers. She stepped closer to the cork board to have a look at the newsletter. The first page had a long message from the president of the organization, presumably the same Ernie she'd already met, thanking donors and volunteers for a successful "winter gala" which had raised $3,525. She had moved on to the article below it entitled, "Stories of Hope" when she heard a voice call out.

"Potowomut!"

She looked to her left to see Ernie standing in the doorway with a smile on his face and hands in his pockets. Chewy stood next to him as his hairy sidekick.

"I beg your pardon?"

"The golf course by Goddard Park. Isn't that where I've seen you before?" As he asked, Chewy walked toward her.

"No, I've never played golf in my life." She eyed the dog and crossed her arms over her chest like she was ready to head down a water slide. But the dog gave her only a halfhearted tail wag before his nose pointed into the air and some scent led him out of the room.

"Don't worry. Chewy's lazy. After he's ruined one outfit, he's over you."

Coco smiled. "Good. I only have one other coat."

"What can I do for you, young lady?" He smiled. "More donations in the car?"

"No. Um, here's the thing." Coco suddenly felt self-conscious and fiddled with the zipper on the purse strung across her body. "I was just wondering if maybe you could use some more help around here."

He looked at the floor and shook his head solemnly, hands fiddling with the change in his pockets. "No."

"Oh." Her head pulled back reflexively, giving her a double chin. She was taken off guard and became instantly embarrassed. "I'm sorry. I just thought—"

"I'm kidding, I'm kidding! Of course! We take as much help as we can get my dear!" He threw his arms in the air.

She was relieved and pissed at the same time. He was a ball-buster but he couldn't have known that his small jest had hit her in the stomach like a cannonball.

"Sorry. I joke. My wife always said it's my worst trait. I can live with that, though. This place survives on volunteers and donations. We never turn down help. Come have a seat." He gestured to the folding metal chairs in front of his desk. "Can I get you some coffee, Chloe?"

"Coco."

"I'm sorry. We only have coffee or soda. Or water."

"No, my name is Coco," she said.

"Oh, right" He snapped his fingers. "You know what they say, 'Happy is the person with the bad memory.'"

"Is that what they say?" She smiled. She couldn't stay mad at this man.

"Can I get you a cup of coffee or some water, Coco?"

"Water would be great."

He disappeared down the hall for a minute and came back with a cold bottle of water in one hand and a cup of coffee in the other.

"Let me tell you a little bit about The Mission of Hope," he said as he handed her the drink and took a seat at his desk.

She settled onto the cold metal seat and listened to Ernie explain the purpose of the charity, all the while spinning the wedding ring on his finger. He expanded on what James had read from the website and then explained some background information including how it had started out in his garage almost thirty years ago. It had originally been his wife Hope's idea, hence the name. Together she, their daughter, and he began collecting linens to dole out to poor families in the area. He pointed to the framed photo on the bookcase behind him when he mentioned his family. His wife was sitting at the top of a blue playground slide with a girl of about five on her lap. The photo was taken just at the moment they shoved off and both had open mouths and raised arms.

Within a year, he and Hope realized the need was much greater than they'd expected, so they began soliciting hotels and private schools for their gently used mattresses and distributing them to needy families. After outgrowing their garage, they leased a small building down the street from their home to store what they collected.

"It didn't matter how many mattresses we amassed, they'd be gone the same week! Couldn't keep the darn things in stock. Once word got around, we'd have people waiting for us at the door when we got over there in the morning."

The desk phone rang and Ernie answered it. After giving a quick set of directions to the building, he told the caller to take it easy. "Now, where was I?"

"Mattresses."

"Right."

"I'm curious, Ernie. Why mattresses?"

He leaned toward her and folded his hands on the desktop. "You cannot underestimate the importance of getting people up off the floor, Coco. Even in the army we slept on beds."

Coco recalled one night in a sleeping bag on a camping trip as a kid. One night was enough.

"We met so many families who didn't have a bed or enough beds for their whole family. It wears away at your self-esteem and your dignity to sleep on a floor. Imagine having to get up off the floor in the morning and head to work or school? So we started giving away mattresses first. We had no idea how widespread the problem was. After people started showing up at the door, we had to get more organized. We moved to this bigger building and work by appointment now. The more things we can collect, the more people we can help. Once we moved here, people started donating other things like furnishings and linens and it made sense to accept everything. Except clothing. We decided to leave that to the other guys who know what they're doing."

She listened closely and wondered if her expression gave away the fact that she was using the hand she was sitting on to count her blessings. She was already looking forward to getting home and explaining everything she'd learned to her family at dinner.

"What's happened to these people that they end up needing your help?"

"Oh, lots of things." He counted on his fingers, too. "We meet abused women who've run away and ended up in shelters. Most times they have young children and are starting all over again with nothing. We've had clients who are refugees and were relocated here. Most of them have one suitcase to their name if they're lucky. Let's see, we also have people who have lost everything because of a medical issue, a fire, or an addiction. Veterans. There's a lot of reasons people find themselves needing our help. And as long as they can show that they have a valid place to stay, we do the best we can to get them off to a fresh start."

"Wow. It must be awful seeing all the despair." She'd never even met a refugee or an abused mother. That she knew of. "It must be hard to forget the stories you hear."

"But I don't want to forget the stories, you see." Ernie leaned back in his chair and held on to the armrests. "Over all these years running this place, I've learned two big things." Then he paused.

"What are those?" she asked because she felt like she was supposed to. Ernie liked a straight man just like her dad had.

"First, that people are mostly good."

She nodded in agreement.

"Second, that there's always positive underneath the negative. It's there. It's always there. You just need to find it. If it's buried, dig it out. Like when a big tragedy happens; an earthquake or a terrorist thing somewhere. We look for the helpers, right? How else are you going to make something good out of something bad? If we didn't have any good, the bad would suffocate us. We can't undo what's happened to the people who come to us, but we sure can help them create a better next chapter. In my wife's words, 'Find the shine.' Like the silver lining, you know? It's always there. Might be hiding and buried, but if you want to, you can."

"Yeah," was all college-educated Coco could manage to say. "I live just a few towns from here and I didn't know about you guys. How do these people find you?"

"Through different agencies when they are looking for help for other things like housing, abuse counseling, food, clothing. We first set up a meeting with them to figure out what they need. Everybody's different. In fact"—Ernie checked the clock on the wall—"our next clients aren't due for another half an hour. Why don't you and I take a quick tour before I meet with them?"

"Okay." She got up from her chair with her purse and water bottle and followed Ernie down the yellow, linoleum-covered hallway. As hard as she tried to focus on the seriousness of what he'd told her, there was a big part of her brain that just kept singing, *I got a job! I got a job!* At some point she would ask herself if it was the type of job she wanted, but for now she was just happy to *be* wanted.

Just beyond the front office on the right was a door labeled "Interview Room" in black lettering on a white slide-in tag. Ernie reached in and flipped the light switch. Coco peeked around the doorway and was instantly taken aback. The windowless room was about twelve feet square. In the center of the floor sat a beautiful and polished mahogany table surrounded by six matching armchairs. The grandeur of the furniture surprised her because Ernie had set the bar so low. *Swanky* was the word that popped into her mind, and she bit her tongue to prevent her mouth from whistling with admiration. A grandfather clock stood sentry in one corner, and a large Oriental rug covered nearly all the linoleum in the room. Just as Ernie opened his mouth to speak, the clock chimed its notes to mark the half hour. He spoke over it.

"The furniture in this room was a gift from the Canadian consulate in Boston."

"You're kidding."

"I kid you not. They found us on the Internet when they were redecorating and needed a home for this set. When people come to us for help, we sit them down in here so we can talk to them about their specific needs. We want to find out what items they don't have and which ones they already do."

"It's a lovely space," she said. *Almost too lovely for a charity*, she thought honestly.

"Probably should have saved the best for last, but I wanted to show you the flow when clients come in. We bring them in here first." Ernie ran his hand along the curved back of the Chippendale chair. "The purpose of this *room* is to have a place to sit down in private with the clients and figure out what they need. But the purpose of the *decor*, if you will, is to have a dignified place to do that."

She nodded.

"We try to make our clients feel safe and respected during a very vulnerable time. It's not easy for any of them. We do everything we can to make sure they are relaxed and not embarrassed or anxious. You see, any one of us could be in their situation, so it's all about compassion and sensitivity. Never any judgment. Who are we to judge, anyway? No one is better than anyone else."

"No."

As they walked back into the hall, Ernie snapped his fingers as if he'd just remembered something. He went back into the room and came out holding a small white rectangular box in both hands.

"This is very important and I almost forgot to mention it."

Holding it against his stomach, he carefully pried one end open. "Remember when I talked about looking for the shine?"

"Yes."

He pulled out a simple four-by-six silver-plated frame. "This was my wife's idea. We give one of these to each client on the day they come here. They can only come here once. If we get their permission, we snap a Polaroid of them at the end of their interview. It's not the best quality, but we want them to know that there's no other copy of the photo on file here. That's why we use the instant camera. We slip it in the box with the frame and they can do anything they want with it. We hope that they take it to their new home and use it to remember that people care about them. I don't know if they do it or not, but I'd like to think they do. We try to remind them to focus on the positive because they've been on a tough journey. Sometimes we all forget to focus on what we're grateful for. If you lose that sense of positive motivation or reflection, it can get really hard to get up in the morning."

She felt like he was referring to a broader truth, and she was aware that it was hard for her to relate to the people he described and the circumstances that deposited them on his doorstep. East Greenwich wasn't teeming with refugees, and those few people she knew who suffered unfortunate events where always able to offset them with insurance or help from relatives. Living without such safety nets was a chilling proposition.

He pushed the frame back into the box and set it on the table. "Some people don't want their photo taken and that's okay, too. They still have the frame as a gift. Something new that's all theirs." He smiled at her and she smiled back. "Come with me and I'll show you more."

Just past the Interview Room was a small nondenominational chapel with six chairs set up in two rows and a beautiful stained-glass window placed in a cutout on the interior wall. Ernie walked in and Coco looked around from the doorway. It was a tiny but peaceful space.

"This room is available to clients and volunteers," he said. She nodded as he moved past her and into the hall. "We don't push any religion on anyone, of course, but those who want can enjoy the space. Arthur, one of our first volunteers, made that window himself."

"Wow. It's beautiful. Do the volunteers come in here to try to cope with the sad stories they hear?"

"Actually . . ." Ernie pivoted toward her with his hands in his pockets. "We come in here and say a prayer of thanks for the people who help us change lives with their time and donations." He shrugged and continued on the tour. Coco felt a warmth in her chest in reaction to his humble words and followed behind him out of the chapel.

The open door across the hallway led to a break room. As they walked in, Ernie told her that the upper and lower cabinets on two of the walls had been donated by his neighbor when she'd remodeled her kitchen. Laminate countertops from one of the big home-improvement stores topped the lower cabinets and supported a microwave and a coffee machine. An old oak conference-room table and chairs sat to the right of the refrigerator, and spread across it were boxes of various snack foods.

Ernie moved to the table and put his hands on the back of one of the chairs. Coco couldn't tell if he did it for stability or if he enjoyed touching the furniture. "A buddy of mine from the service gave me this set when he closed his office. It's seen better days, but we're happy to have it. We keep the room loaded up with treats, as you can see. Since we can't afford to pay you, we try to keep you happy with trans fats. Fridge is full of soft drinks. Help yourself."

"Thanks. So you accept private donations?"

"We do. Fact is, that's all we accept. We don't take money from the state or any other government group. Too complicated that way. We're one hundred percent supported by goods and money donated by the public. Every single dime of that money goes to buying beds and other necessities for our clients. I buy the frames myself, though. And the snacks." He smiled and winked.

She smiled back but wondered how successful that private funding strategy could be when she lived only two towns away and had never heard of them. Her brain went to work figuring out if that was his problem or hers.

As if he read her thoughts, Ernie said, "We have a little trouble getting the word out sometimes. We're a small place. We have a simple website, but we get along mostly by word of mouth."

From the break room they continued down the hallway until arriving at a pair of swinging metal doors with plastic yellowed windows on the top and black rubber kick plates on the bottom.

"We don't let the clients beyond this point," he said as he pushed one side open and held it for her.

"Why not?"

"I'll show you."

Once they were through the double doors, the first room on the left bore the label "Linen Room."

"Morning, ladies," Ernie said as they walked in.

"Hi, Ernie," said an older woman dressed in a blue sweater and black pants as she stood at a tall table folding a green crocheted blanket.

"Morning, boss," said another, who stood on a folding stepladder at the back of the room putting a small box up on a shelf.

"I'd like you to meet Coco. She wants to help out so I'm giving her the ten-cent tour."

"Hi Coco," they said simultaneously.

"I'm Peggy," the woman in the blue sweater said. "And this is Yolanda."

"Nice to meet you."

"How's Boots doing?" Ernie asked Peggy.

"Better. He's on life number seven. They stitched up his face and said the bites on his back leg were just superficial."

"Cat got attacked by a coyote the other day," Ernie said to Coco.

"Oh no. Poor thing. I'm sorry."

"Thanks, love. He'll be okay. Don't let us interrupt your tour, Ernie." She smiled kindly and Ernie returned it with a smile of his own. Coco thought she detected a blush in his cheeks, but it was hard to determine with his ruddy Irish complexion.

"When clients tell us what they need in the Interview Room," Ernie explained, "a volunteer comes in here with the list and the others help pull everything from these shelves."

"The clients can't choose for themselves?"

Ernie frowned and shook his head. "Nope. That's why they aren't allowed past the double doors."

"How come?"

"We used to do it that way, but there is so much stuff that they would end up getting overwhelmed with the decision-making and change their minds four or five times. It can be very stressful for them. They have so little and they see so much in here. But we have to keep in mind the other clients who are coming in after them. Day after day. Week after week. They never stop coming. We can't give it all away at once. They used to ask sometimes if they could take more than they needed and we'd have to say no. That was hard to do. So we figured out it was just easier to pull out all the linens and household items for them while they're looking through the furniture in the Showroom."

Coco nodded as her gaze moved around the room, taking in the substantial amount of bedding and other linens stacked high on the shelves. She felt guilty remembering how much good stuff she had donated to the animals over the years because she had no idea this place existed.

The Linen Room had high wooden shelving units that stretched almost to the ceiling and ran the lengths of three of the walls, connecting in a U-shape. On the right side, the shelves were full of bed sheets folded neatly and labeled with their size on masking tape on the front of each set as well as on the shelves on which they sat.

"We meet with four sets of clients a day; two in the morning and two in the afternoon. That's when we confirm the ages and genders of any children and try to match the colors and patterns of the bedding to them accordingly. I'm not trying to sound sexist, but I don't want to give a little girl sheets covered in fire engines. You know what I mean?"

Coco nodded again. It was a lot to take in.

"Some might think clients shouldn't be so choosy, but we take beds and bedding very seriously. A decent bed supports your dignity, not just your health." He ran his hands along the folded sheets. "We had a client in here last week who needed beds for her three little girls. They'd spent their whole lives sleeping on the floor in sleeping bags. She called us a few days after she was here saying that her daughters are up extra early every day now to make their beds before school."

Coco had never given it much thought. A bed is the kind of thing you just took for granted. *For God's sake, even the dogs at the shelter have beds.*

"See these shelves?" Ernie gestured in a wide sweeping motion. "They were built by Eagle Scouts. They supplied all the wood and spent a whole weekend in here putting it all together. Beats the hell out of the cardboard box towers we used to have."

"Ernie. Language," Peggy whispered.

"Apologies." He grimaced at Coco. "I think the Scouts earned a badge or patch or something, too."

Coco examined the sturdy wooden structures. Shelves on the left-hand side were filled with blankets, comforters, curtains, shower curtains, towels, dish towels, throws, and other textiles. Ernie explained that donated linens were washed in the laundry room. On the far wall, the shelves held small housewares, including toasters, which were purchased with donated money when inventory was low.

"After mattresses, toasters are the next most important things we have. No matter how down and out a person is, Coco, if they have a toaster, the children can have a warm breakfast." Ernie pointed to the wall full of boxed toasters and dishes. "Have a look over here." They walked over next to Yolanda.

He explained to Coco that, when dishware and flatware were donated, a great effort was made to create near-matching sets of four, six, or eight.

"We want them to have as close to a similar set as possible so the kids aren't embarrassed when they have a friend over, or the parents won't feel bad inviting people to share a meal with them. Preserving a person's dignity, Coco—that's what we're all about here. We never just throw stuff at them and send them on their way. Peggy and Yolanda and the other ladies do a great job creating matching sets out of what gets donated."

"That's very thoughtful," Coco complimented.

"Through trial and error we've managed to figure it out along the way."

He went on to explain that once the needed items were pulled from the shelves, they were placed into large trash bags, loaded into metal shopping carts, and pushed to the loading dock where the client's borrowed or rented truck waited. Yolanda and Peggy kept busy as he spoke.

Ernie checked his watch again and ushered her back out into the hall. "Keep up the good work, ladies."

"Bye, Ernie," Peggy said.

"Welcome, Coco," Yolanda said.

"Thank you."

"Next we have our Mattress Room."

Ernie went into the next room on the left and Coco followed him.

He reiterated for the third time that the number-one goal at

The Mission was to get clients up off the floor. In years past, they'd accepted gently used mattresses that their volunteers had persuaded hotels and boarding schools to part with. Within the last four years, though, they had modified their rules, and now a supplier, at a fraction of the retail cost, delivered brand-new mattress sets sealed in giant plastic bags every month.

"Everyone who needs one gets a brand-new mattress, box spring, and frame."

He said that clients were allowed to request twin or full-size mattresses. They didn't have anything larger. New cribs and bunk beds were also available if needed. The wood-framed support structures, which held the mattresses in place on their sides and kept them up off the floor since a flood two years ago, had been built by Eagle Scouts onsite, as well.

Also in the Mattress Room were half a dozen carts, large blue canvas boxes on wheels, similar to the laundry carts in large hotels. Coco learned that these containers were used to transport mattresses to the loading dock, where they were then moved into the client's truck.

Coco and Ernie left the room, and then he reached back inside to turn out the light. She looked behind them and realized Chewy had silently joined the tour. As they continued on, half a dozen people passed them in the hallway smiling at Coco and calling out a hearty greeting to Ernie. He replied to each using their names. She could tell he was well liked just by the way they smiled back at him. Chewy stopped to sniff the hands or crotches of everyone they passed and then trotted to catch up with the tour.

"How many people volunteer here?"

"Probably twenty-five or so. But they don't all work here every day. We have our Monday Moms, our Tuesday Guys, our Thursday Ladies, and so on. Because they all work different days, sometimes they only get together in one place at the same time when we have our big events like the winter gala or the yard sale."

"Funny."

"Indeed."

"Most of them have said to me at one time or another that they started volunteering here so they could give back. But then they realized they got way more than they gave. That's the magic of The Mission." He wiggled his fingers to imply something mystical.

Diagonally opposite the Mattress Room was the Showroom.

"Here," he explained, "we have a sampling of furniture set up to resemble actual rooms in a house." Similar to the previous rooms, this one had a dropped ceiling, linoleum floors, fluorescent lighting, and no windows. "Our clients only have one chance to get what they need here. They can't come back again if they forget something. That might sound harsh, but when you look at it from a practical standpoint, if we allow repeat visits, there won't be enough to go around. So they choose what they need in here. When the room thins out, we bring in fresh inventory from the warehouse back there. See those shelves?"

Along the walls, shelves held various mirrors and framed artwork, mostly posters such as the close-up of a ballet pointe shoe, a panoramic view of Lake Como, and a movie poster from *The Phantom of the Opera*.

"Let me guess," she ventured with a smile. "Eagle Scouts?"

"Bingo! Before, stuff was on the floor and the clients couldn't see everything."

"That's great." The artwork was eclectic at best, but she imagined how it would liven up the walls of a client's new home. Better than nothing, for sure. When she and Rex were packing up their last house before the move, she remembered thinking how dull the rooms looked once the hanging art and mirrors had been taken down.

"Peggy does a great job making this room look like a home.

We are constantly swapping out the furniture as clients choose things in here. So Peggy redecorates almost every week. She's got a keen eye, that one." He smiled and Coco wondered what their relationship was.

Tucked away within the Showroom was a small alcove with a children's-sized table and four seats. A pink, fuzzy beanbag chair sat in one corner and two white pressboard bookcases lined one wall, their shelves filled with children's books and small stuffed animals whose ears were affixed with tags.

"We bring the little ones in here sometimes while their parents are choosing furniture. They are allowed to pick a book and a new stuffed animal to take with them. Some of these little ones don't have anything of their own, you see."

From the Showroom, Ernie took Coco through another set of swinging doors to the warehouse, where the majority of the furniture was stored. It comprised half of the total six thousand square feet of the facility. This windowless space had a twenty-foot ceiling, a corrugated metal roof, and a large garage door that opened to the small loading dock. She could hear a sports radio channel playing somewhere in the vicinity. The broadcasters had a lot to talk about with the Patriots playing in the upcoming Super Bowl.

Coco pushed her hands into her coat pockets to protect them from the chill of the unheated space. She made a mental note to dress warmly next time, and then remembered that her warm white coat was in the dry-cleaning pile thanks to the werewolf.

"Is this warehouse full all the time?"

"Not quite," Ernie said. He went on to explain that the amount of furniture and decorations a client was allowed to take depended on how full the warehouse was at any given time. When it was overflowing with items, it was okay to give clients more, since there was less risk that the next family would go without. There was no method for anticipating the volume of donations. Unfortunately, when inventory dipped, with the temperature or the economy, clients were limited in the number of items they were permitted to take.

"February and March are the worst times for building up inventory, because people aren't usually cleaning out their homes or moving in those cold months. We're about two-thirds full right now. But no matter what, nobody leaves without a mattress and a toaster."

He went on to tell her that, when the economy was good, The Mission of Hope rode the wave. People felt more secure and therefore more generous. When they moved or retired, they donated estate items instead of selling them. The Mission benefited as much as the local landfill.

"The Mission was 'green' before that term was hip." Ernie chuckled. *Dad would have loved him*, she thought. "Because we accept large pieces of furniture and reuse them, we keep them out of the landfills. We're of different generations, Coco. We old folks enjoy seeing the furniture get a second chance."

"Like clients," she offered to please him.

"Exactly! People who are getting another chance are given furniture that's getting another chance," Ernie said as he leaned on the back of a slipcovered armchair.

Sofas took up at least a quarter of the warehouse space, while bureaus and upholstered chairs took up another half. In the remaining quarter, wooden chairs and stools hung on metal hooks to keep them off the floor and make use of the vertical space.

"Do you get any hot potatoes in here?"

"Come again?"

"You know…" Her face reddened and she used her hands to explain. "Peculiar things that no one would ever want. Ugly stuff."

"Right. Peggy and I were just talking about that the other day. The funny thing is, we're surprised all the time by what clients want and what they don't. Beautiful furniture can stay here for so long that it ends up getting pushed to the back, while some god-awful geometric stuff from the '80s gets snapped up the same day it goes into the Showroom. There's no science to it. To each his own."

"So what's the least-popular furniture?"

"Without a doubt, dining room stuff. People donate it here, sometimes they leave stuff outside when we're closed. But clients don't have dining rooms. Hell—" He closed his mouth and looked over his shoulder for Peggy. "*Heck*, most don't have bedrooms or beds."

"So what happens to the dining room tables?"

"Ah! I'm glad you asked." He gestured for her to follow him.

9

After walking thirty feet farther down the warehouse, they reached a small room that smelled of polyurethane and sawdust. The smell of sawdust always reminded Coco of her dad's workshop in the basement of the house in Reading. When she was little, the screeching sound of her dad's table saw would send her running upstairs, hands clamped over her ears. But, when the sawdust settled, the aroma would draw her back to the basement to watch her dad work on whatever project was on his list that day. They would talk about his childhood, her school and friends, and he would patiently explain what he was working on and how each tool was used. He'd often let her try using some of the tools herself.

The windowless workshop at The Mission was about four times larger than her dad's and had three table saws lined up against one wall. Leaning against another wall was a large variety of table legs. A long wooden workspace covered in paint splatters sat in the middle with vises attached on opposite sides. The floor was covered in a fresh layer of sawdust, and a burly man stood ankle deep in the middle of it.

"Coco, I'd like you to meet Sawyer the Magician."

Sawyer, who looked to be in his late sixties, put down the circular saw he was about to use and took off his safety glasses. Sawdust stuck in his gray, walrus-like mustache and clung to his black shop apron and Boston Bruins hat. She wondered if Sawyer was his last name or his first as she closed the distance between them to shake his hand. Then she looked around the room, which seemed to have every woodworking tool and product anyone could ever need.

"Sawyer and the others do great work in here making repairs to the donated furniture before its good enough to be brought out to the warehouse. Mostly it's sanding down scratches or tightening the screws on table legs. We certainly never want clients to feel like we're giving them junk or something we wouldn't put in our own homes."

Sawyer spoke in a low raspy voice. "All those saws over there were donated by the high school woodshop. We also get high school kids in here doing their service hours. Most of them are good kids, if they can stay off their phones." He gave Ernie a look and they both grunted. "Some of them stick around here even after they've worked their required hours."

Coco was impressed by that and wondered if this was something her own kids might be interested in doing. At least they could learn how to fix something.

"These paints and stains in the cabinet were picked up for free at the hardware store before they got thrown away." He gestured for Coco to look behind her.

"And the aluminum ductwork up there was just installed last summer so we can get some ventilation. Right, Sawyer?" Ernie was pointing to the system attached to the ceiling, which resembled the hoses used to vent clothes dryers.

"Yes, sir. Keeps the dust and fumes out of the air for the most part. I prefer cigarette smoke, if something's gonna poison me."

"You need to vacuum that mustache so you don't scare the kids," Ernie said.

"It's my camouflage, Kemosabe."

"Don't call me that. I hate that."

Coco considered commenting on the fact that the big man's name started with the word *saw*, but decided against it. "Why do they call you The Magician?" she asked, pulling her arms tighter to her sides as the chill deepened.

"It's a long story." He flapped his hand dismissively.

"No it isn't," Ernie said turning to Coco. "He cuts tables in half."

"I stand corrected. It's is a very short story, my dear."

"Why?" Coco asked.

"Because it has only a few words."

"No." She smiled, remembering what it was like to deal with James when he was ten. "Why do you cut tables in half?"

Ernie took the answer. "Remember I told you before that we have no use for dining room tables? Well, coffee tables are a popular item because they can double as a dinner table. So each week this old war horse comes in and saws a big dining table in half, cuts down the legs, adds a few new ones, and refinishes the raw wood. Voilà! Two coffee tables." Ernie gestured to a platform where two coffee tables sat in mid-renovation. "Find the shine. Right, Sawyer?"

"Mmm. Sure. Just finished the cutting today. Now I gotta shine 'em up." He winked at Coco.

"How many are you up to, bud?"

"Those up there are numeros ninety-one and ninety-two, if you can believe that."

"You're a good man. I'll help you mov—"

Ernie's phone rang in his coat pocket. He reached inside and pulled out a vintage flip phone that made Coco purse her lips to keep from smiling. "Ernie," he said after flipping it open. "Hello? Okay. On my way."

He turned to the other two. "I have to run up front. The

clients are here. Sawyer, can you finish the tour for me? Coco here wants to help us out. Don't scare her off."

"Will do. Or won't do. Or whatever," he said, looking down cross-eyed and pulling shavings from his mustache.

Ernie walked out of the workshop like a man on a mission.

"That guy is a saint. He's a pain in my arse, but he's still a saint," Sawyer said as they watched him hook a left at the sofas and disappear through another set of swinging doors.

"He's very nice."

"He's had a tough go of it but everyone here loves him. He treats them all like family. C'mere. Let me show you the rest. Have you seen the mattresses and linens?"

"I have."

"Okay. Let me show you some other things. Bang a right."

Coco did as she was told and exited the workshop ahead of him. The next area had three pony walls and a swinging half-door. There were worktables on two sides. The back wall had shelves with an assortment of lamps and lampshades in every stage of repair. Open shelves under the tables held wiring, switches, sockets, electrical tape, lightbulbs, and various small hand tools organized in labeled bins.

"This is called the Lamp Room for obvious reasons. It's where we get all our good ideas," he said as he held a lightbulb over his head.

She smiled again. *Dork.*

"Fred works here, but only on Fridays. He's a retired electrician and inspects all the donated lamps to make sure they're safe before we give 'em away. If they need fixing, Freddie takes care of it. He brings stuff from his basement at home so we don't spend much money. Let's head over to the loading dock and I'll show you the truck."

As they walked through the main aisle of the warehouse to the back of the building, Sawyer went on to explain that linens and small appliances were usually brought to The Mission by individual donors who came to the front door. The truck was used to collect furniture donations from the ten surrounding towns and bring them to the warehouse.

"With money from website donations and the gala, we were able to buy an old four-door box truck with space for up to six volunteers to travel together on pickup days. Some guys—and ladies, of course—can drive, but can't lift heavy furniture. And some of the high school kids can lift the furniture but can't drive the truck. So this makes it possible to have more people go on collection runs, and that increases the warehouse inventory faster."

When they arrived at the loading dock, Sawyer hit the round green button on the wall and the fifteen-foot garage door, with its four small windows, began to rise noisily on its tracks. By the time it was halfway open, it was clear to see that the truck was gone.

"Did you make it disappear?" she joked.

"Dammit! I wish I'd said that." He smiled at her with appreciation. "Guess Bull's out on a run. Let me show you back to the front and we can see what Ernie has in mind for you next."

After Sawyer left Coco in the lobby, she wandered around the front area for a few minutes warming up and looking over brochures and flyers about The Mission. She could hear muffled voices occasionally from the Interview Room. When Ernie still hadn't emerged after ten minutes, she sat down on a chair in front of his desk and checked Facebook on her phone. Chewy moseyed into the room and sat his rear end on the old leather couch while his front paws remained on the floor. He stared at her from under his bangs.

"You ruined my coat, you know?"

The dog panted in such a way that he appeared to be smiling.

"So you *do* know?"

He yawned, bored with the conversation, then moved the rest of his body onto the couch and closed his eyes.

"I know you're not sleeping, you phony."

The door opened and she looked up to see Ernie, a woman in her thirties, a small girl of about four, and a slightly older boy. The woman was wearing jeans, a long brown coat, and sunglasses. But it was plain to see yellow bruising around her left temple and red marks on her swollen lips. Her left arm was in a sling. The little girl clung to her other arm and carried the boxed frame.

"Bonnie, Peggy will start collecting your linens and she'll meet up with us after you pick out some nice furniture." Ernie handed a piece of paper to Peggy, who emerged from the room last, looking stricken. Coco tried to imagine what she had just learned in there that would cause her such distress.

"Okay," Bonnie said quietly. The little girl was swinging her mother's good arm back and forth and looking up at her with lots of unspoken questions.

Peggy gave Coco a broken smile and headed off down the hall with some papers in her hands.

"Momma?" The little girl tugged on the woman's sleeve. "Momma!" she said more insistently.

"Hey, Lucy and Trey," Ernie said, bending down to their level with his hands on his knees. "You two have been real troopers. I know this is boring. Why don't you come with me and we'll go visit the children's room?"

Trey nodded and looked up at his mother for permission. Lucy turned her head into her mother's leg and didn't answer.

"Okay, Lucy. You can stay with Mom. Let's go, Trey." Ernie used the edge of his desk to help himself stand up. "On second thought . . ." He made a mischievous face. "If it's okay with Mom, how about we all get a snack first?" Ernie looked at the mom for permission. Bonnie nodded; processed snacks seemed to be the least of her worries.

"Follow me." Ernie held his hand out to Trey, but the little boy didn't take it. Unfazed, Ernie led his little group of clients down the hall toward the break room. Chewy slinked off the couch and pulled up the rear of the parade. He looked briefly back over his shoulder at Coco.

I knew you were faking it, she thought, narrowing her eyes.

Coco didn't know where to look as they passed her, so she looked at her phone. She couldn't help feeling like an intruder in this intimate situation. Presumably, this woman had run away from someone and had to start fresh all over again. Only after they passed by did she dare take another look at the family. The little girl's shoes were at least two sizes too big for her feet.

She jumped when the yellow door opened behind her and the big linebacker Coco had met the day before walked in with a teenage girl about Charlotte's age.

"Hi," Coco said, feeling like she'd gotten caught doing something wrong.

The girl said hello while the man turned his back to her and hung a set of car keys on a hook by Ernie's desk.

"Are you dropping off?" the girl asked.

"Oh, no. I'm actually going to start working here." The words felt strange on her lips.

"Cool. I'm Daisy. This is Bull." Daisy was a very pretty girl, tall and thin with a creamy complexion, dark eyes, and glossy black hair that hung in a silky curtain past her shoulders. She wore a denim jacket too thin for the cold weather, white jeans fashionably shredded on the thighs, and black combat boots.

"We actually met the other day. Hi, Bull."

Bull nodded. Today he was wearing a red turtleneck with a puffy black vest and the same jeans and boots, still untied.

"I'm Coco. I'm waiting for Ernie to come back and tell me what he wants me to do next."

"He might be a while," Daisy said. "Follow me and we'll see if they need help in the Linen Room."

"Thanks." Coco smiled at Daisy's friendliness and followed

the girl down the hall, leaving Bull behind to sit on the couch cushion Chewy had warmed.

When they entered the Linen Room, Peggy was there but Yolanda was gone. Chewy had arrived ahead of them and made himself at home on a bed in the corner. *This dog has the life*, Coco thought.

"Peggy, this is—" Daisy turned to Coco with a questioning look.

"Coco."

"Right. Sorry."

"Yes. Yes. We met her earlier," Peggy said. "How did the rest of the tour go?"

"Good. It's a lot to take in."

"I know, honey," she said with a grandmotherly smile. "Daisy, lovie, can you please pull me down a toaster?"

"Sure thing." The young woman scurried nimbly up the stepladder and pulled a boxed two-slice toaster off the shelf then added it to the half-full shopping cart next to Peggy.

"How long have you been here, Peggy?" Coco inquired.

"A long time."

"Do you enjoy it?"

"I do. When my Ralph passed on, it was a lifesaver for me to be around all these nice people and helping out. My grandkids told me about this place. One of them is an Eagle Scout who helped build these shelves, you know?"

"Nice," Coco said.

"Do you have kids, Coco?"

"Yes. A girl and a boy. Seventeen and almost sixteen."

"How lovely. They're right around Daisy's age."

"Do you live here in Dover, Daisy?" Coco asked the teen.

"Yup." She snapped a big trash bag open and the noise scared Chewy, who promptly stood up and headed back toward the office. She held it open so Peggy could deposit a stack of sheets before Daisy tied the top and lifted the bag into the cart.

"It's great that the schools urge the kids to get involved in the community," said Coco. "They didn't require that when I was in high school."

"Yeah." Daisy glanced at Peggy. "I'll roll this down to the truck." She turned the full cart around and pushed it out through the doorway into the hall.

"Did I say something wrong?" Coco asked Peggy.

"Not at all, my dear. You know teenagers. They have the attention span of toddlers ever since those little pocket phones got invented."

"Right." Coco shrugged and pulled a new bag from the box.

10

When she got home late that afternoon, after watching Charlotte's team lose to Barrington with a buzzer-beater, the house was quiet. James had gone upstairs and Charlotte had gone out for consolation frozen yogurt with some of her teammates straight from the game. Coco made her usual laps around the house plucking damp towels off the floor and closing closet doors.

Now she stood at the kitchen counter staring at the toaster's red coils as it cooked half a bagel. Her mind traveled back to what Ernie had said about the importance of a toaster. The little stainless steel appliance she'd taken for granted for so many years had earned her respect. She had never considered how something so small and inexpensive could be so important to someone.

When her phone rang, she jumped and dropped the knife she was holding. Her hand went reflexively to her chest as the utensil clanged down on the marble counter.

"*Jesus*, Mary, and Joseph!"

It was Piper. Coco swiped her phone to stop the ringing.

"You scared the heck out of me."

"Hello to you, too."

Coco could hear her friend smiling. "Hi. Sorry."

"How did I scare you?"

"I was staring at—never mind. What's up?"

"You have to talk me into something or out of something, but I don't know which one I want you to do so don't say anything yet." Piper wasn't one for small talk, and often their conversations had no preambles; as if the two women had just paused an earlier conversation and waited to hit the Play button again. Piper took a deep breath on the other end of the line.

"Okay." Coco sucked the fingertip she'd just burned trying to pull the bagel slice out of the toaster.

"So you know that spousal support group I go to in Warwick?"

"Yeah."

Piper's husband Brian had had a heart attack on the Block Island Ferry a year ago. Block Island sat just thirteen miles south of the Rhode Island mainland. People liked to describe "The Block" as Nantucket sixty years ago because it was still unspoiled by wealthy New Yorkers. Brian had been traveling there to meet some old college buddies for a deep-sea fishing trip. The five men had chartered a cabin cruiser and planned to spend three full days on the boat. The other four had arrived on the island early and were waiting at the dock that day for Brian, hoping to upend him with rugby moves for old times' sake. They had no idea the ambulance waiting next to them in the ferry terminal parking lot was for their friend.

Brian had been talking about the trip for weeks. He was packed a few days before he left. He bought a new fishing pole, sunglasses, and a waterproof parka. The day of his departure, Piper dropped him off at the pier in Narragansett and forgot to kiss him goodbye because the cop there had blown his whistle at her and motioned with angry hand signals for her to keep moving because it was an active loading zone. She was too busy cursing out the cop to realize that Brian had jumped out and blown her a kiss.

"Text me when you get there," she yelled to his back through the open passenger window as the cop blew his whistle again. "I'm going, I'm going, asshole," she muttered.

Three hours later, instead of receiving a text from Brian, she received a visit from the state police. They told her that her husband had suffered a major heart attack fourteen minutes before the ferry arrived at the Block Island dock. He was dead before the paramedics boarded the boat with the skills and equipment they wouldn't get to use.

When the police cruiser pulled into Piper's driveway that Thursday morning, Coco had been outside repairing the mailbox that the town plow had bowled over again. Remembering that Brian was away on his trip, she hurried over and walked through the open front door in time to hear Piper's heartbreaking cry, and she reached the living room in time to see her friend fall to her knees on the hardwood floor.

Thirty minutes later, Piper had cried herself hoarse and Coco sank down beside her friend on the sofa to wrap her with a throw to keep her from shaking. Luckily, Katie was still at school.

"But I don't understand," Piper had finally said in a husky voice as she clutched her tissues. "Don't those boats have those . . . those . . . shock machines?"

"Yes, ma'am," the taller of the two policemen had replied. "Defibrillators," he said then looked at the floor.

"So why weren't they able to save him?"

The officers looked at each other then back at Piper. "Ma'am," the older of the two had said, "from what we understand, the unit . . . allegedly malfunctioned."

Seven months later, Piper settled a lawsuit with the ferry company, which was more than enough to pay off her mortgage, fill up Katie's college fund, and start her catering business.

Now Coco cradled her phone between her cheek and her

shoulder as she spread peanut butter on her bagel. "What about your support group?"

"Well, there's this new guy there and he is a real fox."

"I thought you said dating was dumb?"

"That was two weeks ago. I do what I want. Work with me. I've been out of the dating game a long time. I want to call dibs on him, but can I do that?"

"No, you can't," Coco said, shaking her head with a mouthful of bagel. "What do you know about him?"

"Not much. His wife died in some kind of accident. He has no kids and he lives in Warwick. He doesn't talk much, but I was the same way when I started there. And did I mention he's gorgeous? Tall and handsome. I mean there's handsome and there's tall and handsome. They're different."

"Piper, are you stalking a widower?"

"Yes."

"What does he do?"

"Works out of his house. I think he's an accountant. Or an actuary, whatever the hell that is."

"Yawn."

"Shut up. It's sexy. He's smart."

Coco laughed. "If you say so. Are you ready?"

"I think I am."

"I think you are, too. What's the worst that can happen?"

"What if I'm not his type?"

"Let me ask you something, Piper. Do you think he's a fruit washer or a fruit polisher?"

"What the fuck are you talking about?"

"If he wants an apple, do you think he washes it with soap and hot water? Or do you think he polishes it on his pants?"

"I don't know you, weirdo. Probably polishes it on his pants. Does that mean he's my type?"

"It was a trick question. You're everyone's type."

"Are you drunk?"

"No. And you're gorgeous, and sweet, and funny."

"You *are* drunk. I'm not sweet."

"Right." Coco laughed. "Can you ask him out? I'm not sure what the rules are for this kind of thing."

"I know. I haven't dated since the '80s, but I'm a liberated, independ—"

"No, dummy. I mean because he's a widower in a support group. Is that even allowed?"

"How do I know? There's no fucking manual. We're just a bunch of sad sacks who meet once a week in a church basement. Maybe I'll give it a few weeks and let him get obsessed with me first. Thanks, Coco. I knew I'd feel better if I called you."

"Sure," she said, knowing she hadn't helped at all.

"So how did it go in Dover today?"

"Oh girl, how much time do you have?"

"All of it."

So Coco filled Piper in on everything she'd learned about beds, coffee tables, and toasters. Then they discussed the cast of characters including the magician, the sweet seniors, the mysterious teenager, the disheveled dog, and the giant ogre who drives the truck.

"This sounds like a musical. Or a book." Piper laughed. "If you write it, I'll buy it."

"I would, but who would believe it?"

11

O n Coco's first day at The Mission as an official volunteer, she showed up bright and early with a box of coffee and a carton of doughnut holes. It had been a long time since her last first day of work and she figured bribery was the best way to ingratiate herself.

She took an empty parking spot next to the dumpster, locked the car with a chirp, and headed into the main office. This time she remembered to dress warmly in an old ski jacket, turtleneck sweater, thick jeans, James's old baseball knee socks, and warm boots.

"Welcome, Coco." Ernie smiled when she walked through the yellow door. Chewy came right over to Coco, but this time he kept all his paws on the ground. Even so, his head came to Coco's chest. *Sure, crappy clothes don't interest you*, she thought as she held the doughnut holes up over her head.

"Thanks, Ernie. It's nice to be here."

"Need a hand?"

"Yes, please." Coco passed the treats off to Ernie, and Chewy kept his eyes locked on the food.

"We'd better put this up on here for now." He placed the box on a bank of file cabinets next to the couch. "You remember Daisy and Bull?"

"Yes. Hi." Coco turned to the pair seated on the couch and smiled. Only the girl smiled back as the man looked her over from head to toe, arms crossed and expressionless. Daisy elbowed him and he looked down at her.

"I was thinking I could have you work here in the office with me today," Ernie said.

Thank God. Anything but riding in the truck with Mr. Happy, Coco thought.

"You can help with the phones, and we need to stuff a few hundred flyers about the yard sale into those envelopes." He pointed to some boxes on the floor in front of the desk.

"Sure thing."

"If you have any questions, ask anyone. So far it's just the four of us and Peggy today. I'll be right back." He left the three of them alone in the office.

Bull stayed on the couch while Daisy stood up and walked over to the empty chair beside Coco. She took a seat and grabbed the stack of newsletters, tapping them together on the desk to straighten the pile.

"I'll help."

Coco smiled and the two went right to work, Daisy stuffing the envelopes and Coco licking and sealing them one at a time. She thought about getting up to look in the kitchen for a damp sponge to use instead of her tongue, but she didn't want to attract Bull's attention.

"So, Sawyer told me a lot of you students come here from the high school to do service hours," she said to Daisy in between licks. "That's a great program. My daughter had to do volunteer work, too, but she was already helping at the animal shelter so that counted."

"That's good." Daisy shot a quick look at Bull and then picked up one of the boxes of envelopes and put it on her lap.

"So which high school do you go to?"

When the phone interrupted their conversation, Coco was the closest so she grabbed it and answered with a cheery "Hello, The Mission of Hope, Coco speaking." Then, "Uh no, I'm sorry, there's no Milton—."

"Hold up." Daisy reached her hand for the phone.

A confused Coco passed Daisy the handset, which she then passed over her head to Bull's catcher's mitt of a hand. He walked away with what now looked like a tiny toy phone to his ear.

Coco tried to catch Daisy's eye, but the girl went back to stuffing envelopes.

When Bull returned a few minutes later and replaced the phone in its cradle, a smile played upon Coco's lips as she teased, "So, Milton, eh? Is it an old family name? Is that why you go by a nickname instead?"

She watched him plunk his body down on the couch, heard the air exhale from the cushion.

"It's no big deal. Mine's a nickname, too," she said in an attempt at forced camaraderie.

He stared at her.

"I'm sure there's a good story behind the name Bull, right?"

Daisy looked at her big friend and smiled. "Oh, there is."

"Let's hear it." Coco smiled and licked another flap. She wanted to make an inroad with this man, and it would help if he shared something but she doubted he would.

"They started calling me that when I was a junior in high school."

Whoa. That was easy.

"It was a Saturday," he continued. "I was supposed to take the SATs."

Coco nodded.

"I was walking the long way down by the railroad tracks when I saw this van, one of those shuttle buses for the old folks."

Coco wondered what this had to do with his name.

Ernie came back in the room and Bull paused to look at him before continuing.

"The van was stuck on the railroad tracks and the door wouldn't open so they couldn't get out."

"Oh lord," Ernie said plopping down in his chair and shaking his head. Coco glanced at him then turned back to Bull.

"They were all screaming and yelling. I tried to separate the doors, but they wouldn't budge." As he said this he didn't move a single muscle in his body. So neither did Coco. "I went around the bus and checked both ways for trains then I put my shoulder against the back of it and pushed with everything I had. Before I knew it, the bus started moving. That's when I heard the train whistle."

Coco's eyes widened. Ernie was using the corner of his shirt to polish the lenses on his eyeglasses. *He's heard this story before*, she thought. Daisy continued stuffing envelopes, but Coco was on the edge of her seat.

"It was coming so fast," Bull continued. "I took another breath and pushed with everything I had. I pushed that van inches away from the track right before that train went flying past us with its whistle blasting."

Coco eyes were open as far as they could go and her hand was completely covering her mouth.

Bull was looking off into the distance as if reliving the moment. "Then the cops came and all the fire trucks and ambulances. They had to get all the old people water and blankets and whatever because they were all in shock."

"My god."

"When I finally got home, my parents came running out the door yelling at me because the school called and said I never showed up for the test. They were all mad and worried. So I told them my whole story."

"Unbelievable," Coco exhaled.

"Exactly," Ernie said almost to himself.

The silence hung heavy in the room. After a minute, Bull rose with effort off the couch.

"So," she said, "you got the name Bull because you were so strong. That's a better nickname story than mine."

He looked straight down into her eyes and said, "No, new girl. I got the name Bull because I made the whole thing up." He lumbered over to Ernie's side of the desk.

Coco's face turned bright red and she looked away. *What an asshole.*

Ernie kept his head down and pursed his lips. He looked like he felt sorry for Coco, but he also looked like he enjoyed hearing that stupid story again.

Bull nodded at Ernie and said, "Remember my old college bro I told you about? That was his mom on the phone. Needs to borrow the truck to move next week. Is that still cool?"

"Yup," Ernie said efficiently.

"You went to college?" Coco asked, sounding more surprised than she meant to.

"Uh-huh," Bull answered, annoyed. "Why did you assume I didn't?"

Coco looked up at the big man who paused beside her chair. She could feel the flush in her cheeks and the color spread across her face and neck like water on tissue paper. "Um . . . because you said you didn't take the SATs . . . so . . . I figured that . . . you know . . . you probably didn't go to college." For the love of God, why wouldn't the floor open and swallow her?

"I didn't say I never took the test. I said I didn't take it *that day*."

"I see. That's great. Way to go." Coco motioned with a closed fist. Then she tried to get back on track as Bull turned to leave. "Where did you go?" *Why, Coco, why?*

"Excuse me?" Bull asked without looking back.

"Never mind," Coco said.

Bull stopped walking and turned to face her. He leaned down

and put his hands on the desk. "Dartmouth," he said with a straight face.

"You're right. Sorry. None of my business." She looked back down at the box of flyers.

Bull narrowed his eyes to look at her and then slowly shook his head and lumbered away.

She turned to Ernie with a knitted brow and mouthed, *Dartmouth?*

"Yup. Got a perfect score on the SATs, too," Ernie said and went back to his paperwork.

Roll Tide.

For James's sixteenth birthday he wanted to go to his favorite burger place, a pub down by the marina called Topside. If East Greenwich had a gritty section, this small establishment was it. Once inside, visitors left behind the clean salt air only to be smacked in the face with the smell of beer-soaked floors and, if they weren't careful, flying darts.

In the warm weather, patrons had a clear view of Greenwich Bay, filled with dozens upon dozens of beautiful sailboats. But the number of parking spaces shrank dramatically in the winter when the bay emptied out and all the vessels were lifted from their slips and lowered onto supports in the parking lot, all pointing toward the water to begin their long wait for spring. White hulls towered above the parked cars, some enclosed in shrink wrap, some not; most with mast poles stretching thirty feet or more into the air like lollipop sticks. On windy nights like this, the sound of ropes slapping against the metal poles added an eerie quality to this watercraft forest.

Coco and her family had come to this restaurant so many times before, though, they didn't even notice the ringing anymore. After dinner, they walked four abreast back to the Jeep. James called "shotgun" because it was his birthday.

"Do you want to drive home?" Rex asked his son.

"No!" Coco and Charlotte said at the same time from the back seat.

"Why not? He's sixteen."

"He doesn't have his permit yet, Dad."

"Oh please. He's almost done with driver's ed."

"A complete waste of time," James complained.

"Rex."

Father and son looked at each other before Rex started the car.

"Wimps," James said.

"Do you want to live exactly sixteen years, bro, 'cause real driving is not the same as Major Auto Theft, or whatever that game is you play."

"Oh really? I didn't know that, *sis*," James said sarcastically.

"Not even sixteen for a whole day yet and your son is getting a smart mouth. Good parenting, guys. He also told me he's upset that you didn't throw him a sweet-sixteen party."

"Shut up."

"You shut up."

Coco ignored them. "Let's just hold off on the driving lessons until he gets the permit, okay?"

"Mom's the boss." Rex tapped his son's leg with the back of his hand as if to say *Mom's not the boss*. Coco caught the gesture and kicked his seat.

They drove out of the lot and headed along the waterfront before turning right up the hill onto Main Street.

A few blocks out of downtown, Coco suddenly yelled out from the back seat. "Stop! Go back."

"What's the matter?" Rex asked into the rearview mirror, slowing but not stopping.

"Turn around, Rex." She looked over her shoulder out the back window. "Please."

He did as he was told and the kids strained to see what their mother had seen.

"Is it an animal?" Charlotte said, searching the dark road ahead. But all they saw was big blue recycling containers and lots of trash for pick-up the next morning dotting either side of the road.

Coco took off her seat belt and leaned between the front seats, pointing to a spot. "Right there. Pull over by those chairs."

"What the heck, Mom?" James asked, more curious than annoyed. His father pulled off to the side just past a pile of furniture, an old gas grill with no cover, and an empty flat-screen box lying on the grass.

"So this is where Mom left your presents," he said to his son as his wife jumped out of the car. She walked over to the trash and bent down to inspect a pair of upholstered side chairs that had been left out beside the bins and boxes. She pointed at her son, still in the Jeep, and signaled him over with her index finger. He groaned and released his seat belt before slowly getting out of the car. He walked over to his mother, who handed him one of the chairs as she grabbed the other. They walked to the back of the Jeep. When Coco set the chair down and opened the tailgate, she heard the protest from the back seat.

"Oh my god, Mom. What are you doing?" Charlotte looked out the windshield of the car to see if anyone was watching, then she sank down out of sight with her seat belt cupping her chin. "That's so gross. It's someone's trash!"

Coco and her son fit the chairs inside and closed the tailgate. When they got back in their seats and buckled up, Rex said, "Leave Mom alone. They're not that bad."

"Dad! Gross," Charlotte protested again.

"Don't get attached. I'm taking them to The Mission tomorrow."

"Thank God," Rex said under his breath.

"Why would someone trash two perfectly good chairs?" Coco asked in disbelief.

"Why would someone take someone else's *trash*?" Charlotte looked at her mother as if she'd just drowned a bag of flying squirrels in front of her.

"There's nothing wrong with them. Someone could use them. Not everyone gets to go to the store to buy new furniture when they need it, Charlotte."

"Is that how you got my guitar stool?" James was starting to reconsider how much he liked the gift his family had given him earlier.

"Of course not. We got that at the dump," Rex said and winked at his wife in the rearview mirror as she kicked his seat again.

L ater that week, Coco lay low at The Mission and sat at Ernie's desk answering the phone and greeting visitors who came by to drop of donations. She did her best to avoid Bull, who worked mostly in the back unloading the truck he'd been using to collect old furniture.

Ernie, Daisy, and the Santiago family were in the Interview Room with the door open. Some of The Mission's clients were Spanish-speaking and many did not speak English well, if at all. Ernie told Coco that a lot of them came from places like the Dominican Republic, El Salvador, Guatemala, Mexico, and Puerto Rico.

Coco could not speak Spanish, despite taking it for four years in high school, and she wondered how Daisy and Ernie were going to communicate with this family. Perhaps they would convey their questions through charades or flash cards of beds, utensils, and furnishings. She heard the melodic sounds of Spanish and intermittent bursts of laughter coming from the adjacent room and supposed that Ernie's game of charades was doing the trick. After forty-five minutes, the group emerged from the room and into the office.

Coco looked up when she heard Daisy's voice.

"*Por favor siga a Ernie*," Daisy said, gesturing to Ernie. "*Y usted conseguirá su ropa de cama.*"

"*Sí. Gracias*," the older woman said with a grateful smile.

Then, to Coco, Daisy said, "Can you help me pull these things?" She held up the checklist.

"Sure."

Once they got to the Linen Room, Daisy tore the list in half and gave a part to Coco. Both set about collecting items from their own half of the list. After less than ten minutes, they had filled three shopping carts and began double-checking each other's lists. Once they confirmed that they had everything the Santiagos requested, they started pushing and pulling the three carts out of the room and down the hall to the loading dock, where the family's truck waited. Bull was there and wordlessly began moving the carts' contents into the back of the empty truck. Coco avoided eye contact with him until the last cart was unloaded, at which point the women pushed the carts back to the Linen Room.

"Wanna grab a snack?" Daisy asked.

"Sure."

They both walked to the little break room, grabbed drinks from the fridge and chips from a cabinet, and carried them to the Linen Room.

"We can unload these new donations and fold stuff in here if you want," Daisy said. At the foot of the table someone had left half a dozen paper shopping bags full of linens to be washed, folded, and shelved.

"Your Spanish is beautiful, Daisy."

"We speak it at home."

"How long have you been helping out here?"

"Uh . . ." She looked at the ceiling while she counted the time. "About *diez* weeks now." She held up all of her fingers and smiled.

She was a strikingly beautiful girl with a white smile straight out of a toothpaste commercial.

Daisy reached into the first bag. One at a time she removed towels in an assortment of solid colors, and placed them on the table.

"You must be all set with your service hours for school by now, right?" Coco took the towels from Daisy's piles and organized them into sets. Then she turned when the girl hadn't replied. "My kids only have to do twenty hours."

"I'm not doing hours for school," Daisy said without taking her eyes off the towels.

"Wow." Coco was impressed. "That's really nice of you to come here when you don't even have to. A lot of kids could take a lesson from you."

"Right," she said with a snort.

"I mean it. There aren't many teenagers who would give so much—"

"No," Daisy interrupted her. "I came here because I had to."

"Parents are making you? That's okay. Believe me, they're just trying—"

Daisy made a game show buzzing sound. "Wrong again." She smiled. "Look, here's the deal: If I didn't help here, I was going to jail."

"Oh," Coco said abruptly. She was ashamed how fast the young lady had turned from a shining example to a hoodlum. There was a long silence as Coco wondered what to do. Her experiences with Bull made her gun-shy.

"Don't you wanna know why?"

Coco really, really did. But she said, "You don't have to tell me."

"I think you wanna know." Daisy straightened up and took a seat on a stool by the worktable. "I got pinched for boosting."

"Oh," Coco said and looked down at her pile of towels because she had no idea what boosting meant but figured it was drug-related. Coco sensed that Daisy recognized the disappointment in her eyes because the teenager followed up her statement with some defense.

"It was something my little sister needed really bad."

Holy crap! This thug was supplying her sister with drugs?

"I was gonna pay the store back."

Okay, so boosting meant shoplifting. That's a dumb name.

"Anyway, the guy at the store caught me and then he called Ernie."

"Why Ernie?"

"The owner was a client here a few years ago. Ernie really set him up and made a big impression. He eventually got back on his feet and bought the little drugstore. He's from my neighborhood so he wanted to pay it forward I guess. Cut me a break. So Ernie brought me here and told me he could use my help. If I helped after school for a while, the guy said they'd call it even."

"How much longer do you have to come here?"

"Pffft. I was done a long time ago but I like it here."

Coco was getting impressed again. "Good for you. How old is your sister?"

"Fourteen. Her name's Annabelle."

"Well, I'm sure you had a good reason for what you did," Coco fibbed.

The two women worked wordlessly for another few minutes. Finally Daisy broke the silence.

"The kids at school were making fun of Annabelle because of her acne. So I wanted to get her some cream to clear it up. It sounds lame now, but that day I wanted to do anything I could to make her stop crying. I'd probably do it again. She's my best friend."

Coco wondered why Daisy didn't just ask her parents for the money, but knew it was none of her business so she nodded. She also thought of her own sisters and understood that, when you put a face to a problem, it makes it harder to judge. She admired

Daisy's honesty and the guts it must have taken to have everyone know her story.

"So you never got the cream?"

"Pffft. Get real. They found the one in my pocket, not the one in my boot." She smiled and Coco smiled, too.

And just like that, the cards were on the table and Coco felt like she was one of the family because Daisy had confided something so private to her. The shoplifter had brought her into the fold—but that liar Bull was another story.

A t the start of her second full week, Coco arrived to find Bull and Ernie standing in the front office; both smiling with their hands in their pockets. The younger man towered over the older one.

"And that's when I said to him 'I would, but that's my sister,'" Ernie said and threw his head back laughing.

When Bull laughed, too, she wished she'd been in on the joke.

"Morning, Coco," Ernie said.

"Morning." She smiled with a hurried, one-handed wave.

Bull reached into his jacket pocket, retrieved a knit hat, and pulled it down onto his head. His coat was zipped up to his chin and he reached for the keys on the desk. The two men started talking logistics. Bull had to drop off the truck at his friend's house, but needed a ride back to The Mission. Ernie couldn't do it because he was awaiting a client. Daisy wasn't around and Peggy needed to assist with the gathering of bedding and kitchenware for the clients.

"Can one of the guys at the other house do it?"

"Nah. No wheels."

"I'll do it!" Coco blurted out before she realized that she

would have to ride back alone with him. She wasn't afraid of him. Well, maybe a little. But she knew that he hated her. She also didn't know how far they were going to have to go in her car. She didn't know if he'd even *fit* in her car. *Shit. Shit. Shit.* It was no consolation that Bull seemed just as put out by her generosity. He grunted and, as he headed for the truck, he gestured for her to follow him by tipping his head that way.

"You're welcome," she mumbled as they walked in opposite directions.

Thirty minutes later, their caravan of two exited the highway and she was following him down a street in a Central Falls neighborhood that made her double-check her door locks.

Bull eventually parked the truck in front of a red, three-story multifamily house. Coco sat in her Jeep in the pawn shop parking lot across the street where Bull had told her to stay by pointing at her and then the ground when he stepped down from the truck. She understood this meant don't get out, and she didn't need convincing.

"I'm not a dog," she said, stewing.

Several young men with their hoods up sat on the steps of the house and parted like the Red Sea when Bull went up the porch stairs two at a time and rang the bell.

Coco looked around nervously while she waited. A woman pushed an overflowing shopping cart full of belongings down the sidewalk and then stopped to spit on the ground. Coco gagged and looked away. Closed storefronts were protected by metal grates, and a pair of sneakers tied by their laces hung from a telephone wire overhead.

After a minute or so, a few men emerged from the house where Bull waited on the porch. She watched as he and the three other giants went through their ritual of multistep fist bumps and half-hugs. When they were done, Bull handed one of them the keys to the truck, lumbered back down the steps much like she imagined an elephant would, and crossed the busy street to her car. There was no need to look both ways since traffic stopped for him to avoid front-end damage. The closer he got, the more relieved she became.

When he reached the car, he couldn't open the door. Coco fumbled with the locks and, after two tries and a Bull eye roll, she unlocked them. As he got in, she felt the Jeep sink under his weight. She figured it probably looked like a catamaran in a race from the outside now.

Poor tires, she thought.

"Ready to go?" he asked as he pulled the seat belt four feet out of its hiding place.

"Does an oil painting look better at a distance?" She smiled until he shook his head and shot her a look that sent her right hand fishing for the key already in the ignition.

She put the Jeep into gear. As soon as they heard her Aussie guy's first words, Bull stabbed the End Route button on her phone, which she'd positioned on the windshield clip, and directed her back to the main road himself with a superefficient number of words. He was taking up the whole center armrest so she overlapped her hands on the steering wheel at twelve o'clock. Resigned to the fact that he was not going to make small talk, or any talk, she was thinking about what she was going to make for dinner and when she was going to find time to read the last eighty pages of that novel before book club in two days.

When he spoke, it startled her. "Who was that?" he said with a furrowed brow.

"Who was who?" She turned to look at him.

"That dude we just passed? You waved to him."

"No I didn't." She was too nervous around him to explain the Jeep Wave. She'd done it without even thinking, the sight of the familiar grill triggering a subconscious peace sign to pop up. They continued riding along with the radio on so low that she had to strain to make out which song was playing. The only other sounds were Bull's mouth breathing and wind that fought its way in through the seam in the removable roof panels.

"What's that smell?" he asked, crinkling his nose.

"Oh. Pomegranate," she said, defeated.

"Jesus," he groaned. She could feel him staring at her for a good five seconds. Then he turned and looked straight ahead again.

They continued in uncomfortable silence for a few more miles. Then, there it was in the distance coming toward them: the slotted grill and round headlights of another Jeep Wrangler. *Shit*, she thought. Should she deny the oncoming Jeep the wave and preserve the peace, or should she wave and endure Bull's bullshit? The answer was obvious; of course she had to wave. She'd signed Chubby's contract. So she waved and so did the woman in the red Jeep.

"What the hell?" he asked with annoyance, as if she'd just punched him in the neck.

"What?"

"You did it again. Are you pretending to be so nice that you have to wave to total strangers?"

"Shut up."

"You shut up."

"I'm not pretending to be nice any more than you're pretending to be mean. I *am* nice. And you *are* mean." She reached for the radio dial and turned up Taylor Swift's "Bad Blood." *Perfect*, she thought.

After a few minutes Taylor's song finished and, as another pop masterpiece began, Bull reached over and slapped off the radio.

"Hey! My car, my radio!" She used the line previously reserved for her kids.

"Tell me something," he said. She waited, stewing. "Why do you have to constantly put yourself out there hoping other people will like you? Do you think you're that adorable?"

Silence. Shock.

"Is it some kind of social tic?" he continued.

She stared straight ahead as he needled her.

"When you were picked last for kickball—"

"I am *not*! I was *not*!" To herself, she said, *Breathe*. "It's called the Jeep Wave, for your information." He was only mouth breathing so she continued.

"Jeep owners wave to each other when we pass on the road. Not all Jeeps. Just Wranglers; you know, two doors, four doors; hard top, soft top. Doesn't matter. Just a little wave. I mean, sometimes it's a pain to remember, but then we wave to each other and it's kind of fun. Friendly. Like a members-only thing, you know?" She made the peace sign and turned to glance at him. The look on his face dissuaded her from explaining the subtle structure of the perfect wave. A good fifteen seconds ticked by in silence. Then he mumbled something.

"What did you say?"

"Forget it." He looked out his window.

"Tell me. What did you say?" She stole a glimpse to her right and then looked back at the road.

"Okay. You wanna know what I said?" His eyebrows moved up two inches on his forehead. "I said 'dumbest thing I've ever heard.'" Then he shook his head and turned to stare out the window again.

Now she was mad on her car's behalf, too. *What a big, fat, judgmental asshole.*

She considered finishing the drive in silence since they were less than ten miles from The Mission. But the anger bubbled up inside her until it had nowhere to go but out.

"Oh, *really*?"

She'd surprised him with a retort because he turned to face her. He seemed unused to pushback.

"But it's not dumb when you and your friends fist-bump each other and do that stupid rock-paper-scissors thing!" She imitated them with one hand in an exaggerated way with her tongue sticking half out. Then she mocked in a low voice that she hoped sounded tough. "'Yo man. S'up? Nut-in; s'up witchoo? Nut-hin. Cool.'" She could feel her face redden but she didn't care. "You think I'm dumb? You're dumb."

He wasn't speaking. Was he breathing? Was she breathing? She could feel his gaze on her profile. *That's okay. It's fine*, she said to herself. *Now he can hate me but at least it will be for a good reason. I'm over him. Of all the charities in the world . . .* Bull held the grab bar in front of him and used it to turn his considerable mass as far as he could in the passenger seat to face her. The leather creaked. The roof whistled more quietly now because she was decelerating in preparation for ejecting herself. *Here we go*, she thought. *They'll find my body in the spring.*

"I was wrong," he said. Coco couldn't believe he was apologizing to her. *Don't exhale yet*, she told herself. He continued, "Because now that comeback is the dumbest thing I've ever heard."

Against her will, Coco's mouth contorted as she fought the smile that was clawing its way out. *Don't do it, girl. Hold it.* Then, unable to hold it in any longer, she exhaled and her lips made that raspberry sound parents make on their babies' bare bellies. To her surprise, Bull began to laugh, too. It was a sound that seemed to come from inside a cave. His whole gut jiggled and he laughed deep and low like a big, black, baritone Santa. This lasted for a quarter mile or so. When the laughter finally ebbed, the smiles remained, and they continued on in chummy silence.

After another minute, she reached out and pushed the radio knob. Maroon 5's "Don't Wanna Know" filled the car. She took in a shallow breath and sang. "I don't wanna know, know, know—"

Bull slapped the radio off with his big paw and her singing voice filled the otherwise quiet car with one more "know."

"No," was all he said.

They traveled along another five miles before either of them spoke again. The plows and sanders had turned the beautiful snowfall of the night before into a safer but uglier version of itself. Snowbanks along the road were frosted brown with recycled sand, and the white precipitation, which had decorated branches, mailboxes, and power lines, melted in the winter sun. The spray from the road continuously splattered onto the Jeep's nearly vertical windshield and she pulled the wiper fluid lever every mile or so to clean it.

Her mind weighed two possibilities. Should she could dig in, root around, and confront Bull about why he'd been so mean to her? Or should she Febreze the relationship without removing the source of the stink? She impulsively chose the former.

"Why do you hate me?" Her words made contact but her eyes did not.

"Who said I hate you? I don't even know you."

"Well, I just thought since you—"

"I don't *like* you, but that's different."

She opened her mouth to speak and then closed it. *Wait. What?* "Why don't you like me? What have I done to you? We literally *just* met! Is this about that college thing?"

Bull rubbed the back of his giant head with his equally giant hand. "Check that. It's the *idea* of you I don't like."

"Oh, well now I feel better."

"Nah, it's not personal." He watched the houses go by his window. "It's just I've seen your type before."

"Excuse me?" She turned to look at him.

"You know, you live in an uppity town. You vacation on the Cape."

"Okay, Colombo, do you know anything else about me that isn't already a sticker on this car? I'm a Pats fan, too. You missed that one."

"Then how about this: You live in a big house, you have a nice pool with one of those big swan floats, your husband's successful. Right? You have two kids and a dog. You probably make crafts with the kids at school and organize playdates at some paint-your-own-pottery place. I'll bet you have one of those fridges with the digital frames in the door to show all your visitors your perfect life, too."

"Ha!"

He turned his eyes to meet hers.

"I don't have a dog."

"Whatever. Then a fancy cat."

She frowned.

"I'm just saying, you live this cushy life and then you get bored or you feel all guilty for your good life so you put in your one hour a week, do some humble bragging at your Junior League meeting, and everyone thinks you're swell." He said the last two words with a slightly offensive gay accent.

"That's not fair." It would only make things worse if she told him she was trying to save face with her book club.

"I know it's not." He shrugged. "It's just the way it is."

His speech hurt, but she couldn't come up with the words to defend herself. *Did she really care about the clients?* she wondered. Or did charity work mean something different in her town? Sure, the kids were always sent home with notices about can drives or winter hat donations. But, then again, they were also asked to vote for their favorite team to win the World Series by placing their donation in the donation box marked with that team's logo. Or the class that donated the most got a pizza party. Then they'd publish the results in the LISTSERV e-mail. Coco wondered for the first time why the schools felt the need to make charitable giving fun.

They rode the last few miles in silence. When they arrived back at The Mission, she parked and shut off the engine. As she turned to him, Bull got out and pushed his door closed hard.

"You're welcome," she said to the empty car.

15

T hat night Rex was attending a client dinner, Charlotte was next door at Katie's, and James was upstairs playing a video game. If Coco had had the energy, she would have booted him off it and forced him to do something productive. But luckily for James, his mother had had a shitty day and didn't feel like mothering at all.

After fixing herself a big bowl of chocolate chip ice cream with all the toppings, she padded down the hall to the family room in her fuzzy socks, sweatpants, and one of Rex's old hoodies. Houdini trailed behind her with swagger that said, *I know where you're heading and I'll meet you there.*

She had already washed off her makeup, swapped out her contacts for glasses, and put her hair up in a ponytail. Now she sat under a big mohair blanket on the couch in front of the TV. She was still upset about her ride with Bull. Part of her hated him for lecturing her as if she'd done something wrong. Or, better yet, lecturing her like she was some spoiled hedge fund wife. She wasn't. Her parents had made sure of that. Another part of her hated him for not liking her. She'd always felt so likable. He had no reason to hate her. She was helping out. She wasn't getting paid. She was friendly and accommodating. She brought them doughnut holes, for God's sake! He looked like he enjoyed a doughnut hole or twenty. She wasn't even a member of Junior League. But was he right about wanting to brag about volunteering? No. She didn't want to boast about it. She was just happy to fit in somewhere besides her house.

"Fuck him," she said. To herself.

Five minutes later, bratty thoughts were still running around in her mind like tiny ants. *I'm pushing fifty. I don't have to put up with this shit. I don't have to work there if I don't want to. I don't have to work at all. Or maybe I'll go somewhere else and be appreciated. Panera is always looking for help. This stupid mission was a big mistake. Thanks a lot, Piper. Damn you, closed animal shelter. I'll call Ernie in the morning. But, Ernie . . .*

"Damn that old man and his Dad charm," she said aloud. Houdini rubbed his face against her cheek because he thought she was talking to him. A long piece of fur stuck to her lip as she took a big bite of ice cream.

When she heard Charlotte come in the back door, she quietly spooned the next bite and tried to keep her whereabouts a secret.

"Mom . . . *Mom?* . . . Mom!"

"In here," she said halfheartedly with a full mouth. She still didn't feel like mothering. If she couldn't be alone, she didn't want to mother right now.

Coco heard Charlotte drop her keys on the counter and proceed down the hall in her boots.

Charlotte looked like a million bucks with her straight, glossy hair, black riding pants, tall black boots, and bright red pea coat. By comparison, Coco looked like only five bucks.

"Why are you sitting in the dark?"

Coco hadn't realized she'd never turned the television or lights on.

"I'm just relaxing."

"Uh-oh."

Her daughter's concerned face struck Coco right in the heart. Charlotte was an emotional, knee-jerk reactor with a fondness for hyperbole, but she had a huge heart and a sensitivity that was sometimes at odds with her confrontational personality. She watched her daughter shed the coat and boots and made room for her under the blanket.

"What's wrong, Mom?"

"Nothing. I'm fine."

Houdini left Coco's lap and walked across the top of the blanket to Charlotte.

"Yeah, you could probably sell that if you didn't have a gallon of ice cream in your lap."

Coco looked at Charlotte and then down at the bowl, admitting it might be more than the suggested serving size.

"Tell me." Charlotte laid her head on her mom's shoulder and used the spoon to help herself to the melting ice cream in the bowl. Despite her snit, Coco savored moments like this. There had been a stretch in the early teen years when she'd been convinced that her daughter would never again allow any physical contact between them because it was so uncool. Now, they hung out on the couch side by side on a regular basis. Coco wanted to tell every mom of an early-teen daughter to just hang in there because she would come back to you when she realized her peers weren't her entire world.

"It's no big deal."

"C'mon. Spill it." Charlotte used the tip of the spoon to scoop a chip off her chest and eat it as the cat curled into a circle on her lap.

"I think I'm going to find someplace else to help out. This place just isn't a good fit." *There. I said it out loud.*

"But why? I thought you liked it there."

"I did."

"So when did it go sideways?"

"This is going sound dumb, but I feel like I'm the new kid

trying to fit in. I haven't had to do that in . . ." She counted in her head. ". . . a very long time. And there's this guy there. He made up his mind before I opened my mouth that he wasn't going like me."

"First of all," her daughter said defensively, an index finger raised in defiance, "how dare he."

"I know, right?"

Charlotte was getting pissed on her mother's behalf. "Second of all, what's not to like?"

"Right. Everyone else is nice to me. Daisy's nice. Peggy's nice. Sawyer likes me. Ernie likes me, too." Coco felt like the angel on one shoulder was trying to talk her into staying.

"Is this mean guy gay? Maybe he likes one of the other guys and he's jealous."

Coco laughed out loud for the first time all day, visualizing that. "I don't think so."

"There has to be something going on. He doesn't know you well enough to not like you."

"Wait. What?"

"You know what I mean."

Coco continued. "He makes me nervous and I make him mad without trying."

"I've seen you do that."

"Thanks." Coco smirked.

"You're welcome."

"It's not worth it. I don't need this," Coco pouted.

"Oh god, you sound like you're in high school. Who cares about that jerk? He's just one guy. If you were me you'd say, 'Just ignore him.'"

"He's like eight hundred pounds." Coco took a melty bite and wiped her mouth with the neck of Rex's sweatshirt like a five-year-old. Charlotte was right. In the old days, she'd often given her daughter advice for how to get along with a difficult person and make the best of it. Then she'd make a mental note to punish the kid with a small pinecone. At least Charlotte had listened to her advice.

"You know what? You're right. He *is* an asshole. The world's full of them, right?"

Charlotte tried to stifle her laugh and it came out through her nose as a reverse snort.

"What?"

"Sorry." She looked at the cat and tried not to smirk.

"Wha-at?" she said, making the word into two syllables.

Charlotte cocked her head to the side. "When you swear, Mom, it's hilarious. It's like Houdini barking. Totally unnatural. But let's get back to the issue. What can we do to make this Moose guy like you?"

"Bull." She laughed. "His name's Bull. You know what? I don't really care."

"That's a lie."

"No, really. If he doesn't like me, I don't like him, either."

Charlotte licked the spoon clean and held it up to her mouth. Then she grinned at her mother.

"Don't." Coco reached for the spoon, but her daughter was faster.

"Oh, I'm gonna."

"It won't work this time."

"It always works." She laughed, holding the spoon to her mouth. In a low voice she sang the lyrics to Justin Bieber's song "Love Yourself".

"Stop, Charlotte."

Coco tried to keep a straight face. She didn't want to leave her pity party yet, but the pull of the pop song was dragging her out because this off-key Justin Bieber impersonator knew her Achilles' heel.

"C'mon, Mom. You know you want to." Charlotte held the spoon to her mother's mouth and bobbed her head. When she got nothing from Coco, she sang again even louder with her chin tilted up and the end of the spoon pointed at the ceiling. She was a horrible singer.

Coco watched her daughter with amusement. Then she groaned in surrender. She leaned over into the spoon and sang the next line. Out of the corner of her eye, Coco caught the reflection in the French doors of her husband walking toward them down the hall. Together they both sang the chorus about the mother who apparently likes almost everyone at the top of their lungs.

Rex spun on his heel and retreated.

"Coward!" Coco called out, and she and her daughter laughed again.

Charlotte lowered the spoon and said, "And, Mom, you know the song title really means f-yourself?"

"First of all, nice mouth. And second of all, yes."

"Just checking." Charlotte reached for another bite.

"And I *do* like everyone," Coco exclaimed, slapping the blanket and scaring the cat awake.

"Oh, wait." Charlotte spoke into the spoon like a reporter. "What about that kid who punched James in the stomach in school for cutting him in line at the slide?" She tilted it toward her mother for a reply.

"Except him." Coco leaned into the spoon. "I wanted him to die slowly and alone."

"It's only been ten years. I'm sure you'll put it behind you someday," Charlotte laughed and Coco did, too. "Mom," Charlotte said suddenly, spinning to face her.

"Whaaaaat?" She rolled her head back on the couch cushion in dramatic fashion.

"Remember when I was in sixth grade and that kid drew a picture of himself shooting up the school and left it in the locker room?"

"Yeah."

"And most of the parents kept their kids home the next day?"

"Yeah."

"And what did you do?"

"I sent you to school."

"Why? I'll tell you why. Because you said we weren't going to let that crackpot scare us. And you can't let this Bull guy scare you off, either."

Coco stared at her daughter. "I also had lunch plans that day."

"Mom!" Charlotte slapped her arm hard with her mouth wide open. "Are you serious? I could have died!"

Charlotte laughed again. "No. There were like twenty cops at the school. You were safer that day than you were there today!"

"Oh my god."

"But I see what you're saying." Coco appreciated the regurgitation of her advice. "Are you going to tell me to put my bowl in the dishwasher now, too?" She leaned over and hugged her little girl. "Love you."

"You, too. So you're not gonna quit?"

"No." *At least not tomorrow.*

"Atta girl. Oh, Mom, also, you know 'Cake by the Ocean' is about sex, right?"

"Yes, Charlotte." *Now I do.*

"Okay, okay," she said with her hands up. "Just don't want you to have any more awkward Facebook birthday posts."

"Thank you."

"And I really love that pop music cheers you up. You're like those toddlers on YouTube."

"Hee!" Coco tickled her daughter hard and pushed her off the couch onto the floor with her socked foot. "Go put this in the dishwasher."

16

"Hi, Ernie." Coco walked into the woodshop with a coffee in her hand to find him standing on the opposite side of the workbench wearing a thick blue wool sweater, glasses perched on his forehead.

"Hiya, kid."

"Brought you some coffee. And Peggy asked me to tell you that the clients coming tomorrow morning can't find a truck."

"Okay. Thanks. I'll talk to Bull about it."

"Better you than me."

"What do you mean?"

"He doesn't like me."

Gathering a small pile of screws in his open hand he said, "Why would you think that?"

"He told me."

Ernie laughed out loud without looking up. "Don't mind him. He's like Chewy, he's a lot to handle when you first meet him and then he backs off and lets you do your thing."

"I'll have to take your word for it." Coco took a seat on a cold metal stool and tucked her cold hands between her crossed legs. "What are you doing?"

135

The workspace in front of him was covered with a pile of small Allen wrenches, mismatched screwdrivers, bolts, washers, and an old wooden chair.

"Picked the damn thing up." He gestured to the nearly empty red toolbox beside him. "Latch wasn't locked." He took a long sip from the hot cup she'd placed in the middle of the wooden workbench for him. "Oh, that's good."

"Let me." Coco began gathering the washers and trying to remove a few screws that had ended up between the planks of the table, only their heads visible.

"Thanks. If you don't mind, I'll get back to this, then." Ernie flipped the ladder-back chair on its side and worked to reconnect its seat and frame. "So tell me what brings you here, Miss Coco?"

She was a little confused by the question because she'd already been coming to The Mission regularly for about two weeks.

"Just wanted to help out. The kids are at school and Rex is in New York today."

"No, I mean in the bigger sense."

She played with the collection of screws in her hand and stammered.

"Don't worry. I won't fire you." He smiled.

She took a deep breath before meeting his eyes. "To be honest, Ernie, I was having trouble finding a job." She gritted her teeth. "Does that sound bad?"

"Not at all. Why couldn't you find a job? You're a smart lady."

"I've been out of the paycheck game for a long time and didn't even know where to start. I felt like I didn't have any skills anymore."

"Lost your confidence, eh?"

"Sort of."

"Why did you want a job?"

She smiled weakly into her coffee cup. "I don't know. The

kids are getting older and I thought I should probably make myself useful."

"Why weren't you feeling useful?"

She laughed. "If this a therapy session, Ernie, I don't have my checkbook."

"No worries. All my time is free." He turned the chair over on its opposite side, flipped his glasses down onto the bridge of his nose, and began tightening screws.

She drew a breath and continued. "My family is pretty self-sufficient now. Kids are older. Not as much to do for them anymore." She started picking up the larger tools and placing them in the lower part of the toolbox. As Ernie turned the chair, Coco turned the tables. "What did you do for work before you became a therapist, Ernie?"

He whistled a long note. "Want the long version or the short one?"

"Surprise me."

Without stopping his work on the screws, Ernie said, "After high school I enlisted in the army." He smiled at her. "See? Never give an Irishman the option to tell the long version."

"Noted." She was reminded of how her dad loved to tell a long and colorful story, building up to a big finish. "So you were in the army . . ." she prodded.

"For four years. Finished in the MPs. It wasn't that bad because I took my dad's advice. When I was getting on the bus for boot camp, he said, 'Ernie, keep your head down and don't make any eye contact. And don't volunteer for anything.'"

Coco smiled at the irony of his dad's advice, considering what Ernie did now.

"Army wasn't bad, but I didn't re-up after the four years. It was time for a change and I needed to make some good money to keep my new bride Hope living in the manner to which she had become accustomed." He looked up and winked.

"Wow. You were young when you married."

"And immature. Marriage was a big adjustment, but we figured it out. We had a small apartment in East Providence. We had what we needed: table and a few chairs, a bed, a couch and a tiny kitchen. Can you—?"

She knew what he needed before he asked and handed him the pliers.

He took another long sip of his coffee and continued. "One night over dinner at our little table, right after I got out of the service, we both said we had news to share. Ladies first, of course, so Hope told me she wanted to start a family and then I told her I wanted to be a cop. I got my wish that same year." Ernie fiddled with the contents of the repacked toolbox, looking for a something else. She picked up larger pliers from the workbench and passed them to him. He smiled and used them to hold the nut while he tightened the screw. "But Hope's wish was harder to come by. After four or five years, we figured out that maybe a kid wasn't in the cards for us."

Coco nodded with sympathy but then remembered the photo of the girl by his desk and assumed the story wasn't over yet.

"In the meantime, my wife had taken a teaching job down here in Dover. She wanted to be near kids no matter what, so we moved here. Out to the country. Back then it was much more rural than it is nowadays. So was West Warwick where I was a cop. Pretty routine stuff: traffic stops, domestic disputes, shoplifting."

"So you're a retired cop? I wouldn't have guessed that."

"Not exactly. I told you it was a long story." He smiled. After wiggling the chair to test for loose screws, he scratched his chin with the back of his index finger. "One shift I was driving with my partner Vinny, and we heard a call come over the radio about a baby in distress." Coco's eyebrows rose, as she assumed this was the baby he would eventually get.

"We were a few blocks away and got over there fast. A teenage girl was screaming in the front yard. She brought us inside to the kitchen where this little girl, about four, was crying. There was a baby on his back in the middle of the floor. I figured he was a couple of years old, but I was never good at ages."

Coco had stopped what she was doing and sat with her arms crossed.

"The kid's got no pulse and isn't breathing," Ernie said. "Vinny's trying to talk to the older girl to find out what happened but she's still screaming. I'm on my knees looking the baby over to try to figure out what the hell happened." As Ernie told the story, he kept his focus on the chair he was repairing. "Then the little girl says, 'Baby ate the cookie' or something like that and started pointing to the table. I was trying to figure it out because he didn't look like he was choking. So I said to her 'What cookie?' Then the older girl, the babysitter, said, 'Oh my god, the cookies? From my bag? They have nuts! He's allergic. Oh my god!'"

"What did you do?"

"Back in those days nobody had an allergy pen. Vinny went outside to flag down the ambulance because we could all hear the sirens coming. But the kid was turning blue so I did what I had to do."

Coco froze. "What do you mean?" She had her hands tucked under her arms now to bring the blood back to her fingertips.

"I got a knife from the kitchen counter and a straw from a drawer and I did a what-cha-ma-call-it on him." He used the two screwdrivers in his hands to mimic his technique.

"A tracheotomy? Oh my god, Ernie!"

"Right there on the floor. Did it once before in the army. My buddy Mick taught me how. It's not that hard. It *is* very effective, though." Ernie said the last part as if he was telling someone about an obscure new diet he discovered.

"So what happened?"

"The kid got all his color back by the time the EMTs got in there."

"That's unbelievable, Ernie. You're a hero."

139

"Right." He laughed. "Tell that to the department." He grabbed the chair he'd just fixed and set it on the floor. It wobbled slightly so he picked it back up and laid it on the table again.

"What do you mean?"

Taking a seat on a stool opposite her, he said, "Turns out that kind of medical intervention is illegal. At least for cops it is. I lost my job. Well, I guess I quit before they could fire me. All the media attention was getting out of hand. It got to be a big distraction for the department. The big brass finally told me that the city wouldn't press charges if I just resigned. So I did. But the baby lived and that's what mattered."

"Press charges? Are you serious? You saved the boy's life!"

"Tell me about it. I had to wait to see if the parents were going to sue me. That was not fun."

"Did they?" Coco asked. As she watched him draw a deep breath, she already knew it wouldn't be a one-word answer.

"A few weeks later, they showed up on my front steps with their daughter and the baby. I had never met the folks until that day. The little kid was asleep on his dad's shoulder. I'll always remember he had this sweater on that had a brown dog on the back sitting in a red wagon. Hope invited them inside, but I was as nervous as a son of a gun." He pushed the chair aside and looked at Coco. "Turns out they were very grateful and they were upset that I'd lost my job. We talked for hours and hours. They ate lunch and dinner with us that day. The boy woke up and, man, he was a little charmer. By the end of the day, he was sitting on my lap and handing me books to read to him. It was something else." Ernie's hands were still and he stared at a spot on the workbench.

Wiping a tear away she whispered, "That sounds like a movie."

"I know it does. But it's all true. On my mother's grave." He made the sign of the cross on his chest.

Now Coco realized that the baby in the picture wasn't this little boy. "So did you guys stay in touch?"

"Sure did. We all became friends. Hope and Simone, the boy's mom, stayed especially close."

"How long has it been since you've seen the boy?"

Ernie looked up at the wall clock. "About an hour."

"What?" She made a face that said, *Uh-oh, the old man is losing it.*

"I saw him an hour ago." He gestured toward the loading dock. "It was Bull."

Coco tucked her chin to her chest and raised her eyebrows in disbelief. "Bull is the baby you saved?" she said in a voice an octave lower than usual.

"Yup. He's grown since then. Don't think he'd fit on my lap these days." He laughed.

"So is that why he helps out here? Because he feels indebted to you?"

"No, no," said Ernie. "It is quite the other way around. You've only heard half the story, my dear."

She stared at him, expectant.

"We'll save that for another day. Back to what we were talking about before." Coco felt that Ernie had shared that very personal story so she would feel comfortable talking to him.

He snapped his fingers and she jumped. "The Coast Guard House?"

"What?" She laughed.

"That restaurant in Narragansett. We met there, right?"

"Nope. Never been."

"That's a shame. You should go. The shrimp cocktail is delicious." He wore the expression of a doctor who can't determine what's wrong from the symptoms he's told. "I'll figure it out. You have that face."

Coco shrugged.

"So what do you want to get out of your time here at The Mission, Coco?"

For the hundredth time she was reminded of her dad. Always

trying to help. Gently. She took a deep breath and decided to be brutally honest, probably because if she were to close her eyes she might feel like it was her dad across the table from her right now and not Ernie. She exhaled.

"When I started looking for a job—now that's a long story—I thought just I wanted them to be proud of me."

"Who?"

"My husband, the kids, my parents. Even my friends."

Ernie nodded and said, "I don't know them, but I've been around a lot of people in my time. They're probably proud of you without a job, you know?"

She nodded, unconvinced.

"Most times, being around for the people you know is just as important as being around for the people you don't know." He gestured around the room with his hand.

"I agree. That's why I think it's probably something more."

"Go on."

"Now I'm thinking that maybe I'm the one who wants to be proud of me." She shrugged again, showing a hint of embarrassment. She'd been up for hours after eating ice cream with Charlotte trying to figure out if there was anything keeping her at The Mission besides Ernie.

He nodded slowly, watching her eyes. Coco felt like Wonder Woman's truth lasso was wrapped around her. She couldn't stop spilling her guts.

"I feel like we stay-at-home moms get to the point where all the pride we feel is by proxy: being proud of our kids' accomplishments or our husband's achievements, our new kitchen. But that's not the same as being proud of our own accomplishments."

"So you want something separate from being a mother and a wife?" He took a sip of his coffee.

She stared at the full toolbox. "No. But maybe in addition to. I love my family. But I guess I want to be proud of myself at the end of the day. Just myself. Maybe that's why I like to fix things."

"It's easier than you think to do something you're proud of."

"Oh, easy for you to say. You saved a baby with a straw!"

"I know. It was easy." He smiled. "But you can save a person's life in a lot of different ways, my dear. A lot of different ways. Sometimes all it takes is a gesture or a word, and I already know you are capable of that."

Coco considered this for a full minute in silence.

"Here we go!" Ernie flipped the chair over and placed it on the floor beside him. "What do you think?"

"It's beautiful. Thanks, Ernie."

He looked from the chair to Coco and winked. "You bet." He stood up and brushed his hands on his pants. "You should get back out front and warm up, kid. I've got to gas up the truck. Thanks for the coffee. I'm glad you're here." He got up and walked away.

"Me too," she said softly to his back as he headed for the office.

B ook club always took place on the last Thursday of every
month except December. It had started with a small group
of women in the neighborhood and grew and shrank as people
moved in, moved out, or simply lost interest, like Piper.

This month, the book club was meeting at Ava Logan's house,
a gigantic, brick colonial at the end of Goose Lane. It faced out
into the cul-de-sac like a general reviewing his troops; a vast,
multi-columned, perfectly lit and landscaped general. The street's
remaining ten houses faced one another on both sides like
minions. Ava and Johan's house was the best location on the
street because she never settled for less.

Ava had joined the book club when she first moved to Goose
Lane four years ago, and Petra Hingham, from whom Ava had
bought the house, insisted that she take her place in the rotation.
Word on the street was that Ava planned to attend only the first
book club and then bail, but one month stretched into another
and the redhead stuck around. Why was anyone's guess.

Whoever's turn it was to host got to choose that month's
book. On the upside, the book club forced Coco to read books
she might never otherwise have picked up. On the downside,

Coco had learned more than she wanted to know about Nazis, the Armenian genocide, Chinese foot binding, and tiger moms.

True to the stereotype, there was always a lot of gossip and a lot of wine. In fact, whenever it was Coco's turn to host, she always joked that she ended up with more bottles of wine than she started with, as each member greeted her at the door with yet another gift of cabernet, chardonnay, or rosé. It wasn't a complaint, just an observation.

Book club evenings began with an hour or even two of socializing and eating before the selection was even mentioned. Coco had long ago taken on the responsibility of printing discussion questions from the Internet ahead of time. Some months the women were very responsive, spending ten minutes or more on each answer as they went around the room throwing in their two cents. Other months she would read a complicated compound question and, instead of answering it, someone would yell out, "Pass." The interest in complex questions seemed to directly correlate with whether the ladies pre-gamed with one or with two hours of wine drinking before settling down to discuss the story, as consumption and diagnostic capabilities were inversely correlated.

The book Ava had chosen this month was *Gone Girl*, the suspenseful story about a cheating husband and a missing wife with a taste for violence. Coco had finished the book just minutes before ringing Ava's doorbell and, like every time Ava chose the book, all of them had actually finished because no one wanted to make her mad.

Once they ate their share of gourmet appetizers, Caesar salad, and shrimp cocktail in the gigantic chef's kitchen, Ava topped off each wineglass and ushered them into her inviting sunken living room.

The focal point of the room was a twenty-foot-tall fireplace made of stacked stone with a heavy, reclaimed wood beam as its mantel. Above the mantel hung an honest-to-God original

Picasso. A crackling fire danced, its dark-orange and amber flames licking the inside of the large cavity like a paid performer. In front of the fireplace, two oversized white slipcovered sofas faced each other. Genuine mink-covered, down-filled pillows littered the couch with intentional randomness. The paradox of Ava's inviting home and her intimidating personality wasn't lost on Coco. But she envied Ava for her hostess skills and ideal entertaining space.

Sitting between the sofas was a huge distressed-wood coffee table with missing chunks representing knots in the tree from which it was cut. The table held several multi-tiered plates of petit fours, assorted chocolates, and macaroons, as well as fat glowing candles of various heights. Smooth piano music emanated softly from the house's hidden speakers.

"What kind of person takes his dog's medicine?" Marybeth continued her conversation with Sophie as they each chose a seat.

"I'm just telling you what I heard." Sophie picked up a macaroon and an L-embossed cocktail napkin.

"Get outa here," said Coco.

"It's a real thing now. I just saw it online," Ava said, moving Sophie's glass to a coaster. "They get the vet to write a prescription for pain or anxiety medicine and then they take it themselves."

"Jesus," said Marybeth.

"Where's Johan? Is he hiding out upstairs?" Sophie asked.

"He's traveling," Ava said easily, taking a seat on the edge of a sofa cushion and smoothing her pencil skirt. "Visiting his mother. She's been ill."

"Sorry to hear that," Marybeth said.

"That makes one of us. He will be staying with her for a while."

Coco put her wineglass down on one of the abundant coasters and pulled the discussion questions from inside her copy of the book. As she cleared her throat to read aloud, Ava, who had chosen the seat across from her, asked a question of her own.

"Did you ever end up getting a job or was that just a performance darling?"

Coco looked up from her lap and blushed. She hadn't told anyone except Piper about The Mission of Hope, and her friend wasn't here to run interference. She worried what these women might think about how she spent her days now, deep in the bowels of a warehouse full of used bedding and furniture.

"I did find something. It's good. I love it," she said honestly and looked back down at the list of questions. "Okay, first question: In what ways did Amy's background—"

"Where did you end up?" Ava interrupted. "Is it someplace where you can move up the ranks or will you just rot at entry level until you die?" *Typical Ava*, Coco thought. *Always trying to keep people off balance while she ascertains who's creeping up the ladder far below.*

"It's this really great place a few towns over. A nonprofit. Are we ready for a question?" She looked hopefully at the other women, whose full mouths prevented them from saving her.

"So what is it, this nonprofit? I know them all," Ava said, mildly annoyed. After a moment she added, "Don't make me beg, babe."

"It's a . . . um . . . it's a . . . um . . ."

"Having a stroke?" Ava asked with hinted humor. The other women busied themselves by flipping through their copies of the book on their laps and searching for some imaginary passage. No one enjoyed being in Ava's cross hairs, but they did enjoy her tiny key lime mousse cups.

"It's a place that gives people furniture and linens when they are trying to get back to life."

"Dead people?" Ava seized on Coco's poor explanation.

"No. Alive people; refugees, veterans . . ." Coco wasn't doing a good job explaining because Ava was staring at her like a predator.

"So it's a charity?" Ava stated.

"Yes." Coco wondered why this poised creature across from her looked like she'd just stepped out of hair and makeup while Coco was sweating like a fat kid in gym class. "It's called The Mission of Hope."

Ava blinked fast a few times as if trying to center a wrinkled contact lens.

"Piper told me about it," Coco said for some strange reason. Maybe it was subconscious and she was trying to deflect, since those two women were at odds right now.

"Oh, that figures."

Bingo.

"I know that place!" Marybeth flapped her hand. "In Dover, right?"

Coco nodded, grateful for help.

"Yeah. I've been to their yard sale. It was awesome." Marybeth turned to Sophie. "That's where I got that desk you love." She stretched out her arms to explain the width of the desk.

"Good for you, Coco." Sophie smiled kindly.

Ava stared at Coco for five seconds without blinking, while her brow battled Botox in its effort to knit itself in confusion. Then she worked her finger in the air in front of her like she was doing a complicated math problem in her head.

Coco smiled a thank-you to Marybeth and Sophie. Then she felt braver and rested the paper with the questions in her lap. "It's actually really important what they do. It's no joke. They give furniture, bedding, and kitchen things to people who are just getting out of shelters or are down on their luck." Coco reached for her glass. "These people have nothing and The Mission of Hope helps them set up a home. And the best part is they give it all away for free."

"When did you get so charitable?" Ava asked.

Marybeth looked at Ava. Her eyes said, *What the fuck is your problem?* while her mouth said, "Are you charitable, Ava?"

"Oh, honey, I'd show you my tax returns, but I don't want to make you sad. For yourself."

Gulps of wine were heard all around the room. Marybeth added one last thing. "Well, I say they are lucky to have you, Coco. To The Mission of Hope." She lifted her wineglass for a toast.

"Mission of Hope." Ava laughed. "Sounds like *Mission: Impossible*, but whatever."

Coco made a face as if there was a noise hurting her ears that Ava couldn't hear. She leaned forward, put her glass of wine on the table, and sank back, finding some measure of comfort in the hug from the downy cushion. At least she'd gotten that announcement over with. She reopened her folded page of discussion questions.

"But how can they afford to pay you?" Ava couldn't let it go.

Coco closed the paper and exhaled. "They don't. I'm volunteering." She stared at Ava and started to get pissed.

"Oh," Ava said to her in a long and drawn-out way, like, *Oh, you didn't put in the effort to lose ten pounds, you just pulled on Spanx.* "Good job checking that resolution box, Coco." She snorted into her wineglass.

If Piper were here, she'd scratch your emerald fucking eyes out, Coco thought as she stared at Ava. Was it only her imagination or had Ava become meaner lately? The glaring contest ended when the doorbell rang and Ava rose gracefully to her feet in one fluid movement. The remaining women glanced at one another and shook their heads.

"Don't listen to her," Sophie said in what would have been a brave display of solidarity if she hadn't whispered it and looked over her shoulder in the direction of the front hall.

Ava returned to the room with latecomer Tracy, who was

breathless with a story about the family of deer she almost hit on the way to Ava's house.

"He just stood in the middle of the road staring at my headlights."

My spirit animal, thought Coco.

Once the wild animal tales ran their course, and determined not to allow Ava's line of questioning to resume, Coco cleared her throat as a signal and asked the first of her twelve questions.

As the night wound down, she announced her choice for next month's meeting at her house. Then, not wanting to be the last person there with Ava, she made an excuse about having to make sure James had finished his (fictitious) biology project, and fled.

18

"Coco, c'mere for a sec," Sawyer called out as she passed near him in the warehouse. She was pushing a blue mattress cart full of linens to wash and he was holding a brass lamp in either hand like some weather-beaten St. Pauli Girl. She rolled the cart out of the way and walked twenty feet to where he stood.

"Hi. What's up?" She rocked forward on her feet with her hands in her back pockets.

"Can you give me a hand? Fred's not in and I need to fix these. Our lamp inventory's pretty low."

"Sure." She followed Sawyer into the workshop, where he placed the lamps on the bench.

"These cords are not up to code and I have to replace them before they burn someone's house down. I need to strip these wires and can't see 'em too well because I left my glasses at home. How are your eyes?"

"Pretty good." She inspected the lamps and their cords.

He held up a small tool with red rubber-wrapped handles. "This is a wire stripper."

She smiled. "I know."

"Okay. Good." He pushed one lamp in front of her. "I need to use it to cut the plastic casing off the last inch here. Underneath the casing are two wires that—"

"It's okay," she said. "I know. My dad taught me a thing or two."

Sawyer was taken aback. "Oh, really?"

"Really," she said with a smile.

"Well, be my guest, then." He gestured dramatically at all the tools and supplies between them. "Don't worry, whatever you break, I can probably fix." He winked.

"Gee, let's see what I can remember." She squeezed her chin, caressing her imaginary goatee. "It's been a while." She studied the tools and equipment on the big table. Picking up a pair of pliers, she pulled the handles apart with two hands.

When Sawyer opened his mouth to correct her, she said, "No. No. I can do this."

Then she picked up a flat-edge screwdriver and went about detaching the socket by disconnecting the wires from the screws on either side. She used the wire cutters to sever the cord near the lamp's base and pull it out. Sawyer crossed his arms. His big mustache hid his lips, but she could tell he was smiling by the squint of his eyes.

Her hands kept working as she reached for the new cord and split its two insulated wires apart. She used the wire strippers to remove an inch of casing off each of their ends. Then she twisted the ends of the old and new wires together to make a rope and pulled it up through the base. Next, she untwisted them and discarded the old cord. She made a quick under-writer's knot to prevent the cord from being pulled out if it were to be jerked on the other end, and then attached the neutral wire to the terminal screw and the hot wire to the brass terminal and tightened both. After smoothly snapping the socket back onto the stem, she replaced the sleeve and the shell, plugged the lamp into the power strip on the bench, and held her right hand out. Sawyer put a lightbulb into her palm and she screwed it smoothly into place and pushed the power toggle switch.

When the blinding light of the uncovered bulb lit up the space between them, she curtsied and said, "Ta da."

Sawyer removed his baseball cap, smoothed his thick hair back with one hand, and replaced the cap on his head. "Well, look who thinks she's a magician now."

"I told you my dad taught me some things."

Coco smiled, thinking of all the times her dad had used simple and difficult repairs to patiently explain every step to her. Sometimes he would fix something and then unfix it so she could do it herself. Even after she got married, he'd regularly stopped by to repair this or that and Coco always kept him company, observing his technique and his tool usage and making him a grilled cheese afterward while he played with Charlotte and James. Sometimes she would call him on the phone and explain her DIY dilemma and he would talk her through it like a seasoned 911 operator; calm, measured, asking all the right questions. After a while, she knew just enough about plumbing, electricity, spackling, and various other repairs to fix things herself and save a few bucks along the way. "If you have patience, you can do anything," he would say.

When she and her sisters sold the family house last year, her dad's workshop in the basement was by far the hardest room to say goodbye to. Back when she was a young girl, her dad had worked in it every weekend rewiring her mom's favorite lamp, or soldering somebody's broken necklace, or building a bat house and things along those lines. Every tool was hung neatly on the pegboard and every imaginable screw, nail, wall anchor, and washer could be found in his card-catalog-style metal storage drawers.

"He did a good job teaching you."

"Thanks. Ernie reminds me a lot of him. Same smile. Same temperament. Same helpfulness. Plaid-shirt-off-his-back kind of guy. It's such an overused expression, but for some people it's literal. You know what I mean?"

"I do," Sawyer said, turning off the lamp and reaching for the other one. "Mind if I do this one?"

"Go for it," she said, quickly stripping the ends of the wires like he'd originally asked her to do and pushing the tools across the table to him. "Don't worry, whatever you break, I can probably fix."

"Touché." He grinned.

She watched him work for a minute before asking, "How long have you known Ernie?"

"Long time. A really long time," he began. "He married my sister, in fact."

"Really!"

"Yup. Hope and Ernie were high school sweethearts. I was a year behind them."

Coco smiled, thinking Sawyer and Hope were the same age difference as her kids. "So they've been married a long time then. She's lucky."

"Yes and no," he said.

Coco frowned. She couldn't imagine what he could say that would change her impression of Ernie.

"This is no secret so I don't think I'm talking out of school," he said looking through the doorway of the shop and out to the warehouse. He abandoned the lamp repair and sat down on a stool. "Did Ernie tell you about how he met Bull and his family?"

She nodded, "Uh-huh."

"I'm not surprised. He loves to tell that story."

"The cookie. It's unbelievable how those two families came together."

"Yep. Well, his wife—my sister Hope—and Bull's mother, Simone, became really close friends after that. Bull's father, Gus —may God rest his soul—and Ernie were also friends, but they saw less of each other than the wives did. After Ernie left the force, he got a job driving a heating oil truck. That has nothing to do with the story, but I remembered that just now. Anyway, Bull's mother found out about Ernie and Hope's bad luck in the baby department. You know how you women talk to each other about incredibly private and personal things all the time?"

Coco nodded, unashamed. "You guys make us like that because you're not good listeners."

"Fair point," he conceded. "So a few years after Ernie gave Baby Bull a blowhole, Simone told Hope about this sixteen-year-old girl she knew in her neighborhood who was pregnant and looking for someone to take the baby. The family was poor and couldn't afford another mouth to feed. You know how it goes?"

Coco nodded but she didn't know how it goes.

"Hope was beside herself with excitement. It's all she talked about for a week straight. I knew from the minute I heard about the baby they would be adopting it. Ernie was stubborn because he's Irish, but Hope was even more stubborn because you women are unbelievably pigheaded sometimes. No disrespect."

Coco smiled. "No disrespect."

Sawyer went on to describe what Ernie had told him about the first time he and Hope went to visit the pregnant teenager, Cha'relle. Hope had been speechless when she'd seen the condition of the house. Six kids living with their mother in a one-room, fifth-story apartment with no elevator. Cha'relle was the oldest. The youngest was still in diapers. The four littlest ones shared one twin mattress on the floor.

"They had to sleep sideways on the thing so they could all fit. Cha'relle was eight months pregnant then, and she and her twelve-year-old sister shared another twin mattress on the floor. Their mom slept on the couch. It wasn't even a pull-out couch. Cha'relle's dad was gone, but I don't know if he was alive or dead. Hope told me she cried that night to Ernie after their visit. By that point, Ernie knew he was getting the kid. Simone was a lawyer and she helped Hope with all the paperwork. Two months later, baby Vivian was born and they took her home."

Coco smiled. She loved babies and happy endings.

Sawyer continued. "She was the most beautiful baby ever born. Enormous brown eyes, pouty red lips, and these fine-looking long fingers. She was friendly to everyone, let everyone hold her. Even a troll like her Uncle Sawyer. She was the happiest kid I ever knew."

For the next ten minutes, Coco listened to him tell stories about Vivian and how she brightened up everyone's lives. From her part as a spoon in the school play, to her talent for writing, to her habit of bringing home live toads, she was clearly the light of their lives.

Sawyer smiled. "You should have seen Hope's face when she found out they had to buy live crickets to keep Vivian's toads alive! But she did it, God love her. She kept a bag of them in the fridge. Crickets, not toads." He laughed, reveling in the simple memory. "She would have moved a mountain for that angel."

He told her how the mom and daughter were attached at the hip and how Ernie had loved every minute of it. Coco was reminded of life with a little girl and that mother-daughter bond. She had felt the same with Charlotte and still did. Recently she had thought about how she wished she could turn back time and spend a single day each with her children as toddlers. Just one day. Life was crazy back then changing diapers, cooking for picky eaters, baby-proofing the house, and trying to keep it reasonably clean. She would give all the money she had to be able to play with her little babies again; to pinch those fat cheeks, feel their warm breath as they slept on her chest, and hear those silly giggles.

"As happy as Hope was, though, she couldn't forget Vivian's birth mother and her family, you know," Sawyer continued, snapping Coco out of her daydream. "We all spoiled the little darling, but it always made Hope feel guilty. When Vivian was around a year old, my sister bought two sets of bunk beds and a full mattress and had them delivered anonymously to Cha'relle's apartment. And believe me, Ernie and Hope didn't have a lot of money. That didn't stop my sister. When Vivian was old enough to go to school, she and Hope created blanket drives in the schools here in town and collected money to buy mattresses. She always said, 'We have to get these people up off the floor and help bring back their dignity.' She was right, of course. Who wants to get up and go to school or work after they've just slept on a hard, cold floor all night?"

Coco nodded solemnly.

"Anyway, to make a long story short, their efforts doubled and tripled and within a few years, they'd raised enough money to give away more than a hundred mattresses. It was really something."

"Ernie explained something about that to me when I started here," said Coco and wondered how this story could possibly have a downside. "I would love to do something similar to that with my Charlotte. Maybe I could speak with Hope or Vivian someday about it."

Suddenly Sawyer's face became serious and his expression darkened like he'd tripped over a mental wound that was scarred over. His eyes fell to his hands, which were clasped in his lap. Coco couldn't remember at what point Sawyer had stopped working on the lamp.

"What?" she asked softly.

He inhaled, held the breath, and stared up at a corner of the ceiling. When he exhaled, he began again. This time there was no evidence of pride or enjoyment of a favorite memory. "Two weeks after Viv's tenth birthday, my sister took her to the doctor because she was pretty sick; tired, vomiting, confused. Come to find out . . . she had a brain tumor." Sawyer's gaze met Coco's and both sets of eyes began to water. His voice lowered to a whisper and he nodded slowly. "Doctors gave her less than two years; said there was nothing they could do because it was covering her whole brain like an octopus."

Coco bit her lip trying to ward off the blow she now knew was coming. She couldn't think of a single thing to say so she started picking at a splinter under the edge of the wooden workbench.

"She didn't make it to eleven." He shook his head. "That was thirty-six years ago this summer . . . wow."

Coco inhaled sharply and Sawyer paused. She heard the crack in his voice and was struck by the emotion he showed even all these years after losing his niece.

"Little Vivie knew she was going to die. She heard the doctors talking and felt herself melting. That was her word: melting. Such pain she was in. In the end, Ernie and Hope had to be honest with her. She was so smart. My sister used to lie in bed with her and talk about how everything was going to be okay and that she would be happy in Heaven and all the pain would finally go away. Sometimes Vivian was strong and that made Hope strong. But sometimes Vivian just cried and cried and said she was afraid."

"I'm so sorry."

"Yeah. One night toward the end, she told her parents that she would be lonely and scared because she would miss them and she wouldn't know anyone in Heaven. Can you imagine?"

"No," Coco whispered. "What a nightmare."

"And it gets worse," he said staring at the door. "Two days after Vivian died, my sister sat in the running car in the garage with the door closed and..."

"No," Coco gasped.

"She wanted to be with her baby girl. Ernie found her that night when he got home from making Vivian's arrangements at the funeral home. He buried both his girls together three days later. In the same casket. Because that's what Hope said she wanted in her goodbye note to him."

"Oh no," she whispered. As a mother, Coco fully understood the bond and her heart broke for Ernie and his family. And Sawyer. She thought of the decades she'd had with her own parents, but they still weren't enough.

Even just moving out of the house when she was twenty-five had been emotional. Her mom had cried for days and Coco was only moving twenty minutes away. Her dad was more stoic about it. He was happy she was in love, but sad to lose her to another man and another home.

She remembered that weeks before she got married, she'd been watching out the front window of the house in Reading waiting for her then fiancé Rex to come down the street in a rented U-Haul. They were going to move her stuff to their new apartment, which she wasn't going to live in until after the honeymoon. While she waited, her dad had come in the back door from the yard and stopped in his tracks as he looked over the piles of belongings Coco had collected from all corners of the house, half of which did not belong to her. In addition to her own clothing and things, she had commandeered a coffee table and lamp from the attic that had belonged to her grandmother, towels from the linen closet, a portable stereo from the playroom, a painting from the dining room, and a bookcase from the basement. She stood before him, embarrassed, and finally managed to say, "Do you see anything you'll miss, dad?" He looked her straight in the eye and said, "Yes. You."

Coco thought about what Ernie had said about Hope's mantra. It was sad, but completely understandable, that the woman was incapable of finding the shine after her daughter's death. No one would be able to. She shuddered at the mere thought of losing one of her kids.

"Anyway, that's why he officially started The Mission of Hope." Sawyer's words snapped Coco back to the present. "After he lost his girls, he wanted to do something to keep their memories alive. Three decades later and here we are." Sawyer rose and cleared his throat for a second time.

Coco dropped the giant splinter she had pulled off onto the floor. "I don't know what to say."

"Wanna hear the dumbest thing? I think about Vivs every time I see those little three-foot Christmas trees for sale at the store. Cut down before they even had a chance." He exhaled loudly.

She looked up from her lap. "I'm sorry."

"It was a long time ago. Still gets to me, though. My softball buddies tell me I'm turning into a pussy. Pardon my French." He pushed the tools back over to her side of the table. "Why don't you do this other one, show-off? I got to see a man about a horse."

"Sure." Coco watched him walk off in the opposite direction of the restroom and considered the life Ernie led and the losses he'd had to deal with. Yet he still had a positive outlook. It took a special human being, she thought, to carry the emotional load he'd had to carry and still work so hard to improve the lives of others. Maybe his past made him realize what was important. Or maybe since he couldn't help his daughter or his wife, he decided to find the shine by helping others with the charity his wife had started.

19

As was typical in New England in early March, the sun was completing its full descent even before dinnertime. Charlotte was at practice and James was getting a haircut and a burger with his father, so Coco was in no particular rush to get home. She and Daisy were finishing up in the Linen Room before they both left for the day.

Peggy had told Coco the day before that The Mission survived on private donations like those from a couple named Bob and Nuala Sheehy. Each year around their wedding anniversary, they would stop by the office and ask Ernie what they were in the greatest need of. This year it was twin sheets. So, in place of an anniversary present to each other, the couple returned with two dozen new sets of twin sheets. Daisy was now standing on a step stool adding those sheets to the top shelf, where they would wait for their new owners.

Chewy was snoring in the corner on his bed, a futon mattress someone had donated that wasn't up to the quality Ernie required for his clients and had been relegated to a pet bed. Chewy's big hairy body was fully on the bed and only his head was on the cool cement floor.

Coco folded the last of the comforters that had come out of the dryer and labeled them with their sizes on masking tape. Now she was sorting through more of the boxes that had arrived that day. As she pulled out the things inside, she put them into different piles on the table in front of her. The utensils she wrapped into sets of four and six and tied with rubber bands. She pulled out a white ceramic teapot with ivy painted on it, which she placed the on the table with the coffee pots, and a cookie press, which she added to the crate of items for the yard sale next month. Yolanda had told her that anything that wasn't practical for a person setting up a home could be used to make money at the yard sale. They would use those proceeds to buy new toasters and mattresses.

"Yikes," Daisy said as she looked down at the cuckoo clock that Coco pulled next from a box. "That's hideous."

"A hot potato."

"A what?"

"You know, something no one wants so it just gets passed back and forth. Didn't you play that game as a kid?"

"I have no idea what you're talking about."

"Never mind. I'm dating myself." She put the clock back in the box, sealed it up, and wrote "Yard Sale" on the top with a red marker. She opened the next box, which was about the size of a microwave and half as heavy.

"Whoa! Check it out," Coco said as she looked into the box, which had been heavily taped before she used scissors on it.

Daisy climbed down from the step stool and walked over to the table. "What is it?"

Coco carefully set aside the yellowed newspaper to expose a collection of snow globes in varying sizes. "Holy cow."

"Sweet," Daisy said, reaching into the box to pull out a snow globe. She turned it around in her hands. It was about seven inches tall including the base. Inside was a cardinal perched on the end of a branch, his mouth open in silent song.

The two began to remove each one from the box. The *Providence Journal* pages they were wrapped in were dated 1990. Coco smiled when she pressed out the wrinkles and read the headline out loud. "'Mandela is Freed.' Wow, remember this?"

Daisy leaned over the counter and looked down at the paper.

"I was born in the next millennium." She pointed to the date. "So, no."

"That's depressing."

"Yeah, for you." Daisy laughed, showing her beautiful white teeth. "Was he stuck in a mine or something?"

"Mandela? No." Coco grabbed her phone from her back pocket and tried to google the former South African president, but the Wi-Fi connection was too slow. "Never mind," she said as she watched Daisy unpack the rest of the box.

When she'd finished, there were nineteen snow globes on the table between them. The biggest one, about the size of a duckpin bowling ball, had within it a castle surrounded by pine trees. It was also a music box. Coco wound it up and set it down. As the snow fell on the castle, the sweet notes of some classical piece gently chimed away as the globe rotated slowly on its base.

Coco looked up to smile at Daisy but the teen had her gaze fixed on a globe in the middle of the collection. She picked it up with both hands as her eyes grew wide. Inside the glass dome, a family was frozen at one moment in time enjoying a day of sledding on a tiny hill. The mother pulled a snow-suited baby on a sled. The dad was swinging another child in a pink coat around by her hands, her mouth open in a squeal only those inside the dome could hear. The breeze was blowing her dark hair straight out behind her. A small dog was in midstride with his head and tail held high and a pink hat in his mouth.

"Cute," Coco said as her eyes moved back and forth between Daisy and the snow globe.

"It's perfect," Daisy said. Then she seemed to snap out of a dream and placed the globe back on the table. She walked slowly over to the step stool, climbed up, and resumed what she'd been doing.

Coco considered saying something, asking if Daisy was okay, but she chose instead to mind her own business and repacked the snow globes in the box. This collection wasn't exactly what she would consider a hot potato, but she didn't think it was something The Mission's clients would be clamoring for when they came in search of beds to sleep on. She taped the box closed, wrote "Yard Sale" on the top, and pushed it off to the side.

"Eeeeuuwww," Daisy said from atop the stool, pinching her nose closed and covering her mouth with the same hand.

It took a few seconds before Coco caught wind of the dog's fart and then she pinched her own nose closed. She looked at the sleeping giant. "What is Ernie feeding that dog?"

"Today it was a burrito. Yesterday I think it was steak and cheese. Bachelor food."

"Well, no wonder. I'll pick up a bag of real dog food tomorrow."

Bull popped his head in the doorway. "Whoa. Nice work, ladies," he said waving his big hand in front of his face.

"Very funny," Coco replied. "It was the dog."

"Sure it was. Can you two give me a hand?"

Since the Jeep ride to Central Falls, she and Bull had managed to have a distant but professional relationship. She had given up trying to be buddies with him when she realized he only had room in his heart for people who shoplifted zit cream or jammed straws in his throat.

Daisy jumped off the stool and she and Coco followed Bull and his untied boots out the front door. Someone had dropped off furniture and left without ringing the bell while Chewy was on a break, farting up a smokescreen. There were two bureaus, a recliner, a tall curio cabinet, and a few tables outside. It had started to snow and Bull wanted to get the wooden pieces in before they got wet.

"I got the big stuff," he said. "Just grab that table." He pointed to a square coffee table. Its awkward shape required a two-person lift.

"Roger that," Daisy said, tilting her head back, eyes closed and mouth open, to catch some of the big wet flakes on her tongue.

Bull heaved the bureau up on top of his head and headed around back to the larger door.

Daisy reached for one end of the low table as Coco lifted the other. They said "*Ooof!*" at the same time, acknowledging its weight. Coco walked it forward as Daisy walked it backward. It wasn't a bad piece of furniture. Coco examined the top as they inched it to the door. It must have been an impressive table at one time, with its ornate carvings in the corners and on the legs. A big compass rose created by two different types of wood radiated from the center. The finish had been damaged by scratches and water rings, but it was nothing that Sawyer and the guys couldn't fix. Someone was going to love this one. Coco contemplated how they were going to angle it once they got to the front door.

Without warning, Daisy dropped her end. The two legs on her side crashed to the ground and snapped off midway up. Coco yelped as the wooden apron on her own side slipped and scraped her palms and fingers. She let her side down to the ground and looked at her hands. The skin was torn, but they weren't bleeding.

"What—?" Coco looked up at the girl.

Daisy stared over Coco's shoulder into the darkness, her eyes widening as the color drained from her face. Coco knew there was bear behind her. She'd heard stories on the local news about people who walked out to their open garage to find a black bear tearing through their garbage cans. Her adrenaline surged and she eyed the broken table legs on the ground. She leaned slowly down to pick one up and then spun around fast, holding her arms in the air to appear bigger like the anchorman had told her to.

As the dark figure approached, though, it was on two legs, not four. She could make out the shape of a man. Confused for a moment, Coco didn't know if this was a better or worse scenario than the one on the news.

As her heart beat out of her chest, he walked toward them and triggered the motion-detecting floodlight in the corner of the building. When the glow illuminated him, she realized he stood about six feet tall with dark hair and dark eyes and wore a black ski jacket and faded jeans. He had the height of a man, but lacked the bulk. She guessed he was closer to James's age than Rex's. Just a kid.

"Daisy," he said. "I need to talk to you." His impatience held a hint of menace.

Daisy came next to Coco's side and said, "Please, Louie, not now." Her voice was filled with such emotion that Coco's attention pivoted from the boy to Daisy.

He took a step toward them and Coco pushed the girl behind her with her free hand. For each step he took step closer, they took one backward.

"Did you follow me?" the teen asked the boy.

"You won't text me back. You won't answer your phone. God knows you're never home, and we both know why that is, right? You didn't leave me any choice, baby. I need to see you."

"Please. Not now." Daisy glanced quickly at Coco. "I can't talk."

"I don't know what's going on here, but you need to leave. Right now," Coco said in a firm voice as she reached between herself and Daisy for the phone in her back pocket. It wasn't there and Coco cursed the fact that she'd left it on the table in the Linen Room. *Damn Nelson Mandela.*

The young man didn't move. He just stared past Coco at Daisy. The women weren't very scary and he clearly had some unfinished business with the younger one. Coco tried to figure out what to do next. Maybe she'd know if she'd watched more cop shows and fewer reality shows. *Damn* Vanderpump Rules.

"I can't do this right now. Just go. *Please.*"

"Go!" Coco said loudly and she took a step forward brandishing her bear club in the air with her right arm. Daisy held on to the bottom of Coco's sweater.

Louie stared at Coco. He made a frustrated grunting noise before he gave a quick glance at Daisy and, all of a sudden, turned on his heel and walked back up the street.

"And don't come back or we'll call the police!" Coco yelled shrilly.

"Trust me, you won't," he said over his shoulder as he faded back into the darkness.

What a rush. The adrenaline was coursing through her body. She was a little surprised that he'd left, but definitely relieved. She had no idea she could be that intimidating. It felt terrifying, but exhilarating at the same time. Daisy let go of Coco's arm.

"Let's go inside Daisy."

As she turned toward the building, Coco crashed into the middle of Bull's chest. She gasped and bounced off of him, dropping her club as he grabbed her arm to keep her from falling. *Speaking of bears,* she thought, regaining her balance. "Bull! How long have you been standing there?"

"Long enough."

B ack inside the building, the two women sat down at the repurposed conference room table, and Coco blew on her mug of tea. The side of the cup read, "You don't have to be crazy to work here. We'll train you." Daisy concentrated on peeling the label off the water bottle in front of her like she was getting paid to do it while Bull sat on a high stool by the door, drinking from a disposable coffee cup. Chewy sauntered into the room and greeted them with a giant yawn. Coco couldn't decide which end of him smelled worse. He went straight to Daisy and put his head in her lap. She scratched his ears with a serious expression on her face and he lifted his head, sniffing, to see if there was anything edible on the table. There wasn't, so he put a paw on the girl's leg.

"Some guard dog you are," she said.

Coco looked back and forth between Bull and Daisy. "Should we call the police?"

"No!" Daisy said too loudly. She looked from Coco to Bull and then back down at Chewy. Then, in a softer voice, "Please don't."

"Okay," Coco said, holding her hands up in mock surrender. "I just don't want anything to happen to you . . . or me." She laughed weakly. Except for the ticking of the wall clock and the humming of the fridge, the room was quiet for a minute.

"You were pretty brave out there," Daisy said.

"Really? I was scared to death." Coco exhaled and examined the scrapes on the underside of her fingers.

"Me too. I hate being scared." Daisy gently twisted clumps of Chewy's fur as his head rested in her lap. "I never go to scary movies."

"Me neither," Coco replied shaking her head and wondering why Daisy was so anxious to change the subject. "Someone said they should show blooper outtakes at the end of those so you won't have nightmares."

"Really?" Daisy smiled. "What else are you afraid of?"

Coco pushed her lips to one side and thought about the question. "Those eighteen-wheeler trucks with the tiny windshields. Terrifying. Giant waves. Oh, and you know those sobriety tests where they have to say the alphabet backward? I can't do that sober so they'll never believe I haven't been drinking. I practice sometimes when I can't fall asleep. Z-Y-X-W-V- T-U—"

"Nope," Bull said.

"Ugh! See?"

Daisy smiled as she watched the dog leave her in favor of his bed.

"What are you afraid of, Bull?" Coco said, turning in her chair to hear his answer.

Daisy looked at him, too. "Yeah, what *are* you afraid of?"

"Nothin'," he said with a deadpan expression. His arms were crossed over his broad chest and he had one foot on the floor like a bouncer waiting to check IDs.

"Oh c'mon. There's got to be something," Coco prodded.

Bull shook his head slowly with his trademark frown.

"How about needles?" she asked.

"Nope."

"Heights?"

"Nope."

"Public speaking?" Coco said, looking for a smile.

"Nope."

"Bull, everyone's afraid of something," Daisy said.

"Yeah," Coco agreed.

He stared at them without expression, his arms still crossed. "You can ask all night long, but nothing scares me."

"Nothing?" Daisy laughed.

"Nothing." Bull narrowed his eyes.

Turning back around to face Daisy, Coco said under her breath, "Peanuts?"

"What did you say?" Bull asked with raised eyebrows that said *Oh no you didn't.*

"Nothing," Coco mimicked him in a low voice. She rolled her eyes and Daisy smiled with an expression that implied that she knew the story and got the joke.

He grunted and got off his stool. "I have to get the rest of the stuff. You ladies enjoy your tea party." He wiggled the big fingers of one hand in the air to Coco. "Oh look, 'Jeep Wave.'" Then he laughed as he left.

"You're doing it wrong," Coco hollered after him over a shoulder. She looked across at Daisy, who was lost in thought, and said, "Thought he'd never leave."

Daisy smiled, but with her mouth not her eyes. She pretended to be focused on the paper label and the bits she'd already peeled off.

"What's the story with you and that guy out there?"

Daisy stared at her water bottle while her hands spun a coffee stirrer that someone had left on the table. She was waging some inner battle to decide how much to divulge to her new friend.

"It's okay. You can trust me," Coco said with her hand over her heart. She reached across and gave Daisy's hand a quick squeeze. "I have a daughter your age. You will feel better if you talk about it. It usually makes the problem feel smaller."

Daisy didn't speak.

"C'mon. I was a B student in school so they say that makes me a good listener."

Daisy held Coco's eye for a long while and then nodded slightly. The battle had been decided.

"My mom used to clean his parents' house in EG. I drove her to work a few months back because we only have the one car and I needed to get my sister after school. When I came back to pick my mom up at her last house, she wasn't done yet so I had to wait in the driveway. Louie pulled in behind me."

Daisy moved from her chair to join Chewy on his futon. The dog twisted his body and arched his back, offering his stomach for a scratch.

"He came over to my car and started talking to me. He was the cutest guy I'd ever seen. I'd never had a boyfriend so it was kind of nice the way he was looking at me. He asked me if I wanted to go to a movie. But then my mom came out to the car and he left to move his car so we could leave."

She scratched the dog's wiry belly as her mind went elsewhere.

"My mom got in the car and told me to stay away from him because she didn't need him getting me pregnant and making another mouth to feed. He's a junior, too, and the star pitcher for the team or something. Your kids probably know him. He's a player, on and off the field. I knew she didn't want me to end up like her, a pregnant high school dropout. I didn't need any more convincing and I figured I wouldn't see him again, anyway. Boys like him didn't come to Dover."

Coco listened carefully.

"Then . . . one night, when my mom wasn't home, he knocked on our door. He'd gotten my address from his mom. He brought me flowers. I let him in and we talked. I made him leave after a while because my mom was due home from a date. He made me feel good when I was with him so I kept seeing him behind my mom's back. Then, when she—" Daisy stopped herself and looked at Coco. The ticking of the clock replaced her voice.

"When she what?"

"Nothing. I broke up with him and he got mad." A fat tear filled up Daisy's lower lid and she erased it with the cuff of her sweatshirt. "I have to go. My sister—and my mom—are expecting me home for dinner." She rose abruptly, wiped the fur off her jeans, and headed for the door. Coco touched Daisy's arm as she tried to pass.

"Are you sure you're okay?"

"I'm totally fine. I gotta roll."

Coco followed her through the office to the door and watched while she walked to her car, checked the back seat, got in, and drove away.

She couldn't believe that this girl was the same age as Charlotte. Coco felt a surge of helplessness because she couldn't fix this for Daisy. She didn't even know what was wrong. But something was definitely wrong. The only thing Coco could hope for was that Daisy's parents were good listeners and would help her work through this. She remembered something she'd just seen on Facebook: *A man should ruin your lipstick but never your mascara.* She wondered if Daisy's mother ever told her that.

21

The next morning, a skeptical Chewy stood over his bowl watching Coco scoop dry pellets from a bag of dog food and drop them in. Since Bull was out with the truck, she'd had to use a wheelbarrow to bring the fifty-pound bag of food from her Jeep into the office. Chewy's bowl was the size of football helmet. She filled it about a third full and then stepped back.

"Go ahead, Chewy, try it." She gestured with her hands toward the bowl as if she thought he was waiting for permission. "You can't be eating burritos. This is your food from now on."

The dog sniffed the food and then looked up at her with sad eyes that questioned why she would betray him. *Good God, what have you done?* He turned away before she was finished speaking and walked out of the office without looking back.

"He'll be back when he's hungry," Peggy said from the doorway.

It had been five weeks since Coco first set foot in The Mission, and she was definitely feeling more comfortable there. She was making friends and learning more and more each day about the operation. She and Sawyer fixed a lot of furniture and lamps together. And Peggy had an easy laugh and liked to touch people's arms and hands when she talked to them.

"I'll try to keep the Scouts from feeding him pizza, but if it's pepperoni I can't make any promises. He takes stuff off the counter without even jumping," Peggy said.

There were a few unfamiliar pickup trucks next to the building when Coco had arrived earlier. A man in his forties had been directing some high-school-age boys who were carrying two-by-fours from the truck into the building through the loading dock.

"What are the Scouts building this time?" she asked.

"I think it's a rack system in the warehouse so they can store the couches on end. They take up less room that way and it gets them up off the floor in case we have another flood like last Christmas." Rains back in December had left many buildings in the state under at least a foot of water. "Lovie, can you help me move some furniture around in the Showroom?"

"Sure. Let me just put this bag out of the way somewhere."

"You can put it in that storage room in the break room."

"Okay." Coco didn't know there was a storage room there. She dragged the heavy dog food bag into the break room. *He couldn't have been a pug*, she thought. *He had to be the size of a llama.*

She opened the door to the storage closet and found tall metal shelves full of toilet paper, snacks, water, and office supplies. When she pulled the long string attached to the ceiling fixture, nothing happened. The only light in the fifteen-by-ten space was sneaking in behind her from the break room, peeking over her shoulder like a nosy neighbor. She leaned the bag against the nearest wall and rolled the top down, squeezing out excess air, and then looked for a large binder clip to secure it. She moved boxes of paper coffee cups and sugar packets around on their shelves, but found no clips. She pulled her phone out, activated its flashlight, and walked around the back of the unit to search in the bins she could see through the open shelving. Right away she looked down and noticed a phone charger plugged into the wall, its other end resting on the linoleum floor with no job to do. Next to the charger was a paperback book and two half-full water bottles. Coco picked up the book and looked at the cover. There was a drawing of a woman in a long red coat standing next to a horse. The title read *Orgullo y Prejuicio*. The author was Jane Austen. Coco thumbed through the book but couldn't recognize a single word. A neon-pink highlighting marker served as a bookmark in the middle. She returned it to where she found it and looked around the small space. Nothing else seemed unusual except for the absence of dust on the floor behind the shelves, as if someone had cleaned only that eight-foot by five-foot patch of flooring.

She wondered why someone would be charging their phone here when there were plenty of outlets in every other room, including no fewer than eight in the adjacent break room. She walked back to the doorway, took another look around, and then closed the door.

Down the hall in the Linen Room, she found Peggy perched on a stool at the table, glasses at the end of her nose, sewing the seam closed on a gray comforter.

"I think I'm going to bring in my sewing machine from home," she said when she saw Coco. She sounded like a 1940s gangster with the side of her mouth closed around several pins. "This is going to take me all day."

Coco moved closer and took a seat opposite the older woman. "Can I ask you something?"

"Sure, but could I ask you something first?" Peggy said.

"Oh." Coco was surprised and wondered if Peggy had heard about what had transpired the night before. "Of course."

"How do you picture the months of the year?"

"The what?"

"Months of the year. I mean, are they in a circle or a straight line? Or lined up like a calendar? I think we all picture them differently. I see them in my mind all lined up side by side and whatever month it is slides in front of me. Yolanda said she sees them in front of her but they are in a tall line not a wide one. How about you?"

Coco opened her mouth and then closed it again. "I see them in a big oval, I guess."

"What happens when a new month comes, does it slide in front of you?"

"No." She smiled at this revelation. "I actually move around the oval." She'd never considered that everyone pictures months and days the way they'd first learned them in school.

Peggy opened her eyes wide with the pins still sticking out of the side of her mouth, her expression indicating that Coco's was the oddest answer yet. "Well, that's a new one. Okay, your turn." Peggy expertly fed a new piece of thread through the needle.

"How well do you know Daisy?"

"Well enough, I guess. Hard worker. Heart of gold," she said out of the side of her mouth.

Coco reached for the round red pin cushion between them and started returning the loose pins to it. "Have you ever met her parents?"

Peggy took pins out of her mouth, one at a time, and inserted them into a section of the comforter. "I hope I'm not talking out of school, but heard her tell Ernie that she doesn't know her dad because he left when she was very young. I think that's why she hangs around here, even though she doesn't have to anymore. Ernie's like a grandfather to her. And I proofread her essays." She smiled with her lips closed around the pins.

"What about her mom?"

Peggy shrugged. "Come to think of it, I've never heard her talk about her mother. And she drives herself here so I've never met her. I think her mom's a housekeeper."

"That's what she told me."

Coco's phone dinged to signal an incoming text. It was Ernie asking her to join him in the Interview Room. Every time he texted her, she thought it was probably ten times harder for him to type the message out on his flip phone than to just call her, and it made her wonder how Marybeth was coming on her resolution about not texting her kids.

"Ernie needs me," Coco said as she headed for the doorway.

"Is something going on with Daisy?" Peggy asked.

"I don't think so," Coco said, remembering her promise to keep yesterday's conversation confidential and still unsure about what was going on in the storeroom. "I was just curious. She's not a big talker. Teenagers, right?"

"I'll let you know if I hear something," Peggy said with a hint of concern.

"That's okay. Just forget I even mentioned it."

Coco walked down the hallway to the Interview Room and found Ernie sitting at the far side of the table with some paperwork in front of him and his glasses on his nose. He looked up.

"Our Lady of Faith." He pointed at her with his eyeglasses.

"Wow. That's flattering." She smiled.

"The church. You go to Our Lady of Faith, right?"

"Nope. Saint Thomas is our parish." She knew he was confusing her with someone else, but she liked watching him try to remember where he'd seen her before.

"We're in the smallest state in the union and I can't solve this mystery. I'm losing my touch. Come in, come in."

"How's it going?"

"It's going." He looked up at her after a few seconds. "We've got some clients coming in a few minutes and I want you to sit in on the interview with us."

"Great," Coco said earnestly as she took a seat in one of the formal chairs next to him. She'd never been asked to join a client meeting before, although dozens had taken place since she first started.

"Okay," he said as he looked over the paperwork. "They are

the Washington family. Two boys, two girls, mother is disabled with diabetes, and the dad was out of work for a while. He's got a job now, but they lost the apartment when they couldn't pay the rent. Now they're coming off of a five-month stint in a shelter. They've—"

He was interrupted by a knock on the doorframe. A volunteer named Jane stood there. She was in her forties and wearing jeans, a thick chambray shirt, and a tool belt.

"What's up, Jane?" Ernie took his glasses off and set them on the papers.

"Sorry to interrupt. The Scouts are almost done. I put them in the break room and we're waiting on pizzas."

"Thanks."

"They want to know if you want to keep the leftover two-by-fours or do you want them to take it all with them after lunch?"

Ernie exhaled loudly as a person does whose has had to make too many decisions in one day. "We should keep them. Sawyer can do something with the lumber. Ask them to leave it outside by the back door and he can put it where he wants it. Please."

"Will do." Jane slapped the doorframe and disappeared.

"Are you okay?" Coco asked. "You look tired."

He rubbed his face with one hand. "This is just my look. Can't shine a sneaker."

Coco smiled with affection. "My dad used to say that."

Ernie smiled back and then assessed the piles of paper in front of him.

"Seriously, though. You look like you need a vacation, Ernie."

"What's that?" he said.

"You look like you need a vacation," she repeated louder.

"What's that?" he repeated louder.

She smiled. "It's when you go away somewhere and relax; maybe read or fish. No one bothers you and you don't have to boss anyone around."

"You're just making things up."

The bell tinkled over the front door and Ernie got up from his chair to greet the new clients.

Coco stood as well, but remained in the Interview Room. She heard the couple introducing themselves. Ernie offered to take their coats, but they declined. Then they headed into the room.

After more handshakes and Ernie's offer of coffee or water, the thirty-something Washingtons took a seat in the Interview Room across from Coco and Ernie. They explained that three of their kids were in their new school. The youngest, Theodore, was sound asleep on his mother's shoulder with one arm hanging limply at his side and the other holding a thumb in his mouth. He sucked it periodically in his sleep.

With the help of a government housing agency, they had found a two-bedroom apartment a few towns away. Coco knew from The Mission's website that it was a requirement that all clients come to them only through a recognized agency. Walk-ins were not allowed, and most clients had to wait an average of two weeks before their appointment at The Mission. This gave Ernie time to confirm their circumstances and gave the clients time to arrange for a truck.

This meeting was always a big deal. The beginning of a new chapter.

The same agency that had connected the Washingtons with The Mission had loaned them a truck for the day. If clients had trouble securing a truck to move their new belongings, The Mission occasionally allowed the use of theirs. But mostly it was used to pick up donations rather than deliver.

Coco was the most uncomfortable person at the table, Theodore the most comfortable. Ernie was almost as relaxed as the baby, and the Washingtons were anxious but looking more at home each passing minute as they mirrored Ernie's posture.

There was some talk about the impossible Super Bowl win that the Patriots had pulled off after Ernie commented on Mr. Washington's hat. Then Ernie said, "Let's get started. Shall we?"

On the table in front of him, he had, among other forms, a one-page checklist divided into three parts. The top part was for furniture the client might need; mattress amounts and sizes; pieces needed for other rooms, including bureaus, tables, lamps, rugs, and other decor; and even a line item for children's books and stuffed animals. The middle part was for tallying the linens needed for the beds, bathroom, and kitchen. The bottom portion was a list of kitchen essentials, including baking dishes, silverware, and coffeemaker. Coco was familiar with the bottom two parts from times when she'd had to pull these items for previous clients.

Two things stood out to Coco as the interview progressed. First, the reverence and kindness with which Ernie treated the clients. He didn't tell them what they were getting for free. He asked them, slowly and methodically, what they needed. One didn't get the feeling this was a charity doling out used goods to beggars. The impression was one of a benevolent grandfather-figure helping people he genuinely cared about.

The second thing that stood out to Coco was that Ernie did not ask about their circumstances or what had led them to fall on hard times. He already knew this from the form they'd filled out online. There was no need to rehash it in person and risk shaming or upsetting them. Their past was no one else's business. Ernie didn't look down the ladder like Ava did. If he did, it was only to reach his hand down to pull them up. This was a time for a fresh start and positivity. Coco wondered if Ernie thought about Hope and Vivian every time he interviewed a family.

Having established that they needed three beds and a crib, Ernie worked his way through the kitchen supplies.

"Would you like some mixing bowls?" he asked.

"Yes, please," Mrs. Washington said.

"Now, how about a strainer for your pasta?"

"That would be nice. Thank you."

"Oh." Ernie looked up from the paperwork, removed his

glasses, and smiled. "I just found out that we also have a few fun things that came in today." He squinted at a small sticky note affixed to a folder. "Would you be interested in a popcorn maker?"

The couple looked at each other, unable to determine whether this was for real or not. When was someone going to step into the room and yell, "Gotcha!"?

"Um. That'd be nice for when we all watch a movie together." As Mr. Washington said this, Coco observed for the first time that he and his wife were holding hands. That was when the importance of the meeting began to settle down on her like a lead blanket. Couples she knew had experienced the same feeling of excitement when closing on their new house, or enrolling their child in a posh new school. But this couple was finally getting mattresses so their children didn't have to sleep on the floor. It was a life-changing moment for them. Maybe it was the first time they'd sat with strangers who were trying to give them something instead of trying to take something away. A hint of tears gathered on the father's lower eyelids and Coco looked away. She pinched her thigh to keep at bay the emotion that was causing her chest to ache.

"Excellent," said Ernie, as he wrote "popcorn maker" at the bottom of his checklist in the space marked "Other."

Thirty minutes later, Ernie had finished with his questions. He was in no hurry. He went over the list with them again to ensure that he got every detail correct. Of course he had, because Ernie was an excellent listener. Maybe he'd been a B student, too, Coco thought with a private smile. He carefully tore the form into thirds after making folded seams by hand. He kept the upper portion with the furniture needs and handed the other two parts to Coco.

"Please take this in back, Coco, and collect everything."

She nodded and took the torn paper pieces. Then she stood up and pushed her chair back quietly. She smiled at the couple as their son rubbed his face on his mother's shoulder and then turned his head so his other cheek got a turn on her warm sweater. Mr. Washington rubbed his son's back and nodded at Coco while his wife mouthed, *Thank you.*

Ernie clapped his hands together to signal it was time to leave the room, and the baby stirred. "Ooops. Sorry." He smiled and covered his mouth with his hands. The parents both laughed.

"It's okay," the mom said.

"Mrs. and Mr. Washington," he whispered, "we are going to get you started choosing some lovely furniture for your new home, but first, I'd like your permission to take a Polaroid of you, so we can give it to you in this frame."

"Sure," Mrs. Washington said as Coco left the room and headed toward the Linen Room.

As heavy as the situation was, Coco found herself bouncing down the hall. Excited for this family and excited to be a part of their new beginning. Finding the shine seemed easy sometimes.

22

A t the end of the day, Coco arrived home, tired but happy, to find Piper waiting for her on the front steps. Now they sat across from each other at Coco's kitchen table drinking diet sodas from mason jars and eating pretzels shaped like tiny tic-tac-toe boards.

"I called you, but it went to voicemail," Piper said.

"Sorry. Didn't hear it. Hey, do you know a kid at the high school named Louie? Plays baseball?"

"Yeah. He's a douchebag." Leave it to Piper to cut to the chase. "He moved here about a year ago into that mansion over on Cedar Hill. Remember the house you thought was the library?"

"Oh, right."

"Keep Charlotte far away from him, Gabby. I already told Katie, if he walks east, you walk west."

"What's his deal?"

"You know, typical spoiled brat jock. Parents are divorced and enjoying single life. Neither wants to parent anymore so he's left swinging in the wind. But seriously, he's bad news. Might as well be from Barrington."

"You're so bad."

"Just kidding. Why did you want to know?"

"Someone mentioned him at The Mission the other day. Just wondering who he is." Coco pushed the crumbs on the table into a tiny pile. "What's up with you? Why are you smiling like a psychopath?" Coco eyed her friend suspiciously.

Piper sighed and lowered her voice. "Okay, you can't tell a soul. Promise?" When Coco crossed her heart with her pretzel, Piper cleared her throat and blew out a long breath. "I slept with him."

"Slept with who?" Coco's brain was still consumed with the Washington family.

"Now you're making me sound like a slut."

"Sorry."

"The guy I met? I told you about him. At my support group?"

"Oh, right, right, right. Tall, Dark, and Handsome. How was it?"

"None of your business, Gabby. Jesus." Piper sat back in her chair and looked disgusted.

"I'm sorry." Coco was taken off guard. It's not like the two friends had never talked about sex before.

"Oh my god, I'm kidding." Piper slapped the table with her palms and leaned in.

"Oh, I see. Slutty Piper is funny. I didn't know this."

"Bite me."

"And there it is."

"The sex was good. A little awkward, but fun. We were both kinda . . ."

"Okay, okay!" Coco closed her eyes and covered her ears.

"Prude."

"No, I'm not. But I'm eating. I'm glad to see you happy, honey. I know how hard it's been since Brian . . ."

"Died. You can say it now. He died. My group has helped me to work through that word. Died, died, died. See?"

Coco recalled the first time she'd met Brian. Right after they moved in, Rex had been away on business and James had been playing ball with Charlotte in the backyard. Her little first-grader dove for a catch and landed on his open palm with a locked elbow, snapping both bones in his forearm. Coco had been busy in the kitchen cleaning up after lunch when Charlotte's scream reverberated around the entire town. Brian had heard it, too, and came running through the pool gate. James wasn't making a peep, but it was obvious that his arm was badly broken. As she knelt on the grass beside him, Coco was paralyzed by the thought of hurting her son even more if she tried to lift and carry him to the car. Brian had knelt next to James, too, and talked to him in a calm, reassuring way while scooping him gently into his arms and walking carefully to the driveway as the ambulance pulled in. He had held James in the back of the ambulance while the EMTs made a temporary splint before leaving for the hospital.

Brian had been a big mountain of a man and Piper looked like a child when she'd sit on his lap at a cookout or dance with him at a school fundraiser. She'd stolen him out from under the blind date he was supposed to meet at a coffee shop many years ago. She told Coco that she'd spotted him that day when he asked a woman at a nearby table if her name was Heather. That woman wasn't, but Piper overheard and wrote Heather on her own coffee cup and then sauntered over to his table to introduce herself. Soon she suggested they take a walk because she wanted them to be long gone when the real Heather walked in.

Over the years, when Coco would listen to Piper vent about how Brian did this or didn't do that, she knew that Piper's loyalty was deep and unwavering and she was just blowing off steam. Coco recognized that their marriage was as strong as any she knew. They balanced each other well even though they were inverted in size and personality: tiny Piper's colossal personality and giant Brian's calm demeanor, always ready with a sincere compliment or kind word. And while he never made apologies for his fork-tongued wife, he was always the Zamboni who smoothed the ice in her social wake.

His death had sent shock waves through the street, and the void it created was never filled by another neighbor, whether out of an absence of a suitable replacement or a deep respect for Brian's time on Goose Lane. Without his mitigating influence, though, Coco wasn't the only one to notice that Piper had become pricklier. But no one was brave enough to point this out. Or stupid enough.

Coco had often wondered when her friend would be ready to step back into the dating scene and possibly find someone to complement her passionate personality, and now she had her answer.

"I think it's good that you're open to meeting men now. Finding love is nice. Life is for the living, right?"

Piper cocked her head. "Swell TED Talk, Coco."

Coco cleared her throat and smiled. "So are you and TD&H going to see each other again?"

Piper smirked at the nickname. "You're funny. I hope so. I want to get my mojo back."

Coco understood right away what her friend meant. After Brian died, Piper had grown a tough shell. She became less trusting, less open, less fun-loving, and less fun. Courtney the Terrorist knew this as well as anyone when she got pushed in the pool. Piper was definitely not the same person Coco had met in her driveway on move-in day a decade earlier. But everyone who knew Piper accepted this as part of the grieving process. They just didn't know it would last this long.

"Did you remember to shave your legs?"

"Of course! But damn this muffin top." Piper looked down and pinched the flesh around her hips. "Luckily he's—"

The women jumped at the same time as the sound of an electric guitar exploded through an amplifier and nearly knocked them off their chairs. They both turned their heads to the door leading to the garage.

"What the—?" Coco spoke loudly after her heart restarted.

"Jesus Christ," Piper said. "What the hell's he playing out there?"

Coco got to her feet and flung the door wide open. Down in the garage James was sitting on his stool with his guitar resting across his lap. Next to him stood Daisy with James's old guitar slung around her neck. She was looking down at the strings and using complicated finger work to play Black Sabbath's "Iron Man." Very well. And very loud.

Piper put her hands on Coco's shoulders and stood on her toes to see down into the garage. They both listened as the pretty young girl continued to play with skill and passion, her black hair moving in a single sheet as her foot kept time with the music she was making. Coco watched her son watching Daisy. *Uh-oh.* Her friend thought the same thing and squeezed Coco's shoulders. When Daisy finished, the women clapped and both teens turned, surprised by their secret audience.

"Amazing!" Coco said. "I didn't know you played, Daisy."

The girl looked embarrassed. She lifted the guitar over her head and returned it to the stand. "I stopped by to—you left your phone." She dug in the pocket of her jacket and pulled out Coco's iPhone.

"Oh my god. I didn't even realize. Thanks so much, Daisy. I can't believe you drove all the way over here."

Daisy walked over to the stairs and handed the phone up to Coco. "Oh, and Ernie told me to ask you a question. He said you would know what he meant."

"Okay, shoot."

Daisy looked at the palm of her hand where she'd written something. "Briggs Beach clambake-a-thon?"

Coco smiled. "Nope. Never been to that, either."

Daisy shrugged, seemingly ambivalent about not being in on the joke. *Old people.*

"I see you met my son, James."

"Yep." Daisy smiled and turned to James, who flushed completely.

"And this is my friend Piper." Coco pointed her thumb backward over her shoulder. The older and younger women exchanged a smile and a brief wave.

"Hi, Daisy. You sounded great. Do you take lessons?"

"No. I taught myself."

"Cool," James said.

"Didn't she sound great, James?" Piper smiled mischievously at the young man.

"Yep," he replied and tried to look anywhere but at any of the women surrounding him.

Coco suddenly remembered the phone charger and the book she'd found that morning. "Do you want to come inside?" she offered, pointing her thumb again toward the warm kitchen.

"Nope," James said.

"You live here. I was talking to Daisy."

"Aright."

"I can't," Daisy said. "I gotta get back or Ernie will worry."

"Well, thanks again for driving all the way over." Coco realized that was a real Rhode Island thing to say, since The Mission was only eight miles away. "Do you know how to get back?"

"Yup." Daisy held up her cell phone with her map app showing. She took a quick look back at James and then out the big door to her car.

"You can come over and play whenever you want," James said. "Guitar, I mean."

Daisy stopped and half turned toward him. "Okay."

Coco looked at her son and saw an expression she'd never seen before. Hopeful? Smitten?

As Daisy backed out the driveway, Coco said, "I'm going to close the door, buddy. You must be freezing."

"No. I'm good."

"Suit yourself, tough guy."

Piper squeezed her arms again and whispered in Coco's ear, "Well, if that don't get him off that damned Xbox, I don't know what will."

"Shhhh." Coco pushed her giggling friend backward into the kitchen and closed the door. "Let's focus on your love life for now, you little tart."

23

A few mornings later, Coco was wide awake at six o'clock. She hopped out of bed and into the shower while the rest of the family slept. The night before, she'd had a dream about her childhood home and family. As she dreamed, she was vaguely aware that the house wasn't theirs anymore, but no one else in the dream seemed to care. Her parents and sisters were sharing a meal with her around the old kitchen table and laughing about something her mom had said. Coco was seated in her usual chair between her parents, and she tried to use her cell phone under the table to call Rex and tell him they were actually alive and doing great. But she couldn't seem to push the right combination of buttons. Then her dad asked her to put the phone away and finish her dinner.

While she showered, she was preoccupied by her vivid dream but also excited to get to The Mission. Lately, when she found herself missing her dad, she sought out Ernie as a surrogate. She felt comforted in his presence like when she was a little girl, and a not-so-little girl. As long as her dad was around, she knew everything would be okay because he could fix anything.

When Rex and the kids made their way into the kitchen, all

showered and ready to eat, she wished them a good day, kissed her husband goodbye, and headed to the door that led to the garage.

"No pancakes, Mom?"

"Yes, there are pancakes, James. Freezer. Left side." She pointed her fingers in the shape of a gun at them before backing out the door.

The fifteen-minute drive was quiet. For some reason she had no desire to listen to music. The whistling of the wind trying to come in through the space between the roof and the roll bar was the only sound she heard. It was as if her heart and mind wanted to hold on to her family dream as long as they could without the world encroaching.

She'd loved seeing her mom's happy face as she put the bowls on the table so they could eat family style as they always did, instead of filling their plates from the pots on the stove as her family did now. The old way seemed less rushed compared to today. Dinner used to be an event. When Coco was growing up, her mother cooked every meal for the six of them. Dinner was always on the kitchen table at six o'clock sharp, never on the coffee table. Afterward, the tasks of clearing the table, loading the dishwasher, scrubbing the pots and pans, and then drying them and putting them away were divvied up among the four girls and their dad. There was no set schedule, but everyone knew what had to be done. Her parents ran a tight ship, but Jim was usually the first one to roll up his sleeves and dig into the dirty mess in the sink, even after a full day at work. His days on KP duty in the army had stayed with him, and he could put a shine on any pot. There was no such thing as "women's work" in that house, even though the women outnumbered the men five to one. Those ordinary nights of kitchen cleanup were fifteen minutes of chaos that shouldn't have stored themselves in Coco's brain in her "favorite memories" file cabinet, but they did.

Before she knew it, or how she got there, she'd arrived at The

Mission. As she entered the office, she found Peggy and Sawyer rifling through Ernie's desk like panicked substitute teachers. They told her that Ernie was home sick; an event, she was told, rarer than a Donald Trump apology.

"How can I help?" Coco asked.

"I can hardly make heads or tails of that man's writing. Daisy can but she's at school. Is that a *p*?" Peggy squinted and showed the paper to Coco, who tipped her head to the side and squinted, as well.

"I think so. Or maybe a *b*?"

"That makes more sense. He really needs to get a computer," Peggy said as she held a sheet of paper at arm's length. "So it looks like the Bruens are on their way here."

"Get outa here!" Sawyer said with a smile.

"What?" Peggy said.

"The Bruins? Are you kidding me?"

"Not the hockey team." She hit him on top of his head with the paper. "The couple whose house blew up a few months back."

Sawyer frowned, whether it was because his favorite team wasn't coming or because of the explosion, Coco couldn't determine.

"I remember that one on the news," Coco said. "They were so lucky."

"I know what you mean, but I'm not sure if they'd agree. And I'm not sure we're going to be able to do all this without Ernie."

"Yes we can. We have to," Coco said.

"Can you help with the clients today? They're coming in any minute. Then we have another family coming in at eleven. I don't know how Ernie makes this all look so easy. I don't think he's ever had a day off."

"Man needs an instruction manual for this place," Sawyer said, flipping through the inbox on the desk.

"Or an SOP," Coco snorted but Sawyer and Peggy were as unacquainted with the term as she'd been a few months ago.

After clearing her throat, she said, "Of course I can, Peggy." She shrugged off her coat, hung it on a hook, and rubbed her hands together.

"Thanks, doll." Peggy patted Coco on the shoulder as the younger woman seated herself at Ernie's desk.

"Let's get back out there, Sawyer, and make room for that truckload Bull's bringing back."

"Yes, ma'am. Good luck, kid."

Coco smiled nervously and started putting everything back into Ernie's desk. There were books on refugees, AARP magazines, and various large manila envelopes with writing on them. One said "Receipts," one said "Army," and another said "Petty Cash." After tucking everything neatly back inside the desk drawers, she gathered all the things she would need for her first solo client interview: checklist, case file, pen, pep talk. *Don't screw this up, Coco.*

Thirty minutes later and right on time, the little bell tinkled. Coco looked up with a bright smile to see a couple in their seventies in the doorway.

"Good morning," she said. "Welcome to The Mission of Hope."

"Morning." The man followed his wife inside and removed his hat as they both looked around the small space.

The woman was dressed in a dark-green woolen coat that looked two sizes too big for her small frame. She had short gray hair and beautiful blue eyes. Her husband wore a black-and-white plaid wool jacket and black pants. His salt-and-pepper hair was disheveled from the cap.

"You must be the Bruens," Coco said, coming around from behind the desk and extending her hand to each of them. "I'm Coco. Hello. Has it started snowing yet?"

"Not yet," the man said. "Might be too cold." New Englanders understood the phenomenon of *too cold to snow*.

Coco still got nervous meeting new people. She'd never done

a client interview by herself and was still mentally reviewing all the steps. They only got one shot at this. Ernie knew this process like the back of his hand and had a great gift for making people feel at home, the same as her father had. No scripts. No formality. What you saw was what you got. She made a conscious effort to think like her dad and act the way he would in this situation.

"Please make yourselves at home. Can I take your coats?"

When they declined, and passed on her offer of coffee, too, she jumped down her mental checklist. "Why don't we go ahead and have a seat in this room, then." She led them to the Interview Room, turned on the overhead light, and then rushed back to the desk to gather up their paperwork.

Before they arrived, Coco had reviewed their file as fast as she could. Murray and Anna Bruen were from Hope Valley. A gas explosion in the apartment they'd rented over a garage for more than eleven years took all their possessions, including their feathered child, a parrot named Echo. They had no renter's insurance, but were lucky to be alive. The Red Cross had put them up in a motel temporarily and then they'd learned about The Mission of Hope through their church. Mrs. Bruen was suffering from Alzheimer's and her husband had quit his job as an auto mechanic two years ago to stay home and take care of her.

"We don't need a lot," Murray said proudly. "The people at church have been very generous with their clothing and money. Mostly we just need a few pieces of bedroom furniture."

"Of course. Well, let's go through the list just in case to make sure you have everything you need."

Slowly and methodically, as Ernie had taught her, Coco went through the entire checklist. Murray Bruen smiled when Coco reminded them that they would need a bath mat and dish towels in addition to the furniture they would choose in the Showroom. Anna sat quietly beside her husband with downcast eyes, rubbing the material of her skirt between her thumb and forefinger.

Murray did all the talking, but he often confirmed with his

wife when answering so that she didn't feel left out. She sometimes nodded, but in most cases, she didn't react at all.

When the checklist was filled out and double-checked for accuracy, Coco called Peggy and asked if she would come to the room to retrieve the list.

As they all stood to leave the room, Coco grabbed the Polaroid camera on the side table and handed Murray the small boxed frame. "This is for you, and would it be okay if I took your photo so you can put it in this frame? It's kind of a 'silver lining' thing," she said, using finger quotes. "You know, a reminder that things will get better, starting today." Coco could tell by the expression on his face that he wasn't buying it. *How does Ernie make this sound so much better?*

Murray frowned and looked down at his wife. "I don't think so," he said, "But thank you for the frame."

"Of course." Coco got a little flustered. "Whatever makes you comfortable. Enjoy the frame. Maybe you can put a picture of Echo in it." She regretted the words before they even left her mouth. *Roll Tide.*

Anna looked at her as if she'd been slapped. Coco looked to Murray with a silent plea for forgiveness.

It's okay, he mouthed and rested his hands on his wife's shoulders.

Coco led them down the hall and into the Showroom. As she pointed out different pieces to Murray, Anna wandered through the double doors and into the warehouse.

"Oh." Coco watched her go and then said to Murray, "She's not really allowed back there, for safety reasons. There's a forklift and—"

"I'll get her," he said as they both walked through the doors into the much colder space.

As they watched Anna wander around slowly, Murray spoke. "My wife's taken this pretty hard. We don't have children so it's just the two of us. When we lost Echo—" He paused to swallow.

"Well, he was our baby. We'd had him for fourteen years. She asks me about him almost every day. I have to keep reminding her that he's gone and it's like reliving that day and the loss over and over again for her. I'll be damned if I can remember what her smile looks like anymore." He looked away to gather his composure. "I haven't seen it in a long time. But I know it's not gone for good." He wiped his eyes with his coat sleeve.

"I'm so sorry." Coco touched a hand to his arm.

"Thank you. You've been very kind. Everyone has."

They stood for a quiet few moments looking around the warehouse, both at a loss for words.

"Do you see that tall cabinet there?" he said.

Coco followed the direction of Murray's finger to a six-foot-tall curio cabinet against the wall, visible above the other furniture.

"The one behind the yellow couch? Yes." She remembered that it was one of the pieces of furniture Bull had to bring in from the snow the night Louie appeared. It had glass on three sides, four shelves, and a mirrored back to showcase someone's precious belongings. It also had a glass door that locked with a decorative key, which was now affixed to it with a piece of masking tape.

"I know we're not supposed to be in here, but is that someone's or is it something we can have?" he said with embarrassed eyes. Coco could see that he was not a man who was accustomed to asking for anything.

"Absolutely!" Coco tried to elevate the mood with the cheery tone of a game show host. "Let's go take a look." They made their way around the maze of furniture until they arrived at the piece and could see each other reflected in its back mirror.

"She's a beauty." Murray reached out to run his hand along the word work. "We had one just like it before the accident." He looked around to see if his wife was within earshot and lowered his voice. "Anna used to have a collection in the cabinet, but we lost it all."

"What a shame."

"Her grandmother had a similar collection back in Denmark, so I guess it made her feel close to her childhood that way. She never saw her grannie again after she left to come here in 1957. We traveled some before she got sick, and every time we went to a new place, she would buy another snow globe as a souven—"

Coco took a sharp breath. *Oh my god.*

"What is it? What's the matter?" He immediately spun around to make sure his wife was safe. She was. They both saw Peggy pushing a metal shopping cart toward the loading dock.

"Wait here, Mr. Bruen," Coco said abruptly. "I'll be right back!"

"Okay," he said, puzzled.

She ran as fast as she could through the double doors and down the hall, dodging mattress carts and stacks of boxes lined along the walls in preparation for the yard sale. She skidded on one foot as she took a right into the Linen Room.

"Where is it? Where is it? Where is it?" she said, searching frantically up and down the storage shelves and wiping her hands across the surface of the boxes as if she was reading in braille. She shuffled around a few cardboard boxes and rearranged them on their shelves.

"C'mon, c'mon." She dragged the step stool over and searched the top shelf on the other side to no avail. Hopping down from the stool, she pushed it quickly to the next section of shelves and climbed up again, repeating her grid search.

"Yes!" she yelled when she finally found what she was looking for. She stood on her toes to reach the box with the words "Yard Sale" written in her own red block printing. She struggled to move the heavy load onto her head, carefully descended the step stool backward, and gently lowered the box to the ground. Ignoring the goose bumps on her arms, she grabbed the hand truck by the door and steered it over to the box.

When she pushed it through the double doors into the warehouse, she looked around frantically before spotting the Bruens at the opposite end. Anna was in her husband's arms in front of the curio cabinet and he was whispering something into her ear as he rubbed her back with both hands.

"She's overwhelmed. This is very hard. Nothing is familiar to her." He spoke softly to Coco over his wife's head as she approached.

"I have something I think you'll both like," Coco said, pulling alongside them with the hand truck. She knelt down on one knee in front of the box. Murray looked on with interest while Anna kept her head buried in his chest, completely uninterested in what this strange woman was doing.

Coco pulled back the flaps of the box and lifted a ball of paper out, which she then gently unrolled to reveal the large music box snow globe with the castle inside. She got to her feet and smiled as she shook it carefully and held it up between them by its base.

"You gotta be kidding me," Murray said with his mouth agape. He covered the top of his head with his hand and the gesture seemed to force water out of his eyes. "Sweetheart," he said. His voice cracked and he coughed to clear his throat. "Sweetheart, look." He put his hands on her shoulders and slowly turned her away from him toward the snow globe in Coco's hands.

It took her a moment to understand but then Anna's hand rose to her chest and she rubbed her silver cross pendant, which hung on a thin chain, between her thumb and index finger. The cobwebs seemed to fall away and she expressed understanding in her eyes. Memories were flooding into to her ravaged brain. She reached out with both hands as Coco passed her the heavy snow globe.

Until the day she died, Coco knew she would never forget the smile on Anna's face as she wound the music box and watched the snow fall on the castle. Her blue eyes held the wonder of a child and the sparkle that surely was the bright light this man had fallen in love with so many years before when he'd married his Danish bride.

"Is there any way we could have that one?" Murray implored Coco, and the way his eyes pled with hers nearly broke her heart. Coco knew he would have given every last dime he had to get that snow globe.

"One? You can have the whole darn box!" Coco felt the quiver of her lips and knew her tears were on their way. Trying to focus, she said, "Bet you didn't think you'd fill your new curio cabinet so fast." When she laughed at her own words, hot tears spilled onto her cold cheeks.

Anna turned to her husband and carefully passed the globe to him. Then she took two steps over to Coco and pulled her into a tight hug.

"*Dank. Dank je, schat*," she whispered.

"You're welcome." She watched Murray over Anna's shoulder and smiled at the kind man who just stood there shaking his head in disbelief, as if God had just come down and performed a miracle right in front of him. When his wife turned back to him, he had tears in his eyes as he saw her smile.

"Now, let's find you that bedroom set." Coco exhaled heavily and turned away to wipe her eyes with her sleeve.

"Wait." He reached out to touch her arm.

Coco turned around.

He held the box up containing the silver frame and said, "Can we take that photo now?"

Coco nodded at the pair. "You bet," she said before hurrying back to the office to grab the camera.

24

E very two weeks or so, Coco and Rex had a date night. They didn't call it that, but it was an evening out for just the two of them. Sometimes they had a big dinner, other nights just a few drinks and an appetizer. In the summer they'd take a drive down to the beach after the crowds left and walk barefoot until the sun set. Now that the kids were getting older and heading on to bigger and better things soon, they both wanted to make sure they maintained a relationship independent of being parents. A husband and wife could easily love each other, but in order to continue liking each other, they knew it was important to keep dating each other.

This Friday, Rex had arrived home later than usual and was taking a quick a shower before they headed out. The kids and cat had been fed. Coco was all set to go, but had to switch purses. She carried her cute hard-sided clutch with the Union Jack motif into the kitchen so she could transfer some items into it from her everyday purse.

Charlotte was perched on a stool on the opposite side of the island, looking sketchy. Her backpack was beside her and her laptop sat unopened in front of her. It was Friday and that meant no homework, so Coco braced herself for some bad report card news.

"Hi," Coco said slowly.

"Hi," Charlotte replied equally as slow.

"Honey," Coco said digging through her purse for her lipstick, "can you do me a favor and put these dishes in the dishwasher? I know, I know, he should have done his own. I'll tell him for the thousandth—"

"Tell me what?" James said after he descended the hardwood staircase like a herd of bison.

"Dishwasher," Coco said, pointing to his plate and utensils in the sink. "The maid is off tonight. Do your sister's too, please."

As James loaded the plates into dishwasher with one hand while watching some video on his phone with his other, Coco patted his back and said, "Good boy!"

Expecting a sarcastic "ha-ha" from her son, she was instead treated to a hearty bark from Charlotte's side of the counter.

"What the—" Coco spun around toward her daughter. James tore his eyes away from his phone at the same time.

A furry black-and-white face popped up between two paws at Charlotte's side of the island. She was biting her lip and looking from the dog to her mother, trying to decide if she should act shocked that there was a dog in the house. His scruffy fur spiked out in all directions like he'd recently been electrocuted. He had one blue eye and the other was brown.

Coco looked from her daughter to the dog and back to her daughter. "Explain," was all she could say.

Charlotte patted the dog's head and spoke as fast as a voice reading disclaimers at the end of a radio commercial. "Mom, I'm sorry, but he is the sweetest thing. His name's Ducky. I had to take him." She rubbed his ears as the dog closed his mismatched eyes and panted with a smile. "They were going to put him down—"

"I thought it was a no-kill shelter," James interjected.

His sister's eyes threw poison darts at him. "Let me finish, *James*." Her emphasis on his name confirmed that he would pay for this at some future point. He put both hands up in mock surrender.

Charlotte turned to her mother, who stood by the open dishwasher with an open mouth.

"They were going to put him down*stairs* in the cat room because they needed his kennel for a bigger dog. How humiliating is that?"

Ducky whined and sank back down to the floor and out of sight.

"Where was he tonight before he was in my kitchen?"

"Katie's house. Please, Mom, can we keep him?"

"Keep him?"

"C'mon, Mom. I'll take really good care of him. You know I will. He's so well behaved. He's down on his luck. His eyes don't even match. His whole world got turned upside down. He's sad. He has no one. His owner got evicted and she had to move in with an aunt out of state. And it turns out—"

"Fine.

"—the aunt has allergies and said she couldn't—"

"I said *fine*."

"Oh my god." Charlotte froze like a mannequin, with only her eyes moving between her mother and brother. "Are you serious? I had a whole speech."

Coco couldn't figure out if her daughter was in shock or disappointed that she didn't get to finish the pitch.

"Ask your dad. If he's okay with it, the dog can stay. But he's *your* responsibility. I'm not kidding, Charlotte."

"Oh my god. I know. I love you. I promise."

She jumped off her stool and pulled the dog on his leash across the kitchen and toward the stairs. James held up his hand and the siblings high-fived each other as she passed.

"I gotta call Zoë and Katie! Thanks, Mom!"

"I said you have to ask—"

Mother and son heard Charlotte's bedroom door slam.

"—your dad."

"Ask me what?" Rex said, coming into the room with one hand up under his sweater as he tried to straighten out his T-shirt.

"I'll tell you at dinner." She put her lipstick and phone inside the smaller purse and hooked her arm in her husband's.

"We won't be late, James. Do your homework."

"It's Friday." James gave a cheesy double thumbs-up. *Good luck*, he mouthed with an evil smile because he loved it when he wasn't the last one to know something in the house.

25

ARTvark was trendy new restaurant on The Hill downtown. Its exposed brick walls were covered from top to bottom with framed and unframed pieces of all sizes from local artists, all available for sale. The tables were topped with white paper, and a tin of crayons sat in the center of each one to encourage patrons to create their own masterpieces—or hangman games—while they waited for their meals to arrive. Pendant lights in the style of old-fashioned bulbs in little metal cages hung over the concrete bar, and the far wall was an enormous chalkboard completely covered in quotes by famous artists. Coco's favorite one was down in the lower right corner, as if it was the last one to make the cut. It was paraphrased from Vincent Van Gogh: "Great things are done by a series of small things brought together."

The last time they had come to ARTvark, the quote reminded her of the Civil Rights Movement, but now those same words made her think of all the people involved at The Mission.

They had chosen a high-top table by the windows, and now Rex and Coco sat across from each other sharing an order of calamari. Techno music pulsed from unseen speakers and caused them to lean closer over the table to converse. They talked briefly about a few personal income tax matters and the fact that the chimney hadn't been swept in three years. Coco filled Rex in on some news about their old friends that she'd recently learned on Facebook. Rex and James were the only ones Coco knew who did not have social media accounts. Understandable for a middle-aged man, but downright strange for a teenager these days.

"Well, maybe now Carl will stop posting gym selfies and start sharing pictures of this love child."

"Mmmm. Maybe. Maybe not." They both laughed, knowing Rex's cousin.

"I showed the kids how to replace the bag for the central vac today. It was time," Coco said.

"Good. Those freeloaders need to learn a thing or two about basic chores."

"Want me to show you sometime?"

"Yes."

They laughed again.

"How's work going?" she asked, dipping a piece of fried squid into the cocktail sauce.

"Good. Busy. I have to go to Chicago next week for a few days. Hey, I was thinking." He wiped his mouth with the napkin from his lap. "Do you want to go down to the Cape next month? Just for a night. We could leave the kids. Piper can keep an eye on them from next door. Charlotte's old enough to take care of James. She owes us."

"Oh, you have no idea," Coco murmured and reached for her wine.

"Huh?" Rex held a hand to his ear.

"I said, 'that's a great idea.'" They toasted the plan.

Coco and Rex had met on Cape Cod twenty years earlier. They had both worked at the same clam bar in East Orleans. The tourist trap's employee list was comprised almost solely of college students, a large group of twenty-somethings who slept late, hung out on the beach all day, worked the dinner shift, and then headed out to a bar. Rex and Coco were both dating other people when they met. Two years later, they found themselves single at the same time when they ran into each other in the beer line at Fenway Park. Less than a year later, they were married. The Cape was the scene of the original crime and they often returned to their old haunts to marvel at the youth who had taken over their jobs and their favorite corner table at the Land Ho.

"How are things going at The Mission?" Rex asked as the waitress cleared away the appetizer plate.

Coco laughed. "Why are you using air quotes? It's a real place."

He shrugged and smiled.

"It's good." She pulled an orange crayon from the tiny basket and began doodling on the paper in front of her. "Sometimes sad, but mostly good." She looked up and smiled. "We celebrated Sawyer's one hundredth coffee table today. Peggy brought in a cake and everything."

"That's great. Never a dull moment, huh?"

"Never. Ernie keeps trying to figure out how he knows me. It's driving him crazy. Poor guy."

"Maybe he's met one of your sisters. There are a dozen of you."

"There are only four of us, but I don't think so. And even if he did meet one of them, we all look nothing alike."

"Strange but true."

"So what's going on there besides that?"

"There's always so much going on. Every day is different. So many people need help. I never realized it before. It's just so different when you see it in person. These people who come in don't have beds! And they live in the towns around us!" Coco looked over her shoulder when she realized she was speaking too loudly. She lowered her voice and continued. "I feel like I've been living in a bubble, Rex, and I'm trying to figure out if that was by design. You know? Don't acknowledge it and it isn't real."

The waitress brought them their entrées and the two ate in silence for a few minutes.

Coco poked at her pasta Bolognese and then put her fork down. "We had a refugee family in today from Afghanistan."

Rex looked up from his plate. "No kidding."

"They were so nervous in the Interview Room. They had six kids under the age of ten and their English was pretty bad. They brought along a translator to help them understand the questions. I lent a hand choosing all of their linens. That part I loved. We filled up five shopping carts!"

"Six kids?"

"Yeah. I can't imagine being in their shoes. The mom was a doctor back home. A *doctor*, Rex!"

"Jesus."

"I know we've always donated money to places, but I kinda think, in a way, that's like singing a song when you don't really understand the meaning of the words."

"Is this about that 'Cake by the Ocean' post for Father Dave?"

"Shut up." He was still getting a few more miles out of her humiliation, but she smiled because it was still funny. "No. I *mean* when you do things hands-on for these people it feels different. Like you've been let in on a secret. You figured out the meaning behind the song. And it feels good and bad at the same time. You know? I didn't expect the work to be so heavy. It's a far cry from talent shows and book fairs." Coco pushed her half-eaten pasta away and moved her glass of cabernet in front of her. "Everyone has such a sad story. This family was so stoic. I know they're better off now, but they have to be traumatized leaving their country behind and having to rely on strangers for everything."

Rex nodded solemnly.

"A few hours after they left, we had another family come in who lost everything when we had all that rain back in December.

They had no insurance. They're starting from scratch. I really like being a part of such a great effort, but I can't un-see all this stuff now. Sometimes I miss the Coco that thought 'Cake by the Ocean' was about a birthday beach picnic."

Rex smiled at his wife. "Makes our life seem pretty damn good, huh?"

She nodded as she sipped her wine.

"Just two good kids and an old cat," he said and took a big bite of his chicken Milanese.

Fuck. "And a dog."

Rex looked up to meet his wife's eyes. "A whah?" he asked with his mouth full and his hand cupped behind his ear.

26

They arrived home from their dinner date to find Charlotte's friend Zoë's car in the driveway and a blue glow flickering in all four living room windows. The couple walked into the kitchen through the garage and Rex stopped to thumb through the pile of mail on the counter while Coco went down the hall to the living room at the front of the house.

There she found Charlotte and her two besties under blankets on the couch watching a movie. The lights were out and open bags of snack food and half-empty water bottles littered the coffee table.

"You're back. Hi, Mom. How was dinner?" A muffled and halfhearted bark came from their daughter's covered lap and the blanket gyrated as its captive tried to free himself. Charlotte met her mother's eyes with a panicked look.

"It's fine. I told him," Coco said as she shrugged her coat off and hung it on the end of the banister. "Hi, Zoë. Hi, Katie."

"Hi, Mrs. Easton," the young ladies said in unison.

Just as Rex came down the hall with his coat over his arm, Charlotte uncovered the dog. Ducky jumped down onto the floor sniffing the carpet for potato chip crumbs.

"Jesus," Rex said, recoiling. "That's an ugly dog."

"Dad! He is *not*. He's the cutest."

"He'd be cuter if he stayed off my couch." To challenge Rex's alpha dog tone, the dog jumped back up on the couch and dug under the warm blanket, using his snout as a shovel. "What does Houdini think about this?"

"I think he's okay with him already. He sat on the stairs watching Ducky for a while."

"Ducky? *Ducky?* Blech. Let's change his name. How about Otto? Or Gronk? No!" He snapped his fingers and pointed at his new dog. "The Rock!"

"Dad! *No.*"

"Charlotte," Coco said with a serious face. "I know you played the old 'ask for forgiveness instead of permission' game, but next time, for something important like this, you have to ask us *first*. Or I might play the same 'ask forgiveness thing' when I comment on your Instas."

Katie and Zoë snorted and looked down at their phones.

"Message received." Charlotte smiled and saluted her parents. Then she uncovered the dog's head and kissed it. "Seriously, thank you. You'll love him. I promise. You saved a life today. You should feel good about yourselves." She pointed her finger back and forth between her parents.

"Sure," her mother said. "Just take him out before you go to bed."

"Roger that."

"And get him to a groomer, for God's sake," Rex said. "Let's see if there's a better-looking dog under there."

"Boo," Charlotte said, covering the dog's ears as her parents headed down the hall to their room.

A minute later, Rex sat on the end of the bed and kicked off his shoes. "I think this Mission stuff has mellowed you out, babe. You never would have let her off the hook that easy before. Or were you day-drinking?"

"Ha-ha. I'm choosing my battles, that's all," she said as she removed her bracelets and earrings and dropped them on her dresser. "I'm also old and tired, so that's a thing."

Rex pulled his socks off, smart enough to know he should not agree with his wife this time. He reached for the remote as Coco went into the bathroom.

"I figure," she called to him, "we'd been talking for a while about getting a dog, so this—"

She was interrupted by Rex's raised voice. "Coco, get in here! You need to see this."

With her toothbrush in her hand, she walked back into the bedroom in her sweats and followed Rex's stare to the paused television, which was mounted on the wall opposite the bed. He'd been watching the news, and the contorted face of the woman frozen on the screen made it look as if she'd been about to blow a smoke ring. He used the remote to wind back the program a few frames and pressed Play.

The anchorwoman wore a serious expression as she read from the teleprompter.

"Firefighters were called to a warehouse off of Route 117 in Dover shortly after nine o'clock tonight. The building houses a charity called The Mission of Hope. Reporter Emma Davis is on the scene with details. Emma?"

The pretty young reporter was standing with a microphone at the top of Somerville Road in front of a blur of red flashing lights and heavy white smoke. She wore a long black cashmere coat and a turquoise ski hat pulled down to her eyebrows. Her straight blond hair sat on her shoulders and flipped up at the ends to mimic her perkiness. A small square in the lower right corner of the screen showed a satellite map with an arrow pointing to the location of the fire.

"Meghan, according to the police, no one was inside at the time when this two-alarm blaze broke out in the building behind me."

"What about Chewy?" Coco inhaled and then groaned as she stood with a hand over her mouth. "Oh no."

"A witness at the scene called 911 and firefighters arrived in less than six minutes. Everyone we spoke to said this quick response in all likelihood saved the structure from becoming a complete loss."

The camera panned over Emma's shoulder and zoomed in on the scene.

"Look! Look, babe!" Rex pointed the remote and paused the broadcast. They could just make out the figures of two girls and the giant dog standing a safe distance away from the smoking structure, talking to a pair of police officers.

"Chewy's okay!" Coco squinted, standing directly in front of the forty-two-inch screen. "What's Daisy doing there? Who's that with her?"

Rex shrugged and pressed Play.

"Thank you, Emma. The cause of the fire is under investigation and arson has not been ruled out at this early stage. The building's owner could not be reached for comment. If you have any information, you are asked to contact Dover Police at the number on the screen." Spinning in her chair to face a different camera, a smile magically appeared on Meghan's face. "Today, the Red Sox acquired ace starting pitcher Andrew—"

Rex switched the television off.

"I've got to get over there," Coco said as she stalked to the bathroom to put her bra back on.

Rex followed her. "Babe, it's after eleven. There's nothing you can do. It'll be swarming with authorities there right now. We'll just get in the way. Let's take a ride over first thing in the morning and see if there's anything they need."

"You're right. You're right. Oh my god. I can't believe it. I was just there a few hours ago, Rex, and everything was fine. What the hell happened?"

Coco walked into her husband's open arms and he closed them around her as she cried.

"So many people depend on that place," she said into her husband's T-shirt. "What are they gonna do now? We have four families coming in on Monday. And every day after that."

"Shhhh. It's okay. We'll find out more tomorrow."

27

The next morning, Coco dressed quickly, switched back to her day purse, grabbed her keys, and hurried to the car. Rex had offered to go to The Mission with her, but she politely declined and told him she would text him if there was anything he could do.

After she had seen the news story about the fire, she couldn't settle down. When she failed to find additional information on the Internet, she had paced the floor in the bedroom texting Ernie, Sawyer, and Bull. She didn't have Daisy's cell number. No one replied last night, but she awoke to a short message from Ernie in the morning, which read: "Cheesy ok. Smoke damage. No one hrt." Ernie needed to get a real phone with autocorrect, she thought. Sawyer's and Bull's belated texts said mostly the same thing as Ernie's, but Sawyer added: "Park on 117. Somerville closed."

When she arrived, she pulled off Route 117 onto the shoulder along with the other cars she recognized. Somerville was muddy from the water used to put out the fire. Low temperatures overnight had caused the muck to freeze over, and the grass on either side was damaged by the tires of the heavy fire trucks. The smell of smoke still hung in the air, and Coco could see icicles resembling jagged teeth hanging from the burned-out dumpster along the side of the building.

As she walked carefully along the road with her purse strapped across her body, she was able to get a better look at the damage. She couldn't immediately see any destruction, so she deduced it must have occurred in the back. The heat from inside the building gave enough warmth to cause the water from the fire hoses to thaw and run down the tracks of the corrugated roof, cascading to the ground like dozens of small, sad waterfalls. Icicles hung from the gutter, most with beads of water clinging to their ends and then releasing like medicine from an IV drip. Coco wondered if even Ernie would be able to find the shine today.

At the entrance to the building, she tried her best to avoid the streams of water falling into puddles around the concrete step in front of the yellow door. Protected by an overhang, the sign above it was undamaged, and the familiar ring of the bell gave her a small measure of comfort.

Inside, Bull was using a mop and bucket to wipe up the muddy water on the floor. It wasn't as much as Coco had expected, but there was no telling how long Bull had been working at it.

"Hey," she said solemnly, looking around.

"Hey." Bull stopped to wipe his forehead and then leaned with both hands on the top of the mop handle.

"How's Daisy? How's Chewy? Where's Ernie?"

"Take a breath, Coco."

She realized she was talking too fast. She also realized this was the first time he'd said her name.

"Ernie just finished an interview with the reporter and left to go see the dog at the hospital. They think Chewy was inside for only a few minutes before Daisy got him out. Ernie's all torn up because he feels guilty that he locked the dog in here. Chewy inhaled a little smoke but nothing serious."

"Poor thing. How much did we lose in the back?"

"Do you want the good news or the bad news?"

"Good news."

"Luckily Daisy left her phone charger by mistake so she came back here last night with her sister and saw the fire. She's the one who called 911 and saved Chewy."

So her sister was the other girl.

"She and Annabelle did the best they could with the hose until the fire department got here. Most of the furniture was up on those new racks or on their hooks and the water didn't reach them. And the mattresses are sealed in plastic so they're okay, too. If they hadn't come back for that charger, though, we could have lost Chewy and the whole damn place."

"Wow. That really is good luck." If Coco's theory about the storeroom was right, Daisy and her sister were already here when the fire started. "What's the bad news?"

"We had to reschedule all the interviews for the next three days, and all the linens smell of smoke and have to be washed and relabeled."

"That's not so bad."

"I'm not done. Most of the boxes for the yard sale got ruined. If the fire didn't get them, the water did."

Coco knew that the Linen Room's exterior wall was the one next to the dumpster. She couldn't help but feel relief that the Bruens got their snow globes before the fire. *Maybe that's the shine*, thought Coco. But many more people were going to lose out because the proceeds from the upcoming yard sale had been intended to purchase beds and toasters. Bad news was an understatement.

"How did it start?"

"Don't know. They're focusing on the workshop. Can't think of anything in there that would have ignited it."

"But who would have done this intentionally?"

"Don't know. I gotta finish this. The rest of them are out back so you can go see what they need."

"Okay." Coco stepped over his bucket and headed to the Linen Room, where she found Sawyer and Peggy loading the big canvas carts they normally used to move mattresses or bags of linens.

They greeted her in unison and explained that they were divvying up all the textiles and taking them home to be laundered.

They had already been working for an hour to load up The Mission's truck with the smoky linens and then drive it down the road and offload the bags to their own cars. Ernie had sent Daisy out with some cash to pick up more boxes of big trash bags.

Twenty minutes later, Coco was outside when Daisy pulled up, and she walked to her car to help her with the bags. Daisy turned off the ignition and Coco opened the back door to grab the bags. A big overstuffed duffel bag sat on the floor. The bag was bulging with clothes and toiletries, and a towel sat on top. Coco froze. The towel was from her childhood home in Reading. She touched it and felt the dampness, then she quickly withdrew her hand and pulled the shopping bags out of the car. Daisy got out of the car and closed the door. Coco closed the back door, too, handed Daisy a few of the shopping bags to carry, and they trudged toward the door.

"Hey, I hear you were quite the hero last night," Coco said to Daisy's back.

"Yeah," she said with no enthusiasm.

Coco followed her into the office and wondered what the hell she was going to do now. She knew she couldn't ignore the fact that the girl was living at The Mission, or out of her car, or something.

What the hell is going on? Why didn't I just stick to pinecone turkeys?

"I think Daisy's living at The Mission."

"What?" Rex said.

They were sitting in bed Sunday night watching TV with Ducky asleep between them. The wind howled outside and freezing rain pelted the tall windows like grains of sand. Half an hour earlier, a bleary Charlotte had walked down the hall into their room, with Ducky trailing behind her, complaining that the storm was making him nervous and he wouldn't go to sleep. She had swapped him out for Houdini, and now the dog lay stretched out upside down between Coco and Rex, twitching his paws every now and then in his dreams.

"Why else would she be at the building that late at night with her sister, Rex? Doesn't that sound odd to you?"

"Maybe she's just odd," he said, squinting at the television.

"And last week I found some things in the storeroom. A phone charger and a book. A Spanish novel."

"So?"

"So. She speaks Spanish!" Coco said definitively.

"And she charges a phone!" Rex said, covering his mouth with his fingertips in pretend shock.

"Very funny. She must come back when everyone's gone and sleep there. There was a whole area of the floor that wasn't dusty, like she put blankets down or something."

"I think you're taking a big leap, babe." He scratched the dog's belly and clicked off the TV with the remote. "Maybe she—or someone else—likes to take their breaks in there because it's quiet."

"You think Bull is in there reading Jane Austen? In Spanish?"

"Maybe."

"With a pink highlighter?"

"You said he's complicated."

She gave him a nonverbal *Oh c'mon*.

"No, I'm serious, babe. I think your assumptions are sexist and I'm offended on his behalf."

"Shut up."

"Do you see what I have to put up with?" Rex asked the sleeping dog.

"Oh wait! I buried the lead! I also saw one of my parents' bath towels in the back of her car. And it was wet!"

"Probably from the fire." Rex pounded his pillow with one fist and laid his head on it.

"Nope. Her car didn't smell like smoke at all. Neither did the towel. She took it before the fire started."

"Yeah, but she shoplifts so she obviously has no problem with taking things, Coco."

"No, but then I saw it later in the dryer. I watched her put it back on the shelf in the Linen Room today along with a blanket and another towel that she pulled out of a plastic bag. She was cool as can be and pretended that it had just come in as a donation." Coco waved her hand in the air and then held a finger up in front of Rex's face. "But she doesn't know that I know that towel like it's my own kid."

"That's a weird thing to say."

"I think she's living there, Rex. Maybe her sister is, too. But I don't know why." She tapped a forefinger on her closed mouth.

"Wouldn't their mother be wondering why they didn't come home at night?"

"Maybe. Maybe not."

"I'm sure there's a good explanation. Just ask her."

Coco considered his advice and then her mind moved on. "I'm going to donate my parents' desk to the yard sale."

"I thought these people were your friends," Rex joked.

"You are salty tonight."

"Salty? I like it." He smiled and reached for the light on his bedside table. "I have to go to sleep, babe." He leaned into the middle of the big bed, held the back of his wife's head gently, and kissed her on the lips. "My flight's at five a.m. I'll try to call you after my dinner meeting tomorrow night. I love you." He rolled onto his side with his back to his wife.

"I love you, too," she said, turning off her light and sinking down under the covers. Ducky whimpered softly in his sleep.

In the dark, her thoughts stayed on Daisy. The automatic floodlight in the back of the house had been triggered by the wind, and it illuminated the freezing raindrops that now slid down the big windows. *Why would she need to sleep at The Mission? Is her sister sleeping there, too? Where is their mother? Are they surviving on chips and soda?* She thought of her own kids asleep upstairs in their warm rooms safe from the storm and the rest of the world outside. Then she thought of Daisy and her sister curled up on somebody's old blanket on the hard storeroom floor. Alone.

29

Two days later, as Coco pulled into a parking space at The Mission, her eyes were glued to the large red truck taking up two spaces in front of the building. It was the size and shape of an armored car but with white lettering on the side that read "Fire Investigation Unit."

She dropped her phone into her purse and hurried from the Jeep to the front door. When she entered, the office space was crowded with two uniformed fire personnel, Ernie, Sawyer, Peggy, Bull, and Daisy. Everyone was seated, a few on chairs someone must have brought in from the break room.

"Hi, Coco," Ernie said, standing up.

"Hi." She looked around at the gang with calm curiosity.

"Chief Ferraro was just about to tell us the results of his initial investigation."

The chief, a trim balding man of about sixty, nodded at her and she nodded back while Daisy made room for her on the couch.

"From all the evidence gathered, we've determined that the fire started with a faulty lamp in the warehouse."

Everyone looked around at one another. Bull shook his head

at the ground. Peggy and Sawyer shrugged. And Daisy went white.

"But we never leave those old lamps plugged in," Sawyer said. "I test them myself."

"All I can tell you is that the fire started with a lamp. The cord must have been split and caused a spark."

Coco looked sideways at Daisy, whose knee bounced nervously. She couldn't figure out what was going on, but her instincts told her this girl was carrying a load much too heavy. Everyone agreed Daisy was a compassionate, intelligent, and hard-working young woman, but she was struggling with something, and she was doing it alone. Coco realized, of the handful of female volunteers at The Mission, she was the only mother. Daisy was the same age as Charlotte, but she was over her skis for one reason or another. She needed to do something to help this girl, but she'd have to figure out what and how. Maybe Piper could help.

"If this young lady hadn't arrived just when she did," Chief Ferraro was saying, "you could have lost your dog and the whole place, Ernie."

"Don't I know it." Ernie smiled at Daisy like a proud grandfather. "She was something else."

All eyes in the room turned to the teenager. She swallowed hard and slowly began to stand up. Coco looked up at her and knew the next words to come out of the girls mouth might change her life forever.

"I . . . I have to—" Daisy started.

Coco sprang to her feet like she last had on New Year's Eve, unsure what would come out of her own mouth. "I think it was my fault," she said before she could stop herself.

Everyone turned to her, stunned. No one more so than Daisy.

"What was?" Ernie asked.

"The fire," Coco said.

"What!" Bull said.

"No," Peggy gasped.

Sawyer squinted at Coco. His mouth was quiet, but his expression said, *What choo talkin' about, Willis?*

"Not on purpose. I . . . I was working on the lamps the other day—to help out," she stammered. "I must have messed something up with the wiring. I thought I fixed it, but I must have done it wrong. It's really complicated."

So confused was everyone by Coco's words that no one noticed the complete look of shock on Daisy's face. She sank back down onto the couch, mouth open.

"I guess I left it plugged in. I'm so sorry." She stole a glance at Sawyer, who wasn't buying what she was selling. She turned quickly to Ernie. "I'm very sorry Ernie. I will pay for all the damage. I'll pay for Chewy, too. I can't tell you how sorry I am to have caused all this trouble. Especially after how nice you've all been to me."

The room was completely silent with everyone in it looking at one another but not verbalizing any of their thoughts. Peggy wrung her hands. Sawyer leaned on the file cabinet shaking his head. Bull nodded slightly. It felt like a scene from a movie and someone hadn't paused it, but hit the Mute button instead.

Finally, the Chief said, "Miss . . ."

"Easton. Gabrielle Easton."

"As far as I can tell, you're not in trouble. You're lucky this young lady called for help in time. But I am going to need you to come down to the station with me and write up a statement."

"Okay." Coco's face was bright red. She tried to hide her anxiety and slowly took a seat on the couch.

"Now," the chief said.

"Oh." She popped back up, slung her purse on her shoulder, and then pulled it protectively in front of her body.

The chief held his arm out in the direction of the door. "After you."

"It's okay, sport," Ernie said to her back. "We'll sort this all out. Accidents happen."

Coco walked the dozen steps to the yellow door and then turned halfway around to look over her shoulder. Ernie smiled, sad but supportive. The others looked in equal parts mortified, confused, and surprised. Sawyer opened his mouth to speak and Coco hurried out the door before he could.

30

Two hours later, she drove home from the police department with a pounding headache. Not only had she just filed a false report, but she knew now that she'd never return to The Mission again. How could she ever go back after this debacle? What had she done? This was the mother of all *Roll Tides.*

She had a dozen texts on her phone and five missed calls from the people over in Dover. The police had been kind but businesslike. She marveled at how fast she'd gone from pinecones to perjury and was more determined than ever to get to the bottom of Daisy's story; she felt that she'd earned the right to know now. Just as she realized she didn't have the girl's cell phone number, she pulled in her driveway and saw Daisy's car sitting out front.

She stopped her Jeep and shifted into Park. Daisy emerged from her car, thrust her hands into her the pockets of her thin denim jacket, and hurried over. She opened the passenger door and hopped up inside.

"How did it go?"

"You mean lying to the police?" Coco laughed a bit. "It was fine."

"Why did you do it? It was my fault. I started the fire."

"I know."

"You do? Then how come you—"

"You just seemed like you needed a break."

Daisy looked at Coco for a long moment, her thick black hair tangled and oily, and then started to cry. The front door of the house opened and James stepped out onto the porch. Coco held up a finger to signify that she needed a minute. He nodded and then retreated back inside and shut the door.

"What the hell's going on, Daisy? Are you living at The Mission?"

"Yes." She wiped tears with her cuff.

"With your sister?"

She nodded and turned to Coco. "Our mom left. She's gone. We don't know where. I don't think she's coming back but I haven't told my sister that."

"Oh my god," Coco said. This was not where she thought this story would go. "Since when?"

"About a month ago."

"A month!"

"She left a note on the kitchen table and an envelope of cash. She must have taken off with that dirt bag boyfriend of hers. We were okay for the first couple of weeks, but then the rent was due and the landlord kept banging on the door. If I gave him everything we had left, I couldn't buy food or gas. So we snuck away. We had no place to go, so we've been staying at The Mission at night and then showering at my friend's house. I told her our shower was busted at home. I felt safe with Chewy there. He's no watchdog, though."

"Why didn't you tell someone? Ernie? Bull? Me?"

Daisy's head fell back against the headrest. "Because if we told anybody, they'd put us in foster care. I've seen the people who come through there."

Coco assumed *there* meant The Mission. "Their lives are destroyed," Daisy said. "Their families get destroyed."

"But they get put back together, too."

"Annabelle is all I have. I'll be eighteen soon, but she's only fourteen. They'd put her with a family and maybe I'd never see her again. I don't know. I'm her big sister. I'm supposed to protect her." Daisy started to cry again. "That asshole Louie. He knows about it, too. He said if I didn't start seeing him again he'd tell social services with an anonymous call or some shit."

"Okay, it's okay," Coco said, pulling the girl into a hug. After a full minute, they separated. "What happened the night of the fire?"

Daisy sniffed and wiped her face with her sleeve. "He came banging on the door because he must have followed me again. We hid out in the storeroom. After a while, it was all quiet. But I didn't know if he was gone so I didn't want to turn the ceiling lights on. And the storeroom light's busted. I snuck into the shop and figured I'd bring a lamp with us into the storeroom or someplace else without any windows. In the workshop I plugged the light in to see if the bulb worked—and the whole thing went up with a giant spark!"

Coco handed her a tissue from her purse and Daisy blew her nose. She continued the story with the wet tissue in her hand.

"The spark landed on the sawdust and the fire started. I called for Annabelle and we grabbed Chewy and our stuff and ran for the car. But I couldn't leave without trying to help stop the fire. We called 911 and grabbed the hose by the dumpster. We were so scared."

Coco drew in a deep breath and let it back out slowly. "You could have been killed, Daisy."

"I know!"

They sat for another minute, each trying to process the shocking events of the past few days.

Daisy broke the silence. "Why did you cop to it?"

Coco stared out the windshield. "I've been asking myself that all day." She laughed with fatigue. "I apparently have a new problem with spontaneous outbursts. I knew there was something going on with you, Daisy, but I didn't know what. I was going to ask you today, but I didn't have a chance. You were about to confess and I figured there was no turning back if that happened."

Daisy looked at her hands in her lap.

"Besides, I come from a long line of fixers," Coco said.

"What does that mean?"

"When I was a kid, my favorite place to hang out was in my dad's basement workshop. Every Saturday I'd sit on this old wooden stool and watch him for hours. It didn't matter if he was fixing a lamp or carving out some sort of improvised tool. When I was eight I decided to try wood carving for myself. I ended up mutilating a leg of an old desk my mom had in her bedroom."

"Damn," Daisy said staring at Coco's profile.

"Yeah. Damn. My dad noticed it first and knew my mother would freak out. I remember he nudged me and told me he hated the desk, but had to put up with it because his mom loved it for some reason. So he tried to repair the leg himself. Took him forever to get the right matching piece of mahogany. He finally had the wood, but the first day we went to work on it in the basement, we got busted. You should have seen my mother's face. He took the blame for the giant gouge and the cover-up."

"Why?"

"You know, we never talked about it. But I think it was because he knew it would be easier for him to carry the burden than me. I'd forgotten all about that story until I was cleaning off that same desk in my garage the other day."

Daisy drew her eyes away from Coco and stared into the middle distance. "I told Ernie and the rest of them the truth after you left. Everything: the fire, my sister, Louie."

It was Coco's turn to be shocked. "You did? Why?"

"Because maybe it's easier for me to carry the burden than you." She smiled weakly.

"How so?"

"I knew you wouldn't come back there after you confessed. I saw it in your eyes. And they need you. *We* need you."

"You're right. I probably wouldn't have gone back."

"I know."

"What'd they say?"

"Ernie smiled. Sawyer knew you were full of shit. Apparently you're some handywoman guru," she said in an exaggerated way.

"I really am." Coco laughed. "What are you going to do now, honey?" Coco considered offering to take in Daisy and her sister, but she decided one impulsive act a day was her quota.

"Peggy told me we could stay with her until we figure something out."

"That's good."

"Yeah."

"Wanna come inside and get something to eat?"

"Thanks, but I can't. Annabelle is waiting for me at the library. Then we're driving over to Peggy's." Daisy searched for the door handle in the dark car.

"It's up higher," Coco said as Daisy located it and popped the door open.

"Thanks, Coco."

Coco smiled as Daisy closed the door and walked back to her own car.

Rex is gonna fucking kill me, Coco suddenly realized.

31

The next night, it was Coco's annual turn to host book club. She was expecting nine ladies and a special guest. Ava was traveling for work and couldn't attend, so naturally Piper was eager to come to Coco's house and catch up with everyone without guerilla warfare. While Coco was better prepared to defend her work at The Mission this month, she would be kidding herself if she didn't admit that she, too, was looking forward to a confrontation-free, aka Ava-free, evening.

Rex was still in Chicago. She hadn't heard from him since he left, except for a few short texts and a call she missed when she was at the police station. She was relieved that he didn't know about her confession yet. The kids were eating the simple dinner she'd prepared while they did their homework in the kitchen. Appetizers in all forms covered the counter and the women were expected in half an hour.

James sat on a stool and hunched over the center island, supposedly using the calculator on his phone to do his math homework, but Coco was always skeptical if she couldn't see the screen. Charlotte was at the kitchen table with her work spread out in front of her. She wore her earbuds while Ducky curled up on the rug next to her, his chin on her foot. If Charlotte moved, Ducky wanted to be the first to know about it. She had taken him to the shelter that day to groom him and he'd been transformed. The fur around his face was carefully cut, and the shampoo she'd used gave his coat a soft sheen. The red bandana encircling his neck told the world that he was a "good dog."

Coco assembled the layers of her Mexican dip as she listened to her daughter humming along to a familiar tune from the early '80s. She could hear the tinny sound of the song through Charlotte's earbuds as the teen tapped her pen on the textbook. When it came to the chorus, Coco smiled when her daughter sang.

"Hmmmm, hmmmmm, hmmmmmm. Rock the cast off. Rock the cast off."

Charlotte went to dig into her backpack for something while her mother and brother smiled at each other.

"What?" she said in the loud way people using earbuds do.

"It's 'casbah,'" Coco said in a raised voice so her daughter could hear.

"Ha!" James said as he worked the screen on his phone.

"What?" replied Charlotte. She had just pulled one earbud out and was pinching it between her thumb and forefinger.

"The song. It's not 'rock the cast off,' bozo," James said with a snort. "It's 'rock the casbah.'"

Charlotte looked over at her mother, who nodded in agreement.

"Sounds fake, but okay." After a minute, Charlotte asked, "Then what's a casbah?"

Coco shrugged. "Want me to double-google it?"

James, with a mouth full of pasta, said something unintelligible.

"Was that English?" Charlotte asked.

James held a finger in the air while he swallowed. "It's like an old Arab marketplace."

"Really?" Coco said.

"Really?" Charlotte said.

"Really. It was the Clash's third single from their fifth album, *Combat Rock*," he said, twirling his pasta. "The drummer actually wrote the music. But not the lyrics. And it was the first song played by Armed Forces Radio during Operation Desert Storm."

"Nerd," Charlotte said and went back to her homework.

Coco shot her daughter a condemning look.

"How's the fire cleanup going, Mom? Are they going to have to throw everything out?"

"I don't think so, James. There was a lot of smoke damage, but mostly we just have to keep washing all the linens."

"Why was Daisy here last night?"

"Who's Daisy?" Charlotte wondered.

"She works at The Mission. She brought me more linens to wash." Coco realized she was lying like a pro lately.

Charlotte removed her earbuds. "I'm glad Chewy's okay. Do you think they'll catch the people who did this?"

"I don't know," Coco lied again. She wasn't ready yet to explain everything that had happened. Maybe tomorrow.

"Well, all the stuff on the news will probably help more people find out about The Mission, anyway."

"I hope so. Hey, do you guys know a kid at your school named Louie? He's a baseball player."

"Nope," said James.

"Yeah. I heard he's a jerk. Why? Don't tell me he's at The Mission."

"Nope. Someone was just talking about the team today." *Wow. Third lie in less than a minute.* She opened the upper oven and slid in a tray full of frozen lemongrass chicken eggrolls then went over to a cabinet and began pulling out wineglasses.

"Who coming tonight?" Charlotte asked.

"The usual group," Coco said, inspecting the glasses against the pendant light for water spots. "Except Mrs. Logan can't come." Saying this out loud reminded Coco that water spots weren't a big deal if Ava wasn't coming so she stopped scrutinizing them. "Oh, and Mrs. Harper is going to stop by afterward." Coco omitted the fact that Piper was going to bring her new beau after they went out on their fifth date. Mr. Tall, Dark, and Handsome seemed to be doing wonders for Piper, and Coco was eager to meet this miracle worker and shake his nerdy hand.

"Wow. That's news. Katie said it's been forever since her mom went to book club. How come?"

Coco shrugged and opened the drawer next to the ovens to pull out a few potholders. There was some neighborhood drama that Coco saved for herself. She didn't tell her daughter how strange it had been that Piper had quit book club cold turkey last year not long after Brian's death. No apologies. No explanation. She thought she knew her friend better than anyone else, but this was a mystery. When Piper found out through Coco that Ava's flight wouldn't land in time for her to make it to book club that night, she told Coco she would stop by for coffee with her date after dinner. Maybe she didn't want Ava to meet him. Who could blame her?

James brought his empty plate over and tried to sneak it into the sink.

"Dishwasher!"

"My bad," he said, dropping the dishwasher door open and trying to fit the plate into the crowded lower drawer.

The kids made their way upstairs just as everyone began arriving at the front door at ten-minute intervals. They all started out in the kitchen, as usual, eating, drinking, and laughing in small groups as everyone caught up with one another. Coco watched Ducky lick up fallen crumbs and considered that another good reason to have a dog. Around nine, she herded the group into the living room.

A Man Called Ove was the book she had selected. It was about an old curmudgeon who lost his wife and kept trying to commit suicide but was repeatedly foiled by neighbors who needed his help in different ways. Even though only five of the book club ladies had had a chance to read the novel, the conversation was lively and light.

The last discussion question had been about a character who had died in the book and the subsequent funeral. They all chimed in with responses and then the talk inevitably turned to Marybeth because of her morbid-adjacent profession.

Coco said, "MB, tell them that funny story you told me in the kitchen about that last client."

"The one who took a selfie with his dead grandmother?"

"God no. That's not funny. The other one about the fish tank and the home wrecker."

"Sounds like a country song," Tracy joked.

Marybeth proceeded to entertain the group with a true story about a funeral party she and Oliver had been hired to organize the previous week. Apparently the wife and girlfriend of the deceased had both shown up at the pub following the funeral and the ensuing catfight ended when a chair got thrown by the girlfriend at the wife. It missed its target, but connected with the hundred-gallon fish tank built into the wall.

"So lover boy wasn't the only one laid to rest that day," Marybeth said.

"At least he didn't get flushed."

"True. The mistress was held responsible for the water damage and the loss of twenty-eight innocent tropical lives."

Wineglasses got topped off and more inappropriate funeral behavior was discussed.

"Marybeth," Sophie said, "tell them about the Portuguese family who was wailing because the makeup artist at the funeral home"—she started laughing—"because the makeup artist at the funeral home shaved off—" She was laughing so hard she wasn't making a sound. "Because she shaved off their mother's mustache!" She fell sideways on the couch in hysterics.

Marybeth looked at the others and said, "Well, that's basically the whole story."

"No." Sophie had tears on her face as she remained prone. "Tell them the rest."

Marybeth turned to the other ladies. "They were very upset that she didn't look the same as their mother anymore, lying there in the casket. The funeral director thought they might sue him for cleaning the old woman up because that mustache was not gonna to grow back, know what I'm sayin'?"

The women laughed.

"So what happened then?" said Coco.

"He told me he wanted to cover the cost of the after-party as a goodwill gesture to the family. And damn those Portuguese were happy to run that bill up good and high. It set him back a few grand. Expensive mustache but a teachable moment." She clinked Sophie's glass in a toast.

Coco, who had popped into the kitchen, was still smiling when she returned to the room with a tray full of coffee and lemon squares. After the group sobered up a bit, they began asking her a lot of questions about The Mission and the aftermath of the fire. It had been on the news again several nights that week.

"Turns out it was an accident. Faulty lamp," she said. She didn't want to say more at the moment.

"Really?" Marybeth said.

"Yes. The stuff inside wasn't insured, either."

"If there's a silver lining, though," Sophie offered, "at least more people know about you guys now than they did before."

Coco enjoyed being included as part of the term *you guys* more than she thought she would have a few months ago.

"You're right. Hopefully we'll see more donations now. We could really use them. If you have anything you want to get rid of for the yard sale, too, just let me know and we'll come over and get it."

As the night wound down, Sophie and Marybeth stayed to help Coco clean up. By comparison, book club cleanup was a hundred times easier than pasta dinner cleanup. They moved the food and wine to the kitchen and continued their conversation. Coco checked her watch, a little disappointed that Piper hadn't stopped by as planned.

"I'd better head out soon," Marybeth said. "I've got a ton of laundry waiting for me."

"I can't combine all our family's laundry loads anymore. Ever since thong-static-cling gate," Coco confessed.

Sophie's snort laughed her wine into her hand. "No! Poor James."

"No, no," Coco corrected. "Poor Rex."

"Oh no!" Both women gaped.

"Oh yes. At the airport."

"You're shitting me." Marybeth laughed.

"I shit you not."

They all had a good giggle at Mr. Easton's expense about the embarrassing conversation with the helpful elderly woman in the priority boarding line who peeled the thong off the back of Rex's pants and tucked them in the pocket of his sports jacket with a wink.

After Sophie and most of the others left, Marybeth and Coco were sitting at the counter drinking ice water when they both heard the front door open and a familiar voice call out, "Yoohoo! Anybody home?"

"Oh my god. They're here," Coco whispered loudly.

"Who?" Marybeth asked.

"Piper and her new guy."

"What? Oooo," Marybeth said. "Juicy."

Coco hopped off her stool, smoothed her hair, and checked her reflection in the widow over the sink. She'd only get one chance to make a good impression on this beau.

Piper and her nerd made their way down the hall to the kitchen.

"Hi," Marybeth said as Coco turned around with a big smile to greet her friend.

When Coco saw Piper, she let out a big, "Hey girl!" and hugged her, while over her shoulder she caught her first glimpse of the new man.

What the fuck?

"You're Gabby?" Bull said with his open jaw doubling his double chin.

"Oh my god! You're Tall-Dark-and-Handsome?"

"Thank you." He held his arms out at his sides.

As Coco processed the shock, she had to admit that he did look handsome. He was dressed in a black leather jacket, a white dress shirt, and dark-blue jeans with black cowboy boots. Piper looked pretty in a red quilted jacket and winter-white dress pants. Coco searched Piper's eyes with a look of betrayal that her neighbor didn't quite understand.

Ducky rushed over to sniff the newest visitors.

"Oh, lookie here. This must be the dog you don't have," Bull said sarcastically as he reached down to pat him.

"He's new."

"Sure he is."

"How do you know Milton?" Piper said to Coco with a look of surprise as she shrugged off her red coat.

"This is Bull!" Coco said, pointing at him but looking at Piper.

"This is Cocopuffs!" he said, pointing at Coco but looking at Piper.

"Wait? *What?*" Coco said to Bull and dropped her hand.

"*Oh my god!*" Piper doubled over laughing. "Are you shitting me? This is the funniest thing I've ever heard."

"Cocopuffs? Seriously?" Coco looked up at Bull with her hands on her hips.

"Now I feel bad because you think I'm handsome."

"No I don't! Oh my god!"

"Guys, guys," Piper said when she composed herself. "This is fucking *hilarious*!"

"Is it?" Coco said to Piper, crossing her arms tightly. "What's hilarious is that you think he'd eat an apple. Polisher, my ass. He calls me Cocopuffs and you didn't figure it out?"

Piper doubled over laughing again. "Gabby, it didn't even dawn on me!" More laughter. "I thought it was because he thought some lady at work was crazy like that bird in the cereal commercial. Oh—"

Bull smiled self-consciously.

"Gee, thanks. That sure makes it better." Then Coco blushed, remembering all the details Piper had shared about TD&H. Blech. She turned to him. "You never told her about working at The Mission?"

"We've only gone on four dates."

"Five," Piper said.

"Five dates. And I do have a real job, too, you know."

"You do?"

"Yes!"

"Wait." She inhaled sharply. "Are you seriously an *actuary*?"

"We gonna do this again?"

She knew he was referring to the fact that she didn't think he took the SATs or went to an Ivy League college.

"I just meant that I didn't know you enjoyed math," she lied.

He shrugged. "Yeah, and I didn't know you lived in a big house with a pool and a dog—oh, wait. *Yeah, I did.*" He flared his eyes at her.

Coco slid to her right to hide the digital photo frame on her refrigerator door.

"Can't you just admit that we both prejudged each other?"

"Wait. Why does she call you Gab—"

"No you wait—"

"Shut up! Shut up! Shut uuuuuup!" Piper yelled with her eyes closed.

Coco and Bull turned to her in shock.

"This isn't about you." She gestured between Coco and Bull. "This is about us." She pointed to Bull and herself.

"Fine. You're right. Wine?"

"Yes. Thank you. I can get it." Piper grabbed a couple of glasses from the cabinet herself. She filled them and handed one to her date.

"Cheers," she said, her smile returning. "Cocopuffs," she snorted into her glass.

"Hi. I'm Marybeth." She reached out smiling to shake Bull's hand. Everyone else seemed to have forgotten about the stray book club member. "It looks like you guys have a lot to talk about. So I'm gonna go." She gathered her coat, purse, and book. "It was nice to meet you, Milton. Bye, Piper. Thanks, Coco." She blew a kiss to the hostess.

"Bye," the other women said in unison.

"Night," Bull said to her back.

Marybeth made a hasty exit down the front hall. Almost immediately, Coco realized she must have forgotten something because of the sound her shoes made on the hardwoods as they carried her back to the kitchen. She looked around for the cell phone or something else that Marybeth left behind.

But it was Ava and not Marybeth who appeared in the kitchen doorway.

"Hi," she said, swinging her purse casually by its long strap. She wore a dark pantsuit under a matching Chanel coat that was knotted tightly around her slim waist. She looked around the kitchen cautiously from the doorway like a guest who just walked into the wrong wedding. Or wake. "I caught an earlier flight and saw the lights still on. Did I miss everything?"

"Not quite," Coco said. "Can I get you a glass—"

"We have to go," Piper announced abruptly and fed her right arm back into the sleeve of her coat.

"You do? *Why?*" Coco said. "You just got here." She handed Ava a glass of wine.

"Yeah, why?" Ava repeated into her glass, not seeming to care one way or the other.

"You're right." Piper started to remove her coat again. "Why should I have to leave? *You* should leave." She stabbed her finger in the air at Ava.

"Piper, what's going on?" Coco searched her friend's face for an answer.

"I think the cook is drunk," Ava said as she took a sip from her glass.

"Fuck you," Piper said and took a step forward. Bull's nervous eyes darted around the room, the way big dogs do around little ones.

"Piper! Ava!" Coco said, holding her arms wide like a referee in a boxing ring. "Let's just all take a deep breath and calm down." She looked from one woman to the other and then to Bull, who shrugged his shoulders and shifted his weight uncomfortably.

"I will not calm down, Gabby! I only came here because you told me *she* wouldn't be here."

"You did?" Ava looked at Coco with an expression full of hurt. Then she turned her attention back to Piper. "Oh my god, are you still hung up on those stupid texts?" she said, rolling her eyes. She tried to look bored but only managed to look tired and sad.

"You know it is, bitch."

"You need to let it go, girl. Move the fuck on."

Coco looked at Ava then Piper. "What texts? Let what go—"

"Hey, Becky With The Good Hair, you have a lot of fucking nerve telling me what to do."

"Piper, what the hell's going on here?" Coco said.

"Uggggh!" Piper growled in frustration and turned to Coco. "This one was texting my husband. She fucked up her own marriage and then she tried to fuck mine up, too!"

"Shhhh," Coco said looking at the ceiling upon remembering her kids were upstairs. "What are you talking about?" she hissed.

"She was texting Brian right under my nose!" She lowered her voice in response to Coco's expression. "They gave me all his stuff at the hospital. I went through his phone a few days later and this one was all over it."

"You and your hyperbole. Annoying, really."

"Take some goddamn responsibility, Lurch."

"Responsibility for *what*, you lun-a-tic? We had half a dozen texts! They were innocent, but Ms. Jealousy here can't wrap her little brain around that." Ava took a long drag from her wineglass.

"Oh my god." Coco looked at Ava in shock. Bull tried to bend down to pat the dog, but as he reached, Ducky rolled on his back to expose the stomach he wanted scratched and Bull couldn't reach him. The dog lay belly-up at his feet looking at him hopefully; two males who would rather be anywhere else.

"There was nothing going on and you know it. Brian was sweet but I'm, well"—she laughed abruptly—"out of his league, don't you think?"

Piper's chin dipped and her tone was full of menace. "Ava."

"Maybe you could have been nicer to him. But, pffft, look who I'm talking to."

Piper lunged at Ava. Bull caught her around the waist and swung her flailing body away. Her limbs kept moving like a small dog who's held over water. The taller woman stood her ground without flinching. Coco marveled once again at the woman's cool.

"No wonder Johan left you!" Piper yelled as she hung from Bull's grip. "Maybe you should have spent more time paying attention to your own husband instead of mine and he wouldn't have gone looking for that smoking-hot arm candy!"

"Don't," Ava said.

"Hey, I heard he knocked her up, too!"

If a pin had dropped, everyone in the kitchen would have heard it.

Coco made a tent over her mouth with both hands as Bull lowered Piper back down on her feet. Ava's eyes showed sadness for a second and then a mask slipped back down over her face. She pursed her lips, put her glass carefully back down on the marble countertop, brushed a crumb away with the back of her hand, and picked up her purse.

Meanwhile, Ducky ran upstairs as fast as he could, turning back halfway up as if inviting Bull to run away with him. Bull watched him go with longing.

Ava took a few steps toward the hallway then stopped and turned around.

"You know, Piper," she said softly. "You should clean your own side of the street before you worry about mine. Your rage has been a problem for a long time."

"Ava, for God's sake, just go!" Coco said.

Ava looked at her with hurt in her eyes that Coco had never seen before. "Wow. Thanks, friend. Great book club." She turned back around and walked down the hallway and out the front door.

3 3

The three stood in the kitchen in silence, each leaning against a different section of the U-shaped counter with crossed arms.

Coco turned to her friend. "How come you never told me? I didn't think we kept secrets."

"Oh really? How about the fact that you wanted to go back to work? I found that out when everyone else did."

Coco gave her a look as if to say, *Oh c'mon now.* "That's not the same thing and you know it. First of all, I was drunk. Second of all, at least you knew before my kids did. And before Rex. And I sleep with him!"

"But why didn't you tell me your feelings about not working?"

That was an excellent question. Coco stared at her friend. "I guess I didn't tell you out of pride. And embarrassment."

"Ditto." Piper raised an eyebrow and gestured a quick toast with her glass.

"Well, maybe it *is* the same thing. Wait, don't turn this around. This is about you. You were hurting. I could've helped."

"How?"

"Well, for starters by reminding you how much Brian loved

244

you. And by pointing out that, while she can be a bitch, Ava wouldn't have hurt you, either."

Bull cleared his throat and both women turned to him as if just remembering that he was there.

"We should go."

"We should. I'm sorry," Piper said to Bull as he hung her coat on her shoulders. "And I'm sorry to you, too." She took two steps toward Coco and the women embraced.

"That's okay, you weirdo. Go home. I love you."

"I love you, too, Cocopuffs."

"Get out."

34

B right and early the next day, the kids went off to school while Coco filled her travel mug with coffee and headed to The Mission. She felt a little apprehensive about going back since the whole fire confession fiasco and the scene in the kitchen, so she brought Ducky along as a personal support dog. As much as she wished they had made a decision as a family to add a dog to the mix, she had to admit he was very smart and well behaved.

From the minute he walked through the yellow door, Mr. Confident made himself at home; first by greeting everyone he met with a sniff and a lick, then by drinking all the warm, saliva-soaked water out of Chewy's bowl, and finally by leading Coco to the Linen Room and curling up on the giant dog's futon mattress. Peggy and Bull were already in the room working in silence.

"Hello love," Peggy said to Coco.

"Hi Peggy. Bull." Coco smiled at Peggy and shot a brief glance in Bull's direction.

"Hi," he grunted without looking up from the box he was taping shut. Coco knew he would never bring up the scene in the kitchen the night before and, for once, she was grateful he was the strong but silent type.

If Peggy noticed a shift in the room, she didn't let on. Instead she explained the process of pulling down boxes from the shelves, opening them to figure out their contents, and writing it on the outside of the box. After the boxes were resealed, they should be carried to the loading dock for the yard sale, which was only two days away. The more boxes and furniture they could remove from the Linen Room and warehouse, according to Peggy, the more room they would have to accept practical donations for their clients; and the bigger profit they made from the yard sale, the more toasters and mattresses they could buy to give away.

No one mentioned the fire so neither did she. It was probably small potatoes considering what the volunteers dealt with here every day. She liked that about the place: Drama didn't stick.

The yard sale prep plan this day was to organize everything into three categories: home accents (including artwork), electronics, and furniture too impractical for the clients, such as grandfather clocks and large china cabinets. Thanks to Coco, most of the boxes had only the words "Yard Sale" on them and had to be reopened and examined for their contents.

When Coco looked at Peggy for direction on where to jump in, the older woman's face was pinched in concentration.

"What are you thinking about, Peggy?"

"You know when you mail someone a wedding gift and you don't get a thank-you note back and you think they're bad-mannered?"

"I guess."

"But what if they never got the gift and they think *you're* bad-mannered?"

"Did you find someone's wedding gift in here?" Coco asked, kneeling down and pulling back the flaps on the box that sat on the floor between them.

"Nope. You just asked me what I was thinking about," she replied with a shrug.

"Oh." Coco nodded slowly and the two went back to work opening boxes to inspect them.

"Next year, we should probably write the contents of the boxes on the outside as soon as they get here to save time," Coco said on her knees as she sealed up another box of vases, German figurines, and doilies.

"Next year, huh?" Peggy smiled. "Does that mean you're going to stick around until then, lovie?"

"It does." Coco smiled up at her and the older woman patted her shoulder as she stepped over the box she was closing up. Coco couldn't believe that she'd actually considered not returning.

"I'm going to grab some coffee and take a break. These old muscles aren't what they used to be. Does anyone want anything?"

"No thanks," Coco and Bull both answered.

Left alone, the two worked in silence for another ten minutes. Bull reached the top shelves without the help of the step stool and placed boxes on the floor, and Coco opened, labeled, and then resealed them by folding in the flaps to save on packing tape. After six or seven boxes had been handled in this way, Coco could no longer ignore the big brown elephant in the room.

"So Piper's complicated, huh?" she said in a lame effort to broach the subject.

Bull put down the box in his hands and looked at her as if she'd just said Shaq O'Neal is tall.

"Complicated. No. The space shuttle is complicated," Bull said in a calm voice. "That one," he said pointing with his entire arm toward the door for some reason. "That Piper is bat-shit crazy."

Coco grimaced and an awkward silence hung in the air. She knew Piper would be upset if he dumped her over the disaster the night before, and she felt the blame was on her by unintentionally allowing Piper and Ava to be in her kitchen at the same time. And in front of Bull.

"She's not crazy," she defended.

"One hundred percent she is." He paused. Then he looked up and said, "I didn't say I didn't like it."

"Okay, then." Relieved and grossed out at the same time, she shook her head in an attempt to clear the image, as if her brain was an Etch A Sketch.

"She's definitely not your average white suburban housewife." He looked in her eyes as if to say *like you*.

"I'm still recovering. First, it was a shock to find out about . . . well, *you*."

"Tall, Dark, and Handsome." He smiled, pointing to himself. "Piper told me you started that."

"Oh my god, no I didn't. She did!"

"She did?" He smiled wider. "Hmm," he purred.

Coco shivered. "Then I find out about Ava and Brian. Then I find out about Ava and Johan. I had no idea, and I talk to Piper every day."

"Sometimes you do what you have to do to when you're dealing with something private." Bull pushed some of the boxes together with his big-booted foot, more to have something to do and less because it had to be done.

It was then that Coco remembered how Bull and Piper had met.

"Hey, I'm sorry about your wife."

"Yeah."

"What happened, if you don't mind me asking?"

"I'm surprised you controlled yourself this long. About two years ago, on her way to visit my mother, she caught a patch of black ice and . . . hit a tree."

Coco flinched. "Jeeze."

"She passed away a few months later."

Coco wanted to know more, but she also knew her audience. Still, she pushed a little.

"What was her name?"

"Grace." He reached into his back pocket for his phone and pulled up a photo. He handed the phone to Coco. In the photo, he and his late wife were bundled in heavy coats and sitting on a wall at Narragansett Beach. It was winter and the sand was mostly covered with snow. The sky was a clear blue, but the beach was deserted except for one surfer in a wet suit visible over Grace's left shoulder. Bull was obviously the photographer of the selfie.

Coco spread her fingers diagonally on the touch screen to enlarge Grace's face, then handed the phone back to him. "She's very pretty."

Bull took the phone without looking at the photo and put it back in his pocket. "I was supposed to go instead of her that morning. To my mother's. But I came down with something."

Coco looked up at him, surprised but grateful that he was giving her more than she asked for.

"My mother was going through chemo and I had to stay home so she wouldn't catch my virus."

"Oh wow." Coco was almost afraid to ask. She remembered that Bull's mother had been the one to help Ernie and his wife adopt their baby girl. "Is she—"

"She's good." His head bobbed up and down.

"I'm glad."

"Me too." He actually smiled briefly at the floor when he said it. Coco considered for the first time that he was actually someone's son. She had to admit that there was charm buried deep, deep down under all those layers of flesh.

"Did she—"

"Nope, Oprah. We're done here." He bent down and stacked four boxes before picking up the whole load from the bottom and heading for the door.

"Okay then. Good talk," she said to his back.

"Wait." He stopped in the doorway and turned back to her, holding the boxes like they were empty.

"What?"

"I don't want to mess this up with Piper. Any advice?"

Her mouth formed a slow smile and she nodded. "With Piper? So you need *my* help now? Wait, you want someone to like you? You want to be liked? You should be ashamed of yourself. Is this the first time this has happened?" She stood with her hands on her hips.

"First time since Grace. You know her better than anyone else. C'mon, Coco, help a brother out."

She squinted at him for a long moment then said, "Fine. First, don't ask her to cook for you. She hates cooking."

"But she's a *caterer*!"

"And those people are paying her. Are you paying her?"

"No."

"Then don't ask her to cook for you. She will if she feels like it."

"Aright. What else?" He stood holding the heavy boxes like he had all the time in the world.

"She's allergic to roses."

"Okay. That works. What else?"

"Take her to a Providence Bruins game and sit behind the net. Her grandfather used to bring her every year on her birthday and they'd always sit there."

"Really? Cool. Thanks." He nodded and smiled at her genuinely for the first time since they'd met.

"You're welcome."

"Oh wait," he said. "So when's her birthday?"

"Sunday."

"What?" He dropped the boxes. "When were you going to tell me that? Shit. I gotta go make a call."

She'd never seen him so flustered or move so fast. As soon as he left, Sawyer poked his head in the door.

"He almost flattened me in the hall. My life flashed before my eyes."

"He remembered something important he had to do." Coco glanced at Sawyer, expecting a conversation to begin about the fire. But, with a combination of good humor and respect, Sawyer's expression let her know that he didn't need to talk about it, and she was grateful.

"Can you help me?" she asked.

"I'm afraid not to."

"Funny."

For the next two hours they moved box after box to the loading dock. The boxes were full of all colors and types of vases and clocks as well as small electronics, purses, wallets, fancy dishes, serving platters, silver-plated flatware, crystal decanters, and jewelry boxes. Many of the one-of-a-kind items such as the Underwood typewriter, the dress form, and the five-foot-tall, tuxedoed basset hound butler holding a tray, were left outside at the door when The Mission was closed. Before they started holding yard sales, those items had been given to the Salvation Army or Big Brothers Big Sisters, but then Peggy had floated the idea of a yard sale a few years ago. Now this annual event was one of their biggest fundraisers.

Coco worked with Sawyer to attach red tags on any piece of furniture intended to be in the sale. As they walked around the warehouse, Coco asked him questions about how the sale worked.

"It works the same as a yard sale you'd have at home. Peggy put a few ads online and in the local *Patch* and other sites like Nextdoor. We also sent out all those flyers you stuffed a while back. Peg always adds some photos of our showstoppers, like that pool table or the grandfather clock over there."

According to Sawyer, at the previous three sales, the public had turned out in good numbers in equal parts to support The Mission and to also find a bargain. This year they had far fewer items to sell thanks to the fire and they were also painfully low on furniture. Unfortunately, those were the things that always seemed to bring the crowds. He said that he was worried, but not panicked. Yet.

"Strange thing is, the publicity from the fire will probably bring more people here than any other year because they want to support us. Some people didn't even know The Mission existed until they saw it on the news. People also love dogs, so the Chewy angle helps," he said.

"I know. Charlotte showed me some viral posts about him."

"Yeah, but to be honest, it doesn't matter how many people come if we don't have enough things to sell to them. Fewer big-ticket items means less money no matter how many people show up to shop. I'm a little worried, to be honest, but Ernie doesn't seem to be."

"Where is he? I thought he'd be here today."

"I dunno." He shrugged. "He and Daisy drove off a few hours ago."

They finished tagging the furniture and then dragged out a few folding tables from the back wall and leaned them against the boxes, ready to set up the next morning.

"Did Bull pick up the desk from my house yet?"

"He did." Sawyer smirked under his mustache.

"What?" she said, trying to establish eye contact.

"The thing is, Coco . . ."

"What?"

"It stinks. It smells worse than a medieval fishmonger's armpits."

"I know. I thought a year in my garage would air it out. Sorry."

"Don't be sorry. I figured we can salvage those mahogany legs and use them for a coffee table if you don't mind."

"Okay," she said.

"Are you sure?"

A little part of her felt a guilty for destroying a piece of furniture that had been in the family so long. The truth was, no one would want it inside their house, and at least the legs would make it into a new home. A second chance for three original legs and the one her dad had made to save her ass. She felt like she was signing an organ donor card.

"I'm sure. Are those all the tables we have?" she asked with her hands on top of her head. "Doesn't seem like enough." She rotated at the waist, looking around the warehouse.

"Yup and yup. Most years we have more furniture than furnishings, but not this time."

"Where are we going to put all the boxed stuff? We can't put it on the mud. Wait! I know where I can get some tables. I'll be back."

"See ya, kid."

Coco grabbed Ducky from the Linen Room and headed home.

35

In Piper's garage later that afternoon, the two women struggled to free a plastic table from under piles of stainless steel cooking equipment. Coco stood high on a heap directing her friend on how to shift and cajole a stack of chairs so she could lift one end of the table out from underneath the pile. Piper balanced, wedged between the hood of her late husband's old Volvo and the chairs, with one foot on the front bumper for leverage.

Coco called out orders. "Just move it an inch to the left. Your right!"

"I'm right?"

"Your right. My left!"

"What are you saying, woman?"

"Move it to *my* left, *your* right."

"Shit. Am I mind reader? Wait!"

"What?"

"My foot's stuck."

"Jesus, Mary, and Joseph, Piper. Stop. Stop. I'll do it." Coco held out her hand. "Help me down."

The two women struggled for a bit longer with the heavy

stack before they gave up. Piper walked to the refrigerator and pulled out two cans of Diet Coke, and the women sat on the hood of the dusty car to drink them.

"How are we going to get those out?" Piper said.

"Gee, if only we knew a giant who could help us . . ." Coco looked at her friend sideways.

"I can't just call him when I need a mover. We're not to that point in our relationship yet. Why don't *you* call him?"

"I'm *not* calling him. Wait—did you say relationship?" Coco turned to her friend and elbowed her hard.

"Ow! I guess. Who knows? I'm, like, middle aged so I don't know what I'm supposed to call it. Are we courting? Banging? Do they still say *hooking up*?"

"Don't look at me." Coco took a sip from her can and patted the hood of the car beneath them. "Are you going to sell this? Or hold on to it for Katie?"

"I don't know. Most of me is trying to move on, and then some of me is trying to hold on, you know?"

"Yeah."

"Hey, Gabby, about last night. I'm sorry I freaked out."

"You don't owe me an apology," Coco said twisting the tab on the top of her can and waiting for an apology nonetheless.

"I'd been holding on to it for so long, and it felt like the right time to tell you had long since passed."

"So standing in my kitchen in front of your new guy seemed like the right time?"

Piper shrugged. "As good a time as any. I swear to God I felt like a pressure cooker. It felt so good to let it out." She exhaled deeply, mimicking the feeling. "She was just so goddamn smug, standing there in front of me in all her statuesque glory. Evil Julianne Moore. I know she thinks it was nothing. But she doesn't get to decide."

Coco nodded.

"I mean, I was already reeling from losing him, then I look

through his phone a few days later and I had to deal with anger and betrayal on top of grief. I hated him. I hated her. It was too much."

"You don't really think Brian would have done anything with her, do you?"

"That fucking mannequin," she muttered. "He probably wouldn't have. But we will never know."

Coco rubbed her back. "I'm sorry, honey. It must have been hard because you couldn't confront him, only her. But next time, please let me in. When something upsets you, if you say it out loud, you take away its power."

"Oh lord." Piper turned to Coco.

"What?"

"Look at me. Look at me! Have you been watching that crackpot again, Gabby? You promised me no more Dr. Phil."

"No matter how flat you make a pancake, it's still got two sides," Coco imitated the television psychiatrist in her best Texas twang.

Piper leaned back on the car. "What the hell does that even mean?"

"Don't look at me. I'm not a super-fan. Sometimes I'm just too lazy to change the channel."

"You're full of shit."

"Opinions are like assholes. Everybody's got one."

"Stop. Please," Piper groaned. "I'm begging you."

"How about I will stop if you call your boyfriend to come over and help us?"

"He's not my boyfr—"

"You're fat. Don't sugarcoat it 'cause you'll eat that, too."

"I don't want to. Stop. Puh-leeeeeeze."

"Sometimes you make the right decision. Sometimes you make the decision right."

"Okay! *Okaaaay!* Shut the fuck up!" Piper covered her friend's mouth with one hand and pulled her cell phone out of her pocket with the other. "I'm calling. I'm calling."

Coco sipped her soda smugly, but her celebration ended when she was forced to listen to Piper's sugary voice, knowing who was on the receiving end. "Hi, Boo . . . thanks, Boo . . . you, too, Boo." *Blech.* When she couldn't stand it any longer, Coco reached over and covered her friend's mouth while Piper squirmed and laughed.

She ended the call and then, in her most seductive voice, said, "He's coming."

"Oh god. Puke!" She pushed her friend and they wrestled until both slid off the hood of the car laughing onto the garage floor.

After they composed themselves, Piper said, "Gabby?"

"Yeah?"

"I think I just peed a little."

"Me too."

They clawed their way back to standing and brushed off their pants.

"By the way, Milton said to say hi to Cocopuffs for him. So, *hi*."

"Hey, that's hilarious. Let's go inside and make some peanut butter cookies to thank him."

"What a great idea!"

"Thank you for your service, Caleb," Ernie said to the fifty-year-old man across the table from them.

"You're welcome, sir," Caleb said as he, Ernie, and Coco rose to their feet to shake hands. The Mission's newest client held the Polaroid photo of himself and his new frame in his other hand.

Caleb Browning was a Marine Corps veteran who had fought in the first Gulf War. A leg injury from an IED had led to multiple surgeries, which led to painkillers, which then led him on the predictable path to heroin. After a dozen years on the street and his third overdose, he'd found himself in a methadone clinic in Providence. Upon discharge, he was placed in a shelter for a year and was now ready to begin again. He'd shown up at The Mission an hour earlier dressed in jeans and a green flak jacket. His skin told the story of years of drug use, but his smile was genuine and, by his attitude, it was obvious to see that he was eager to turn the page.

The three walked out of the Interview Room into the office area, where Yolanda was waiting for the paper Ernie handed to her and off she went to the Linen Room, humming some jingle from TV. Since Caleb lived alone, the list of things he needed was short; maybe just one shopping cart full.

The next stop was the Showroom, but Ernie continued to talk with Caleb in the office for a few more minutes about their shared experiences in the military.

"I was stationed at Pendleton for a while, but was able to serve my time in between wars. Got out before Vietnam."

"Some guys have all the luck."

"I'll say." Ernie walked around behind his desk and pulled open his bottom drawer. After digging around a bit, he grabbed that big manila envelope with "Army" written on it that Coco had noticed a week before. He reached inside and pulled out an unframed three-by-three photo, curled at the white edges, which he handed to Caleb.

"Man, you were one skinny-ass corporal," Caleb said.

"Nope. That's not me. I'm the other one. But my buddy Mick and I looked an awful lot alike."

Coco wanted to leave to help Yolanda in the Linen Room, but waited for a natural break in the conversation. She glanced nonchalantly at the black-and-white photo in Caleb's hands. From her upside-down vantage point, she could make out two uniformed men standing side by side with MP armbands, white belts around their waists, and pants tucked into their short black boots. They were both holding pistols aimed at unseen shooting range targets, each with one eye closed as they aimed. She felt a weird click of familiarity in the back of her brain and asked to see the photo herself. Caleb handed it over and she rotated it in her hands. Fortunately the chair behind caught her as she sat down hard and fast, shoulders rounded and her mouth in the shape of an *O*.

"You okay, kid?" Ernie asked. "I wasn't that ugly, was I?" Ernie walked to Coco and looked over her shoulder.

All she could manage to say was, "It's my dad."

"No shit. Mick—I mean Jim, Jim McTeague—is your dad? Son of a gun! That's why you're familiar!" He smacked his forehead with an open hand.

But Coco didn't hear him. She ran her fingers over the photo. Yellowing cracks where the photo had separated from the backing along the edges were hard to her touch, but there was no mistaking it. She'd seen a copy of this photo when she was packing up her parents' albums last summer. She remembered what her dad had written on the front of his own copy: "Mo and me, 1960." Neither she nor any of her sisters had been able to determine who "Mo" was.

Ernie called Bull on his cell phone to come to the office and take Caleb to the Showroom and help him with the furniture selection. Bull lumbered into the office in less than a minute. He looked at Ernie then down at Coco, confusion written all over his face.

"Go along with Bull and I'll catch up with you in a bit," Ernie said with a pat on Caleb's shoulder, and the veteran followed Bull down the hall.

Ernie walked around his desk and took a seat in the empty chair next to Coco.

"Kid, do you want some water?"

"No, thank you," she managed.

"I can't believe Mick is your dad. I tried to track him down early on, but without the Internet it was impossible. How the hell is he?"

Coco looked up and handed the photo back to Ernie. "He passed away last year."

"Oh no."

"On my dad's copy it said 'Mo and me.' How did you get that name?"

"Ugh. Our sergeant, a jackass named Collins, started calling me that because I wasn't the fastest runner in the unit. He called me Mo Lasses. Your dad was the first friend I had in boot camp."

"Really?"

"We were both New Englanders and we'd look out for each other; covered for each other with the sergeant, did the obstacle courses side by side, laughed with each other through those cold nights camping out on bivouac. Then we both went into the military police together. There wasn't a lot of running there, so I liked it."

Coco smiled, happy but unsurprised that her dad had had such a good companion.

"Damn, I wish I could have tracked him down. People used to think we were related, you know?"

"I thought of him the minute I met you. What a small world. When was the last time you saw him?"

He scratched his head, stared up at the ceiling, and blew out two lungful's of air. "It had to be a few months after this photo was taken. Right after the accident."

"What kind of accident?" Coco asked with a furrowed brow.

"Your dad never told you about the accident in the woods? With the Jeep chase?"

Coco shook her head and widened her eyes. Her dad had talked a little about the army, but he never saw any action so she only heard stories no more exciting than those about bad food and tough drill sergeants. She knew that her parents had gotten engaged the day before he left for boot camp, when her dad proposed in his car outside a pizza joint. The only other thing she knew was that her mother had talked him into the army instead of the air force because she'd had a premonition that he would crash his jet. To please her, he'd agreed to keep both boots on the ground. But Coco had only half listened to her parents' stories while growing up. She'd always thought she would have more time to hear them again.

"What happened in the woods?"

"Let's grab some coffee and go into the other room."

A few minutes later, cups in hand, the two settled down next to each other in the comfortable chairs in the Interview Room.

"Your dad and I were MPs together. Not a bad job on the base. Mostly we just did target practice for medals and pulled the drunk soldiers out of the bars when they were causing trouble in town. We'd patrol the base at night with—"

"With a full canteen hanging from your wrist, right?"

"That's right." Ernie smiled.

"I remember that part of the story from my dad."

"When they were full of water they were heavy, so it helped strengthen your shooting arm. Never shot anything for real, though." He laughed softly. "Anyway, we thought we were such bad asses. On our long night shifts, we'd talk all the time about our girls back home: Hope and . . ." He snapped his fingers to jar his memory.

"Mary."

"Right. Mary. Sorry, it's been a while."

As Coco listened, she searched her brain for some crumb of memory about Ernie or this story. It felt like Ernie was talking about a stranger.

"But then one night, a private—his name was Kevin. No, Kenny! He went AWOL in one of the Jeeps from the motor pool. He drank a bottle of cheap whiskey and drove off into the woods after he got a letter from his girl telling him she'd married his best friend. So Sergeant Collins sent your dad and me on an unofficial mission to haul his ass back to the barracks before our lieutenant found out. None of us wanted to walk down the Heavy Hallway."

"Wait," Coco said. "My dad used to say that when my sisters and I were growing up. I thought it was just his name for the hallway to his den that we had to walk when we were in trouble. I thought he made it up."

"Nope. In the service, it used to be the place enlisted men had to walk when they get called to the offices of the brass. Maybe it still is, I don't know. It's 'heavy' because of all the medals the bosses wore on their collars and uniforms. Anyway, no one wanted to be there."

Coco shook her head. "Nope."

"It wasn't easy driving around in the woods at night sober, never mind when you're loaded. We tracked the kid down to where he'd wrapped himself around a tree before the Jeep threw him out. Those army Jeeps didn't have any doors or roofs like yours does."

Coco nodded.

"His leg was ripped up bad and he wasn't breathing. Poor bastard swallowed his chewing tobacco when he hit the tree. Or maybe that's why he hit the tree. Who knows? We couldn't get the thing out of his throat and he was bleeding like a garden hose from his leg. Your dad was tending to the gash. He ripped off his own jacket and was trying to make a tourniquet to stop all the bleeding and yelling to me about how to open his airway. Did you know your dad trained to be a medic before he changed his mind and went into the MPs?"

"No, I didn't. So this is what you were talking about when you said you'd done a tracheotomy before Bull's?"

"You are a good listener, Coco."

Cheers to all the B students.

"How did you do it in the woods without a straw?" she asked, half joking.

"Your dad talked me through it. Cool as a cucumber. Told me to use the knife on my belt and the pen from his pocket. He threw it at me. I took the ink part out, like he said, and used the empty tube. The whole thing was over in a matter of minutes. When your dad got the tourniquet on, he radioed for the medics."

"Wow. I can't believe he never told us that story."

Ernie waved a dismissive hand. "Different generation, my dear. We weren't braggers like the kids these days who think everything they do is interesting. Don't get me started on Facebook posts. Boy, we got in a shit—uh, a boatload of trouble, though." He laughed a little.

"For the tracheotomy."

"Nah, they didn't give a damn about that. It was because we broke the rules."

Coco reached for the photo again and studied it.

"Anyway, the last time I saw him, we were standing in the Heavy Hallway. We couldn't talk to each other. Just stood with our backs against the wall, facing forward, waiting and waiting for the lieutenant to hand down our punishment. They loved to keep you waiting."

"What'd they do to you?" Coco asked, more out of concern for her dad than Ernie.

"Sergeant Collins got demoted. I think Kenny got booted out after he got out of the hospital. Can't remember now if it was because of the Jeep, the leg, or the hole I put in his throat." He laughed again at the distant memory. "Sorry. I don't know why that's funny."

Coco shook her head.

"I got stuck with sixty days of KP duty and your dad got sent to Fort Dix in Jersey, I think. He probably got KP duty, too. They wanted to split us up. They did a good job of it because I never saw him again. He was my best friend then."

"I can't believe—"

"Oh *jeeze*! I just remembered!" Ernie sprang up from his seat and hurried out of the room. Coco, with her mouth still open, assumed he had to run and check on Caleb and Bull, but he was back in ten seconds with the big manila "Army" envelope from his desk. "When I downsized to my house years ago, I brought all my paperwork here because I didn't have another place for it at home." He pulled the contents out and spread it on the table in front of them, sifting through until he found what he was looking for. Still standing, he held it to his chest with his palm flat to shield it from her while he spoke.

"A few days after the accident in the woods, another buddy of mine at the hospital on the base gave me a bag with Mick's— your dad's—uniform jacket in it. The coat couldn't be saved with the blood and all, but he had this in the pocket." He turned the square photo around and handed it to her. "I didn't know how to get it to him. I held on to it and then I kind of forgot I had it. I guess I should have tried to track him down online all these years, but I had a lot going on and I'm not so good on that machine."

Coco took the photo from his hand and her breath caught. In it, her parents were leaning on the hood of a light-colored car with a shiny grill and giant headlights. His arm was around her waist and his knee was bent while one foot rested on the bumper behind him. He was wearing dark pants and a white short-sleeve shirt over a white T-shirt. Her mother was wearing cropped pants, a light blouse tied in a knot at her waist, and a scarf around her neck. Her short dark hair was blowing in the wind. Dark sunglasses hid her eyes, but nothing in the world could have hidden her smile.

"I've never seen this photo before. It's beautiful. I can't believe you kept it all these years."

"He said Mary gave it to him the day he boarded the bus for basic training. They'd gotten engaged the night before he left. He used to smell it all the time. Turn it over."

Her mother's uniquely angular handwriting filled the back. "Counting the days. Yours, Sweets. 1960."

Coco was overcome with emotion. The first thing she wanted to do at that very moment was pick up the phone, call her parents, and say, "You're not going to believe this . . ." It was the first time in a while that she'd had the urge to do that. Realizing she couldn't always made her feel the way she did when she woke up from one of those dreams about them: with a heart that was full and broken.

She wiped her eyes with her sleeve and Ernie touched her other arm with his warm hand. He left it there for a long moment until she covered it with her own.

"I don't know why I'm crying. They had a long, happy life together. They were married for more than forty years."

"You miss 'em. That's why. Photos are powerful. That's why we want to give them to our clients."

"Yeah."

He reached behind his chair and then slid the familiar white box in front of her. "How about a frame?"

She laughed so hard she snorted. "Thanks, Mo Lasses."

At that moment, Bull knocked gently on the doorframe of the room. Neither Coco nor Ernie knew how long he'd been standing there. "Uh, sorry to interrupt." He looked confused and uncomfortable and Coco enjoyed that. "Caleb's all set. His truck's getting loaded up."

"Okay, thanks. I'll be right there."

As Bull nodded and started to walk away, Coco grabbed Ernie's sleeve and said, "Wait. You said my dad taught you how to do a tracheotomy?"

"That's right."

"So he taught you how to save Kenny *and* Bull."

"Yup."

She jumped up from her seat. "Wait! Bull! Guess what?" she hollered with a big smile as she ran to catch up with him.

"Shine on, Miss Mick," Ernie said as he watched her go.

38

When Ava swung open her thick arched door, she found Coco dressed in jeans, a black shirt, and white puffy vest, standing on her front step holding a foil-covered plate of chocolate chip cookies up in front of her chin with both hands.

"Oh," Ava said disappointed. "I thought you were the movers." She looked past Coco into the empty driveway. Stunning as always, Ava wore a 1960s-style rolled-neck cashmere sweater in sky blue and expensive black tapered pants cropped above the ankle. She was barefoot with newly polished toenails in pale pink.

"*Movers?*" Coco frowned and looked past Ava down the long hallway. "Can I come in?"

Ava studied Coco's face for a moment and then looked down, stood aside, and gestured for her to enter with an expression that said *whatever*. She closed the heavy door behind her.

The sound of Coco's shoes on the marble floor echoed off the walls as they walked otherwise silently along the main hall to the kitchen. *Talk about a Heavy Hallway*, she thought. This was the place where all of Ava's photos with celebrity clients were displayed, each of the oversized black-and-white photos in identical matte silver frames lining the two walls like a museum. Coco often thought they were strategically placed there so each guest could get gradually more intimidated as they followed Ava into the house, as Coco was now doing. Dozens of new, flattened boxes were stacked on either side of them as they walked. Unopened multipacks of neon-pink duct tape kept the boxes company on the floor. When they reached the kitchen, Coco put the plate down on the massive island and turned to face Ava.

"Where are you going? Oh god, you're not moving because of what happened?"

"Do you mean the soap opera scene in your house or my lurid affair with Brian?"

Coco was caught off guard by the confession and her mouth hung open.

"I'm kidding, you moron. I told you, nothing happened between us. I may be a lot of things, but I'm not a cheater."

Coco closed her mouth and tried to remember an instance to contradict that characterization, but couldn't.

Ava turned her back on Coco and busied herself pulling glasses down from a cabinet. "Besides, you bitches don't have the power to make me move, Coco. You can't even find a piece of fruit in your car that's the size of a baby's head."

Coco raised an eyebrow but had no retort. *Wow*, she mouthed to the redhead's back and wondered which one of the book club members had dimed her out.

"Look, Ava, I'm sorry about what I said. I didn't know you were going through anything. I'm private, too, and I get it. I just wish you'd maybe reached out so you could have leaned on me. Or someone."

"You mean I should have told you all my business that's none of yours?"

"No. Well. Yes."

"Did I miss something? Because I never thought we had that kind of relationship. And you were already paired up in your clique of two." Ava started wrapping glasses using a big pile of bubble wrap sheets on the counter in front of her.

"I'm not following."

Ava stopped what she was doing and turned around. "Well, for starters, I know Piper's been saying shit and she's your 'BFF.'" Ava used air quotes. "Then, proving my point, you take her side and kick me out of your house."

"Piper never said a word to me about Brian and you until the other night."

If Ava was surprised by that news, she didn't show it. "When have you ever called, texted, or stopped by to see me?"

Coco scanned her memory database in desperate search for one single example but came up empty.

"I also think I scare the shit out of you."

"What?" Coco attempted to sound shocked and futilely tried to smooth the creases in the aluminum foil covering the cookies. "Yes. Yes, you do. I just didn't know that you knew that." She tried to laugh but it sounded fake.

"I'm in fucking PR, Coco. It's my business to read people." Ava retrieved more glasses from the cabinet and, as she reached on her tiptoes, her T-shirt rose up to expose a bare portion of her pale lower back. Coco noticed for the first time that Ava had lost a substantial amount of weight. This wasn't something that happened overnight. How could she not have noticed that her neighbor and fellow book club member was wasting away?

She felt her face redden. "All I'm saying is that you could have opened up to me. Or any of us. We're your friends."

"Controlling who I told was the only power I had." Ava let the words hang before continuing, still with her back to her guest. "So I chose to tell no one. And seeing someone once a month and New Year's Eve doesn't exactly make us best buds."

Coco felt bad that she'd never given this woman the impression that she could come to her if she needed a friend. On the other hand, Coco would never have gone to Ava. But that's because she had Piper. Maybe Ava didn't have a Piper.

Ava kept working as she talked. "I get it. We both have things the other one wants but doesn't have." She added another wrapped glass to a box beside her on the tile floor then turned to Coco with her hands gesturing around the room. "I have the nice house and the career. You have the great marriage and the kids—"

"Wait." Coco stopped her. "I have a nice house, too."

Ava mouthed, *Okay*, and then turned back to the open glass cabinet. "Nothing ever happened between Brian and me. I'm sure you've heard an earful from Piper since the other night, but she's wrong about whatever she's saying. She has a better imagination than Walt Fucking Disney and—"

Coco looked up. "I thought you didn't want any kids."

"What?"

"You said that I had the husband and the kids."

"Why would you think I didn't want kids?" Ava turned around again. "Why else would we have bought this big house?"

Coco was embarrassed to say that she just assumed it because she thought Ava got whatever Ava wanted. She said nothing.

"You want some dirt for the next book club? Grab your bucket," Ava said. "I couldn't get pregnant, so Johan found someone who could. Simple as that. He knocked her up and left. Jesus, even that lesbian Sophie could get pregnant. But not me. So I got lonely and I liked the attention from Brian. End of story." She shrugged. "Johan had checked out of our marriage a long time ago. Brian complimented me sometimes and made me feel good."

Coco nodded, a dozen questions swimming in her head.

"But I never would have taken it to the next level. And, for the record, Brian never would have, either. He was such a sweetheart, and for whatever reason he loved that little nut job. He was just being nice to me because no one else was. I really was out of his league, though. I mean, c'mon. I know that little lunatic didn't want to hear that but it's true. It was just harmless texting."

"The thing is, though, it wasn't. Not to Piper," Coco said, and Ava dropped her arms to her sides. "I think she felt as if you had everything and then you were trying to steal her husband, too. I know how she felt. I used to be a little jealous of you."

"Used to be?" Ava laughed dryly. "But not anymore, right?"

"I still think you're pretty," Coco said with an awkward grin, hoping for a smile from Ava that didn't come. "So, um, where are you going?" she asked to change the subject.

Ava took her time answering. She put her hands on her bony hips as she looked around the room, and her fingertips nearly met at her belly button.

"My friend in London made me an offer a few weeks ago that I can't refuse. My life can't get any worse, so I'm going to get the fuck out of EG, RI, and the USA and help with her new start-up. I need a goddamn fresh start. You housewives make me want to scream most of the time."

Coco wanted to run, but a part of her couldn't let her relationship with this woman end like this. "Do you need help packing?"

"No. The movers already dropped off the boxes. They're coming back to get started sometime today. I'm just doing this right now because, if I don't keep busy, I'll go out of my fucking mind."

Coco watched her neighbor for a full minute as she stood on her tiptoes again to reach into the half-empty cabinet. She watched her pull down the wineglasses she always put out for book club, giant globes with shiny silver stems and bases.

Find the shine, she told herself. "I'm sorry, Ava."

"For what?"

"For thinking you were a bitch."

"I am a bitch." She shrugged. "But at least I own it."

Ava pulled her hands out of the cabinet and turned around.

273

"And are you actually sorry? Or are you just trying to make yourself feel better because you know I'm leaving?"

As usual, Coco was stymied by Ava's confidence and confrontational style. Her mouth hung open for ten more seconds before Ava broke the silence.

"Let me ask you a question." She leaned on the counter like a sinewy cat. "Why is it that when someone seems to have the perfect life and they're a bitch, people are offended by them all the time? But if someone's struggling and they're a bitch, people don't seem to mind?"

"I don't know what you mean."

"Piper!" she said, pointing in the general direction of the Harper house. "People have been walking on eggshells around that nut job for the past year. Why does she get away with that?"

"Because her husb—"

"Oh, don't give me that crap. People croak every day. I know why. Because you all wished you were me and that's why you couldn't tolerate my bullshit. But you are all so happy that you aren't her. That's why you *can* tolerate her bullshit. Because Piper's been a bitch since Brian died and *no one cares!*"

Coco struggled with how to defend her best friend, wondering if Ava was going to take any of the responsibility for Piper's mood. Ava held up her hand like a Stop sign, letting Coco off the hook.

"Hey, I get it. I told you. I know I'm a bitch, too! I can't help it. I was raised that way. And I also know my husband didn't die. *Unfortunately.* I probably could have been nicer to Piper, but I'm just not that way. I'm no girl's girl, as you know by now."

Coco's eyebrow rose in agreement.

"I was hard on you, Coco. I was jealous of the pieces you have that I don't."

"Are you kidding? I'm a mess," Coco said in genuine shock. "That pomegranate's been rolling around for three months!"

"I know. Why can't you fucking find it?"

"It's not that I *can't*. I just *don't*," Coco said, and this time they both laughed.

"You'd better get your shit together because I won't be around to scare you anymore." Coco's face transitioned into unease as a sheen came over Ava's eyes. It was the closest Coco had ever come to seeing her cry.

"It won't be the same here without you, Ava."

"No shit. You boring bitches need to step up your game. If I can leave you all with just one piece of advice, it is this: Use coasters, for God's sake."

"You really are a fucking bitch, though."

When Ava laughed, her cheeks rose up and forced the tears to spill over. She used the heels of her hands to pull the salty water away from her lower lashes without disturbing her eye makeup.

"See? See? Shoot! Why? It was the perfect time to use that," Coco said, looking around in disbelief. "Why does my swearing make people laugh? Fuck! Fuck! Fuck!"

Ava kept laughing and then held up her hand. Coco approached and hugged her for the first time ever. Ava's red hair enveloped Coco's face. She felt the softness of the blue cashmere under her chin.

"You can't swear for shit. You need to get *that* the fuck under control. Jesus."

"I know." Coco squeezed her friend's bony frame and blew Ava's hair out of her face. "I can't help it. I was raised that way."

Both women smiled over each other's shoulders as Ava closed her eyes.

"Okay," Ava said after a bit. "Now get off me."

39

That night, Coco drove over to The Mission to drop off an extra cash box she'd found in her craft closet from when she was in charge of the Ice Cream Social for Charlotte's fourth-grade class. She'd also come across a few packages of round colored stickers she thought they might be able to use to write prices on and affix to some of the smaller items. It was almost dark when she pulled down Somerville Road. An East Greenwich police car was parked in front of The Mission, and her first inclination was to put the Jeep in reverse and get the hell out of there. *They found out I filed a false report. Shit, shit, shit!* She pulled alongside the cruiser and made eye contact with the officer in the passenger seat, who tipped his hat to her and looked back down at the paperwork on his lap.

This is when he looks at the APB and realizes my faces matches, she thought. But he didn't look back up at her, so she quickly parked her Jeep in an improvised spot and hurried in the front door.

Greeted by a burst of warm air and the stubborn smell of smoke, Coco watched all heads in the room turn toward her, and the bell sounded two feet over her head. She felt as if she'd just interrupted a mob meeting, so intense was the atmosphere.

Sensing she'd been too flip about her freedom, she'd nearly put her wrists together in front of her so they could slap the cuffs on.

Ernie sat on the edge of his desk with one leg dangling and the other foot planted on the floor in front of him. Bull stood between the door and Ernie with his arms crossed tightly, forcing his biceps to appear even larger. His expression was very serious. An armed police officer dressed in a dark-blue uniform and puffy winter jacket stood to the left with his hat in his hands. When Bull turned to look at her, Coco could see then that seated in one of the two chairs in front of Ernie's desk was Louie. The kid was dressed in a red custom-made ski jacket that probably cost more than all the beds in the Mattress Room, and he was leaning backward in the metal chair with a cocky look on his young face.

"Coco." Ernie acknowledged her with a solemn nod.

She briefly studied the faces of the three older men in the room. "What's going on, Ernie?" she asked with the expression of a person who doesn't quite understand the joke they just heard, but is willing to have it explained to them. A big part of her was relieved that the joke wasn't on her.

The police officer, who looked to be in his late fifties, said, "I gotta go, Ernie. Let me know if he gives you any trouble." He put his hat on and tipped it to Coco as he passed by without a word.

"Thanks, JT," replied Ernie. "I appreciate you picking him up so fast."

"I owed you one," the officer said as he exited the building.

Bull wore a blank expression as usual, and Coco couldn't help remembering how Piper had called him Boo on the phone earlier. *Blech.*

"Seriously, Ernie, what's going on?"

"Yeah, Ernie," Louie said with punky smile, "what's going on?"

"Well, it seems Louie here has quite a talent," Ernie said. "What's that they say—your strikeouts put the 'K' in 'Kent County'?"

The young pitcher smirked and watched Ernie with amusement. "That's right, pops. Want an autograph?"

"Nope. Because I'm more interested in your talent for starting fires."

Louie assumed the air of a student listening to the principal explain to his parents that they think he cheated but they didn't know how. "You're out of your mind, old man," he said and rose to his feet. Bull, who outweighed the teenager by at least two hundred pounds, grabbed him by the collar of his coat and pushed him down into the chair. "I didn't start any fire." Coco noticed a nearly imperceptible change in the teen's tone.

"Oh really?" Ernie reached behind his back for the remote on the desk, aimed it at the TV on the wall, and pressed a button.

The screen was grainy for a few seconds, then a black-and-white image appeared from the point of view of The Mission's roof. It showed the bright headlights of a car coming down the road. At the last minute, the headlights went out and the car rolled to a stop ten yards from the front of the building. A figure emerged from the dark SUV with his hood concealing his face. He ran toward the right of the building, triggering the motion-sensing floodlight on the corner of the roof. The person in the video looked up at the light. Ernie pressed Pause, and East Greenwich's star pitcher's angry face was plain to see. Everyone in the room turned to Louie.

"Fuck," Louie said under his breath as he closed his eyes and leaned his head back.

"Fuck is right," said Bull, looking down at him.

The date and time stamp in the upper-right corner of the screen read "21:06:04." The date was March 24—the night of the fire. *I'm so confused*, Coco thought with one hand over her mouth and the other wrapped around her middle. *How many people are going to be on the hook for this damn fire?*

Ernie pressed Play and the video continued.

Louie reached for a rock and, with the precision of someone

who knew how to hit his target, he nailed the floodlight on his first try. The image darkened, helped now only by the ambient glow of the streetlight a hundred feet away. A few minutes passed, and Ernie fast-forwarded through the footage. The next image was of the vehicle's brake lights glowing as the driver put the car in reverse. Then it retreated backward with headlights off, up the street and out of view. Within a minute, a bright white glow could be seen in the lower-left corner of the screen. The fire had begun.

Everyone in the room watched in silence as the glow doubled in size. Then Ernie pointed the remote at the TV and pressed Pause for a second time.

"Whoa. Wait a minute! I did not start that fire! I just came here to talk to Daisy." Louie looked back and forth rapidly between Ernie and the television. "You can't pin this on me. They just said on the news that it was an accident. Some bad lamp or something."

"That's just what we told the authorities to protect you. They don't know about the video."

"Protect me? From what?"

"Being charged with vandalism and arson," Ernie said.

Coco looked at Ernie the way she used to look at her seventh-grade math teacher's worksheets named for pro golfers. *I am so confused!*

"I didn't start any fire, old man."

"Where was the camera?" Coco asked stupidly.

"The owl," Ernie said without taking his eyes off Louie.

Owls are assholes. "I thought that was for woodpeckers."

"It's a brick building, Coco," Ernie said, finally turning to look at her.

"I know. But I—"

"I swear to God I did *not* start a fire. I never even went inside. I just came to talk to Daisy but she never came out. Did you know she was hiding here?" Louie thought telling on her would get the heat off him.

"She wasn't hiding. I asked her to keep an eye on the place and the dog," Ernie lied.

Louie looked like he was starting to realize that getting out of this might not be as easy as he thought. He had a one-man conference on the mound and chose his next pitch. "So you're gonna call your cop friend back in here and have me arrested? Go ahead," he taunted. "I'm not even eighteen. My old man will have me out with a slap on the wrist before you finish watching *Jeopardy* tonight, gramps."

Bull growled down at Louie, and Coco knew the grandfather reference had stung more than Louie could have known.

"No, son. I definitely don't need the police anymore," Ernie said with finality.

Louie looked nervous for the first time. He glared back over his shoulder at Bull. "Oh, so you're going to have your bouncer mess me up? That's original." Louie tried to be flippant, but the unease he was starting to feel was creeping into his tone. Bull nodded, and Louie shifted in his seat.

"Ha!" Ernie smiled. "Don't be so damn dramatic. You're not that important, you little snowflake."

"Oh, so what, you're gonna tell my mommy?" Louie put his hands over his heart in mock disbelief. "She only cares about her designer wardrobe and figuring out new ways to get more alimony. Go ahead. Tell my mother. All she'll do is take my Amex away for like a week," he said with a snort. "She won't give a shit."

Ernie shook his head. "I'm not telling your mother, either."

"Then what's your game, old man?" The young man's confidence was returning.

Ernie leaned close and looked in Louie's eyes for a long moment. "Speaking of game, I think I'm gonna tell my friend at Barrington High, Coach Olson, that you started a fire here and tried to kill your ex-girlfriend and my dog. What do you think of that, Comet?"

Coco gathered that must be his nickname on the team.

Louie scoffed and his eyes narrowed as he worked out whether Ernie was telling the truth.

"Oh, I just bet he'd love to share that tape on social media and get you kicked off the team and maybe even kicked out of EG High. Those folks in Barrington will eat this up. They hate EG. Did you know that?"

Oh snap, thought Coco.

Ernie continued, "How do you think the team would do without their star pitcher? And you? No school, no baseball. No baseball, no college baseball. Shame, really; I hear you're pretty good on the mound. Maybe even good enough to go pro, they say. Right?"

Louie went white. "No. I didn't start that fire. You *can't*," he pleaded.

"Oh yes I can."

Louie's eyes filled with tears. Watching Louie's face crumple triggered the mom reflex in her and Coco actually felt a little bad for him. Especially because she knew he had nothing to do with the fire. Then she remembered Daisy and all the emotional harm he wanted to inflict upon her.

"I'm sorry for whatever it is you think I did. C'mon. Baseball is all I have."

"Hey, here's one for you, Mr. Jeopardy." Ernie smiled as he leaned closer to Louie. "The category is 'Louie's Sorry.' Here's the $400 clue: None." Ernie hummed the *Jeopardy* theme song. "Ding. Time's up. The question is, How many fucks do I give?"

"Please don't send the video. I'll do anything you want." Louie's voice cracked.

"Okay, let me think for a minute." Ernie chewed the inside of his cheek and pretended to consider a few scenarios. "All right.

Here's the deal. I'll keep this video to myself for now, but you're going to do something for—"

"I'll do anything. You name it."

"You can start by not interrupting me again." Ernie extended his index finger in the air in front of Louie's face. "Jesus, your parents have done a terrible job."

Louie listened from the edge of his seat.

"I will keep this video quiet," Ernie began again, slowly, "and you're going to keep your mouth shut about Daisy and her sister. Don't tell your mother, or your friends. Don't even talk about it in your sleep." He straightened his back.

Coco looked from Ernie to Louie to Bull and back to Ernie.

"Okay. I promise I will. I mean, I won't. *Jesus.* I swear. I promise I won't tell anybody about Daisy and her sister."

"No you won't." Bull moved closer to Louie with his arms still crossed.

Coco watched Louie's Adam's apple bob down and then up. She shifted from side to side. Confrontation always made her antsy. She'd pay money to watch Ava and Ernie go at it in a cage match, though.

Ernie looked irritated. "I'm not done. I've got a few copies of this tape at my bank and other places, so don't think of doing anything stupid. Or anything *else* stupid." Ernie stood up to poke his finger into Louie's chest. "And if I ever, *ever* hear anything about you mistreating a girl again, any girl, this video will be the very least of your problems, superstar. Are we clear about that?"

Louie nodded.

"Are we clear about that?!" Ernie shouted.

"Yes, sir!" Louie hollered back. "I never meant to hurt Daisy and her sister. Or the dog. I just—"

"Get outta here." Ernie gestured toward the door and stood up. He walked around the desk to signal that he was done with this issue and ready to get back to work.

Louie turned to leave.

"Wait," Ernie said, and Bull grabbed the boy's collar.

"How much cash do you have on you?"

Louie looked at him like he didn't hear the question. "Oh. Uh . . ." He dug into his back pocket and pulled out his wallet. He removed a stack of twenties and held them up.

Jesus, thought Coco. *Charlotte was thrilled to have a comma in her bank account. This kid probably has one in his pocket.*

"Give it to me."

Louis handed over all the cash.

"We're going to use this money you lost at *Jeopardy* to buy some toasters. Thanks for the donation."

"You're welcome."

"Get out of here."

"And no receipt." Bull escorted the boy to the door by dragging him by his coat collar.

"Wait!" Ernie said and Bull lifted the kid off the ground by his expensive jacket again.

"Here's twenty for a cab." Ernie gave the boy back one of his own bills. "Now go."

Bull released his grip and Louie scampered out and the door as fast as he could.

Ernie shrugged at Bull. "What? I'm not an asshole."

"I know, but have you heard of Uber?"

"Nope."

The three of them paced around the small space after Louie left.

"I actually do watch *Jeopardy*," Ernie confessed.

Coco looked slowly from Ernie to Bull trying to form a sentence. "I don't understand. We all know he didn't do it. He didn't start the fire. Daisy did," Coco whispered.

"Yeah, but he doesn't know we know that he didn't do it."

"Come again?" Coco said.

"That kid's on a slippery slope," Ernie said as he straightened the top of his desk. "Daisy told me what she told you. She also showed Peggy bruises she had on her arms from him. When she told me he was over here harassing them the night of the fire, I checked the owl cam to see if we could nail him with something. If Daisy goes to the cops about him, they'll want to talk to her parents and then they'll find out about her and Annabelle's situation. I can't let that happen."

"I don't understand."

Bull said, "This way, that little shit will be afraid to step off again because of the videotape."

Ernie said, "He has no way to prove he didn't start that fire, or explain what he was doing here that night. So he'll have to leave the sisters alone so that I don't release the tape. It looks bad for him because the fire starts right after he leaves. We have his face plain as day on the tape. It may not shut him up forever, but I just need to buy enough time until Daisy turns eighteen and can become her sister's guardian. Who knows? Maybe the mother will come back before then."

"That's pretty smart," Coco said.

"I'm no Stephen Hawking, but I do okay." Ernie winked at her. "What I do know is that you never know what people are going through." He looked down at the photo of Hope and Vivian by his desk. "But you also can't hurt other people just because you're hurting."

"Yeah," she said, looking at Bull.

"I gotta go home to Chewy. I have to admit, I like having someone to come home to." Ernie pulled his coat off the back of his chair and folded it over his arm. "Can you guys lock up?"

"Sure," they said.

"See you tomorrow, bright and early. Get some rest. It's going to be a busy day." Ernie left with a salute.

Left by themselves in the office, Coco straightened the two chairs in front of Ernie's desk and dropped some empty coffee cups into the trash while Bull switched off the overhead lights and turned down the heat. They walked out the yellow door together, and Coco waited beside Bull while he turned around and locked it.

"That was a nice thing you did for Daisy. Taking the fall. Stupid, but nice," he said.

"Gee, thanks."

They walked side by side, her shoulder in line with his chest.

"Why do you work here, Bull?" Coco had her eyes on the ground in front of her as the motion detector triggered the floodlight.

"Same reason you do." He looked down at her.

"So you can brag at Junior League?"

He smiled at that. "Because it feels good to help. We're like a family here and I'm grateful."

"Aw. Am I part of your family?" She smiled up at him.

He exhaled loudly and blinked slowly. "I suppose."

"Really? Like your cool younger sister?"

"Like my nerdy old step-cousin."

"I'll take it."

They walked until they reached her Jeep and she turned to face him again.

"Ernie told me how you and he met." She found herself again looking for the tracheotomy scar but it stayed hidden under the rolls of his neck.

"He tells everyone that story. I don't mind. He's like a second dad to me."

"He's good at that." She didn't mention that she felt the same way. What a strange family they would have made.

"Do you know why he never remarried or had more children?" This time it was Bull sharing personal info. "He said he never wanted to be in the position where he couldn't fix it again. Said there's nothing worse than feeling helpless. I'm here to remind him of a time when he did fix it. And here, the work he does, he fixes. That's what makes him happy. Just like tonight."

"Do you think he's lonely?"

"Nah. Too many of us around who care. Including you."

"Including me." She nodded and turned to get into the Jeep.

He walked over to his Toyota and opened the door. "Hey! Nerdy step-cousin."

"Yeah," she said, with one foot inside the car and one still on the ground.

"Stop doing that stupid wave." He gestured to the Jeep. "Even you ain't white enough."

"Shut up."

"You shut up." He laughed as he folded himself inside his car and waited for her to pull out of the lot in front of him.

40

Coco was cleaning out the fridge and frowning at the amount of groceries that had gone bad since she'd been working at The Mission. Dinner was warming in the lower oven and Houdini sat on the tile floor in front of it enjoying the hot air blowing on him. Charlotte was in her room with Ducky, and James was hopefully up typing an essay that had to be submitted to his history teacher online by midnight. The sound of the garage door was Coco's cue to get out a pair of plates and cutlery. It was after nine o'clock and Rex was just now returning from his trip to Chicago. The garage door began its descent as Rex opened the door into the kitchen. She smiled at her weary traveler and met him halfway across the room.

"Welcome home."

"Hi, babe. It's good to *be* home." They kissed then hugged with Rex's garment bag still strapped to his shoulder.

"I missed you. How are the kids?" He dropped his bag to the floor and emptied his pockets of keys, a boarding pass, lip balm, and a phone.

"Good. Everybody's good. Go change and I'll serve us up." Rex headed down the hall with his bag, followed closely by Houdini, like the cat had something to tell him in confidence. Coco pulled the shepherd's pie out of the oven and put it on a trivet on the counter. She had arranged two place settings side by side on the center island, and poured two glasses of club soda on ice with a splash of cranberry. Rex returned barefoot in less than ten minutes, his face freshly washed. In his old jeans and white T-shirt he looked ten years younger than he was.

He sat down, put a napkin across his lap, and swallowed a big bite before speaking.

"Mmmm. That's delicious. Sorry I haven't had a chance to check in the past few days. The meetings were just back to back to back. Did that chimney sweeper ever call?"

"Yeah." She pointed her fork at him. "He's coming next week. Tuxedo, top hat, and all."

"That's funny. What else?"

"Well, let's see." She twirled her forkful of mashed potatoes and looked up at the ceiling as if trying to recall if anything interesting had happened while he was gone. "Ducky got groomed. He looks great."

"Finally."

"Oh, and James has a crush on the shoplifter."

"I—"

"No. I'm not done. Also, Piper is sleeping with Bull. What else? Ava's moving to London and she and Johan are getting divorced because he has a pregnant girlfriend."

Rex opened his mouth to speak and then closed it as his wife continued.

"And I was right. Daisy and her sister *were* living at The Mission since their mom took off. Turns out Ernie and my dad were friends in the army and he has a photo of them together before they saved a guy's life. Oh! And I confessed to the police to setting the fire at The Mission before Ernie framed Daisy's ex-boyfriend for it." She took a bite and then pointed at him with her fork. "How was your flight?"

As the sun came up the next morning, Rex slept in and Coco headed over to Dover to set up for the yard sale. She and Rex had talked late into the night about everything that had happened since he left for Chicago.

"Remember the good-old days when I'd come home from a trip and you'd tell me that they'd changed the drop-off pattern at school or someone in Charlotte's class had lice?"

"God, was I ever that young?" she'd joked. They'd laughed, remembering all the silly things they used to think were the end of the world. Around one a.m. they'd both fallen asleep, spooning safe and sound beneath the heavy comforter.

Now Coco was on the move again, shifting gears to prepare for a busy day.

Early April was a risky time to plan an outdoor event in Rhode Island. The backup plan was to have the yard sale inside the warehouse, but it still smelled like a wet ashtray and that option was slated as a last resort. Luckily the mercury climbed to the lower sixties, a temperature New Englanders considered warm, and the sun stood backstage waiting to make an appearance.

Thanks to Ernie's charm, a Dunkin' Donuts van had agreed to park in The Mission's lot and hand out free coffee and doughnut holes to the yard-sale shoppers for the first few hours, but it hadn't arrived yet so Coco grabbed a cup from the break room before heading back outside.

She and the other volunteers were carrying items out of the warehouse and depositing them on the tables anywhere they could find a space. The tables were labeled with sheets of paper taped to the front: "Under $10," "$10–25," "$25–50," "$50+," and so on. The furniture prices were attached with painter's tape. Haggling was allowed, but Coco hoped that, because people knew this was for charity, they wouldn't be too aggressive in their bargain hunting.

Sitting outside in the light of day, the inventory looked even skimpier than she expected. Chewing on her bottom lip, she walked over to stand beside Sawyer and Ernie.

"How are you guys doing?" she asked.

"Well, I'd be lying if I said I wasn't disappointed."

"Maybe we could bring out some of the other furniture from the warehouse."

"We'd only get pennies on the dollar, though, and I'd rather that practical stuff be saved for the clients."

"How about a kissing booth?" Sawyer said with a straight face.

"Yeah, that would sure solve—"

Ernie was interrupted by a piercing, repetitive beep, like an expired oven timer. They all looked up to see a giant black tractor trailer backing very slowly down the pothole-pocked road.

What the hell? Coco thought as she walked on the grass along the roadside until she came even with the driver's door.

The driver's windowed lowered and Coco heard a hearty, "Howdy, ma'am" from the young trucker, who tipped his STP baseball hat. He parked the rig to stop the beeping sound. The truck shuddered and exhaled. "Name's Chip," the driver said, looking down at Coco from his window.

"Howdy yourself, Chip," she said, shielding her eyes from the sun with her hand. "Are you sure you're in the right place?"

"Yes, ma'am," he said with a Southern drawl. He held up some paperwork and said, "This is The Mission of Hope, correct?"

"Yes, it is, but—"

"I got a delivery for you, darlin'. I'm coming back. Can y'all make sure everybody's out of the way, please?"

"Okay," Coco said. "C'mon down." She looked back toward the building and caught Ernie's eye to see if he knew about this. They both shrugged at the same time. He shepherded some volunteers out of the way and waited.

The driver slipped the truck into reverse and continued to slowly move backward toward the building, beeping the whole way. Coco walked alongside him for fifty yards or so until he came to a stop. When he killed the engine, the vehicle hissed again and then fell silent. After a minute, Chip pushed open his door and jumped down onto the dirt road in one big leap. He was a cowboy the likes of which Rhode Islanders rarely see: suntanned face, ponytail, and lots of denim.

He walked down the length of the trailer and unlocked the tall doors. By now a crowd of volunteers had gathered to see what was in the back of this giant truck. Coco hoped it wasn't horses. He swung the doors open, first the left then the right, and secured them with sliding bolts to the sides of the trailer. Then he hopped up into the small empty space at the back edge of the truck and started untying the straps that attached a forklift to a hydraulic platform.

Peering around to look inside the truck, Coco stood in shock at what she saw. The entire forty-five-foot-long space was filled with tables and chairs of every size and shape, shrink-wrapped couches, headboards, floor and table lamps, recliners, rugs, clocks, crated artwork, and dozens upon dozens of boxes sealed with neon-pink duct tape. She recognized enough to know that this was almost the entire contents of Ava Logan's beautiful home.

Holy shit!

"Are you Coco?"

She nodded up at Chip and he handed down a copy of the manifest and an envelope taped to a plate.

"Then this is for you, darlin'."

Coco tucked the manifest under her arm and looked at the envelope. It had her name handwritten on the front. She pulled it off the plate she recognized from her own kitchen and carefully slid her finger beneath the flap and removed the piece of paper inside. She unfolded it and read it to herself.

Dear Coco,

The movers loved the cookies, but to be honest they were a little dry. Here's your plate back.

I thought you guys could use this stuff for the yard sale or whatever. I had planned to store it all, but changed my mind after you stopped by today. It's all part of my old life and I need a fresh start. I hope Johan cries when he finds out I gave away all of his mother's shit. Tell Piper she can come back to book club now. And tell her I'm sorry. If you find yourself in London someday, look me up. The Picasso's not in the truck. I'm generous, but I'm not stupid.

And for what it's worth, Coco, I'm proud of you. But STOP GIVING A FUCK what people think!

—Ava

Coco folded the letter, smiling, and looked up to the back of the truck as Chip, who was now joined by Bull, discussed a plan for unloading it.

I'll be damned. Even Ava can find the shine, Coco thought.

A few hours later, every inch of grass was crowded with furniture and decorations. Ava's beautiful pieces added a real sparkle to the sale inventory, and Coco experienced a tingle of excitement like she used to feel just before Charlotte's ballet performances or James's at-bats during playoff games.

At eleven o'clock, an hour before the yard sale was scheduled to start, Coco rushed home to shower and change. James offered to return to the sale with her. Whether it was out of the goodness of his heart or with the hopes of seeing Daisy, she wasn't certain, but she didn't care either way. She did notice that he had his contacts in and smelled great.

Coco was thrilled to see how many cars were clogging up both sides of Somerville when they returned. She was less thrilled when she and her son had to make the long walk along the soggy grass with her shoulder bag throwing her off balance. When they finally got to the parking lot, there was controlled chaos. SUV drivers were backing up at various angles with new purchases blocking their sightlines through their back windows. Dozens of early-bird bargain hunters were milling around with their free coffee and doughnuts trying to find a steal before everything good was slapped with a "Sold" tag. Sawyer, dressed up as a clown, was strolling around making balloon animals to keep the kids entertained while their parents haggled with the volunteers. No one haggled with Bull, but he was relatively happy to carry their purchases to their cars.

People were shoving money at Peggy and Ernie at the makeshift cashier's table. The metal box was overflowing and Peggy was making change for a couple and their young kids. The mother was guarding two slipper chairs upholstered in a rich watermelon silk, looking around at passers-by with eagle eyes as if they might pick up her chairs, not her children, and run off with them. Coco knew those chairs. She had sat in those chairs at Ava's house many times.

"Hey guys," Coco said in a chipper voice as she approached.

"Hello there, lovie."

"Well, good morning." Ernie was quick with his usual smile.

Chewy popped his head up from behind the table.

"Look who's here!" Coco was happy to see the scraggly Wookiee who'd been the very first to welcome her at The Mission back in January. He walked under the table toward her. Remembering his penchant for greeting new people, she placed herself between the dog and her son.

"How does he like his new digs, Ernie?" She rubbed Chewy's ears with both hands.

"He sleeps like a baby at my house. A snoring, farting baby. He even prewashes the dishes I put in the sink. Right, Chew?"

The dog wagged its impressive tail.

Peggy gave Ernie a stern look and he shrugged.

"This is my son, James. James, this is Peggy and Ernie."

They all shook hands.

"Nice to meet you," James said sincerely as Coco eyed him with pride.

"Aren't you a handsome fella!" Peggy swooned. "So tall. Isn't he so tall?" Peggy said to Ernie.

"We've heard a lot of nice things about you, young man."

"Thanks," James said, because what else did someone say to that? Then he shifted around and scanned the crowd.

"James, honey"—Coco pointed to Sawyer—"could you run over there and help the clown with that armoire? It looks like they need help with the geometry. Pretend it's the dishwasher."

"Sure." He smirked and walked over to the SUV upon whose back bumper one end of an expensive cabinet rested. Bull held the other end up effortlessly as Sawyer and another man sat on their haunches working out the angles.

"It's good to finally meet him." Ernie smiled at her. "Nice kid, but that's not a surprise." He winked at her. "Did you tell him I knew his grandfather?"

"I told the whole family. They'll all be here today at some point. I'm so happy Chewy is okay." The dog had settled beside her and leaned against her leg so she could reach his ear.

"You and me both," Ernie said, looking down at his adopted dog. "Didn't know how much I liked that big bag of fur until I almost lost him."

"I know this sounds dumb, but I feel like he and I have something in common," Coco said.

"How so?" Ernie tilted his head to the side, amused.

"You're both very friendly and enthusiastic," Peggy said kindly.

Coco smiled her thank-you. "And we both just showed up here hoping to fit in."

"Coco," Ernie said. "I've been meaning to tell you something. I heard about what you did for the Bruens. Murray wrote us a beautiful note about what a difference you made for him and his wife. He said she stares at those snow globes for hours at a time and just smiles. He's getting another parrot for her birthday. He said he's going to name it Coco."

"Ha-ha. Really?" Coco snorted.

"Really. I'll show you his note. It's in my desk. We're gonna put it in the next newsletter. I told you it wasn't hard to find a way to make yourself proud a hundred times over."

"Yes, you did. Thanks, Ernie."

"Don't thank me. You're the lifesaver now."

"Well, it was no tracheotomy, but the day is young." They all laughed. "So how's it going here?"

"We can't keep up, in a good way. We had to bring out inventory to satisfy the crowd. Your friend's donations are causing quite a scene. Remind me to get you a receipt to give her."

Coco didn't know how to reach Ava and figured a tax deduction was the least of her worries right now, but she nodded instead of explaining. "Okay. Has anyone seen Daisy?" she asked, looking around.

"She was out here a minute ago." Ernie squinted at the crowd.

"Your glasses are in your hand," Peggy said.

"Right. By the way," Ernie said to Coco. "I spoke to the fire chief and explained that we figured out that Daisy was actually the one who started the fire by accident. I left the details kind of foggy, but at least your name won't be associated with the fire anymore."

"Oh. Thanks." Coco smiled, trying to act cool, but secretly crippled with relief. The rule-follower's record was clean. Well, except for letting her dad take the blame for the old desk leg incident, but the statute of limitations had surely run out on that.

The three of them watched as two women circled one of Ava's settees until one of them plunked down on it and reclined sideways to claim it as her own. Musical chairs sans music.

"Uh-oh. Stand by for a catfight," Ernie quipped.

"How's she doing? Daisy?"

"She seems relieved about the whole Louie situation being over with." Ernie took a pile of money handed to him by Peggy and put it under the tray in the cash box and closed the lid. "So far, he hasn't had any contact with her. I'm hoping he holds his tongue, for Daisy's sake. But part of me just wants to nail his balls to the wall."

"Ernie!" Peggy said.

"Sorry, ladies. I told you, you can't shine a sneaker."

Coco smiled on hearing her dad's expression. "Did you know about all this stuff with Daisy?" Coco asked Peggy.

"I did not." She frowned gravely and shook her head. "But I'll tell you, those girls are model roommates. What's the sense in living in a big house if you're all alone? The idea of those two girls fending for themselves brings me to tears," Peggy said in a soft voice. "And they are great company. So spunky."

Coco smiled. "You are a sweetheart. Is she inside?"

"She must be. Hasn't been out here lately."

"Okay. I'll be right back."

"Take your time, lovie," Peggy said sweetly.

Coco walked into the building, through the main office, and down the hallway. When she passed the Linen Room, a movement caught her eye and she backed up a few steps until she was even with the doorway. She watched unnoticed as Daisy pulled box after box down from the shelves, peeked inside, and then returned them to their place.

"Want some help?"

Daisy jumped and turned around from her step on the ladder.

"Oh. Hi." She backed her way down to the floor with an expression of desperation Coco recognized from the night Louie surprised them in the parking lot.

"Is everything okay?"

"Yeah. I was just—"

"Is there more to put out? I thought we got everything this morning."

Daisy fiddled with the zipper on her sweatshirt and continued to look around the room. "Are you sure all the boxes went out?"

"Pretty sure."

"Even the one with the snow globes."

Coco nodded.

"Are you positive?"

"Actually I am. A hundred percent. I gave that box to some clients who came in a last week."

"You did?" Daisy looked crestfallen. "Why?"

"Sorry. Was I not supposed to?"

"Don't worry about it." Daisy passed her hand in the air as if swatting a mosquito. "I'd better get back outside and help." She put her head down and tried to walk past Coco.

"Wait," she said with her hand on the girl's forearm.

Daisy stopped but tried to use her curtain of glossy black hair to hide her face. Coco shifted her shoulder bag in front of her so that she could dig into it. "I got you something."

The young woman seemed uninterested and tried again to escape. "Thanks, but I have to get back out and—"

She stopped and looked at Coco's outstretched hand. In it was the snow globe with the family sledding. "Oh—" She covered her mouth and nose quickly with both hands, looking from Coco to the snow globe and back again.

Coco wordlessly encouraged Daisy to take the globe from her hands. "The clients lost everything in a fire, including their old snow globe collection, if you can believe that." She smiled as she watched the wide-eyed girl's expression. "But I couldn't let them have this one. This one's yours."

Daisy clutched the globe to her chest with one arm and patted it with the other as if it were a newborn bunny. Then she stepped forward to hug Coco.

"I can't believe you did that," she said, her voice cracking. "I haven't been able to stop thinking about it since I saw it. I was waiting until today to buy it for my sister. When the box was gone . . ." She pulled away and looked down at her gift. "I can't believe its still here. Thank you."

She shook it and they both watched the happy family with the dog in the swirling snowfall.

Daisy's eyes were on the globe, but her mind was inside it when she spoke. "My mom used to tell me that, before my dad left, we would do normal things like a real family." She rotated it slowly in her hand to see the back of the scene. "We'd go to the beach to find sand dollars, we'd sing songs in the car, and we'd sled on the hill at the bottom of our street."

"That sounds nice."

"My sister and I were too young to remember, but I want to think that this is the way things were back then." She tipped it back and forth again, upsetting the settling snow. "Seeing it frozen in time is how I'd like to think we were. Just a perfect family on a perfect day. And time can't change it. Lucky family."

Coco couldn't think of a thing to say. And she'd learned from her mom that sometimes the best thing was to say nothing at all. After a long minute, she cleared her throat and said, "Hey, let's get back outside. I think there's a tall guitar player out there who's trying not to look for you."

"Okay." She smiled.

43

W hen they walked out of the building side by side through the loading dock door, the first person Coco saw was her husband. He stood a head above everybody else and was easy to spot in a crowd.

"Rex!" she called out, waving her arm.

"I'll see you later." Daisy smiled and walked off toward the snack table, the snow globe sitting snugly in the big front pocket of her sweatshirt.

Rex made it over to Coco and gave her a kiss on the cheek. "Hi, babe. How's my favorite pyromaniac?"

"I'm good. Thanks for coming." She wrapped an arm around his waist as he slung one of his over her shoulder.

"Wouldn't have missed it. Impressive turnout." They both glanced around at the crowd.

"So far, so good. This is going to translate into a boatload of toasters and mattresses. *That* I know for sure. Thanks to Ava. She really saved us. Her stuff and the publicity from the fire. What a weird week."

"Yeah."

"That's Ernie over there at that table." She pointed with her chin and smiled.

"Ah, the Papa Jim of Dover." They both watched him for a few seconds. "I see what you're saying about the resemblance. Would have been nice if he could have seen your dad again."

"I know."

"And that must be his lady friend."

"Yup. That's Peggy. There's something going on with those two, but baby boomers flirt in such a weird way it's hard to catch them." She squinted at the older pair just as Ernie lifted Peggy's hand and kissed it. Then they both looked around quickly to see if anyone had seen.

"How cute are they?" Coco sighed. "But the owl's gonna rat him out, too." She pointed up.

They both looked up at the roofline to the silly-looking over-sized plastic owl camera with the wide-eyed expression fixed on his flat face.

"Owls are assholes," Rex said and they both laughed.

"Speaking of lovebirds. Don't look yet. Okay, now." Coco gestured to her left with a nod and Rex looked over her shoulder to see James and Daisy standing a few feet apart.

"Atta boy."

They both watched their son take a big box from Daisy's arms and the two walked over to a table where he put it down. Familiar with his body language, Coco and Rex knew he was dying inside, but Daisy was too distracted by whatever he was saying to notice.

44

L ater, after Coco helped a woman carry a pair of Ava's ridiculously expensive lamps to her minivan, she caught sight of Rex and James lugging a coffee table toward their Jeep. He caught his wife's eye and gave her a thumbs-up and then pointed to the table with a big grin. Of course he had no idea it was one Sawyer had made from the severed legs of Coco's old desk. Poor Rex. He'd been so happy when he found out she'd given away the old smelly thing. She gave him her own thumbs-up and watched the guys carry it toward the street.

A half an hour later, she noticed Charlotte and Ducky coming down Somerville Road toward her.

"Hi!" Coco yelled and waved at her beautiful daughter in her faded jeans and black sweater.

Charlotte waved back and Ducky's tail wagged as the pair made their way down the road among all the parked cars and potholes. In addition to the leash she had looped around her wrist, her daughter was carrying a six-foot-tall wooden coatrack with metal hooks in one arm and a shadeless brass floor lamp in the other.

"Sorry I'm late. You wouldn't believe how far away I had to

park," she called out as she got closer. "I'm out on 117. This is crazy. Look at all these people." Both women looked around at the crowd of shoppers.

People were talking over cups of hot coffee as they stood and watched their children run around with balloons in their hands. Others walked to their trucks and SUVs with their new bargains as if they had to leave quickly before someone told them it was all a mistake. Rex was now collecting used cups and napkins and putting them in the trash bag he carried around with him. Daisy was next to James looking at something he was showing her on his phone. At the same time, they both burst into laughter before James put the phone back in his pocket and they walked toward the doughnut truck. Ernie was working the crowd, encouraging purchases and shaking hands.

"Is this a casbah?"

"Very funny. What have you got there?" she asked when her daughter was steps away.

Charlotte put the coatrack and lamp on the ground and shook out her sore arms. "I saw these dumped at the end of someone's driveway on the way over here. Can you believe that?"

"Charlotte Elizabeth Easton!" Coco said with her hands on her hips. "Did you pick up someone else's trash?"

"I did!" she said proudly with her mouth open showing the best teeth money could buy.

"That's my girl!" Coco playfully punched her daughter's shoulder and bent down to scratch the dog's head. "Hi, Ducky. I think Sawyer or Fred will have to check out the lamp first, but let's get this nice coatrack over there and put a price tag on it."

"I was thinking about something the other day, Mom," Charlotte said as they walked toward the building. "People throw away furniture like they throw away their pets, even though they still have a lot of life left in them."

"Yeah, you're right. I hadn't thought of that before."

"And you guys are like the shelter because you give the furniture and bedding to people and both sides win. You save the furniture and you make people happy."

Her mother nodded. "That's an interesting comparison."

"You really change lives here, Mom."

Coco stopped walking and looked at her beautiful girl. "You're very insightful, Charlotte." She felt the tingling in chest that always preceded tears. "I can't take all the credit, though—"

"I'm really proud of you. Here." Charlotte reached into her pocket and handed her mother a flat wrapped gift about half the size of a CD case.

"What's this?"

"Open it."

Coco pulled the paper off to reveal a clear plastic three-by-five frame with a magnet on the back. Pressed inside the frame was the neon-orange sticky note from New Year's Eve. It still had some of Houdini's fur squished between the two sides like a lab sample going under a microscope. On the note, in Coco's drunken handwriting, were the words: "My mission: Find good work." Coco's eyes welled up.

Charlotte stepped forward and hugged her mother. They rocked that way for a few seconds and Coco closed her eyes to savor the feeling.

Just as they were ready to break the embrace, they heard someone yell, "Incoming!" at the same time that Chewy threw himself at them to form a group hug.

"Easy, big fella," Charlotte said, struggling to keep her balance as Ducky ran in circles, jumping up and down at the other end of his leash and trying to decide what to do.

"This is my life now." Coco laughed.

"Cheeeewwwy!" Bull called for the dog. Chewy dislodged himself from the hug and ran full speed back. "Sorry, ladies!" Bull hollered with a big toothy grin and a wave.

"Is that the guy my momma don't like?" Charlotte said,

turning her back to him and lowering her voice. "Does he like you now?"

"He does! I broke him." She held her arms high in the air in victory. They both laughed, picking up their items and walking into the crowd.

4 5

The next morning Coco returned early to The Mission to help clean up. Exhaustion had set in the night before and everyone left as soon as it got dark. There was barely any evidence of the crowds of the day before aside from the flattened grass and all the tire marks. As she got out of the Jeep, she noticed Sawyer bent over on the loading dock struggling with something at his feet.

"Need a hand?" she called out as she shut her door and walked toward him.

"Uh," he said, looking around as if caught red-handed.

As she drew closer, she realized that the thing he was wrestling with was the top of the old desk from her parents' bedroom.

"Sorry, kiddo," he said as he straightened up. "I was trying to get rid of this before you got here."

She regarded the severed desk top and felt a pang of sadness mixed with guilt.

"Is it my imagination or does it smell better now?" she asked hopefully.

"It's your imagination."

She let out a big sigh. "Let's just get it over with." She lifted one end while Sawyer raised the other to hip level. Swinging to the count of three, they rocked the desktop and finally let it fly into the dumpster below. But gravity had other plans and the wooden piece missed clearing the opening by an inch. It hit the edge hard and smashed to the ground and into dozens of pieces. They both stared motionless for a full five seconds.

"Damn," Sawyer said eventually. "That wasn't how I pictured that going."

"Well, I guess that settles that."

He jumped the three feet to the pavement below and offered his hand to her. They walked over to the mess and started tossing the broken wood into the dumpster. It seemed impossible that all of the pieces had been a single unit thirty seconds earlier. While sifting through the debris, Coco bent down to investigate a spot of color that had caught her eye.

"Careful for nails," Sawyer warned.

When she straightened up, she was holding a small blue box in one hand.

"What's that?" He looked from the box to her face and back to the box.

"Oh my god." A flash of a memory appeared before her like a childhood friend jumping out from a doorway to surprise her. The snowstorm, the dining room, the tea party, the covered dish, the blue box.

"What?" He moved closer and scratched his mustache under his nose.

She held the box in the palm of her left hand and used her right to lift the cover. It creaked open and, confirming her suspicion, the truly spectacular ten-point star-shaped diamond pin sat there as patient as a monk. It was small, no larger than a silver dollar, but much more beautiful than she remembered. As the sunlight hit every diamond, the piece sang out with brilliance; a genie liberated from a bottle.

"What the hell?" he said leaning in on the balls of his feet.

"I cannot believe this is happening." Coco covered her eyes with one hand and started trembling. She made a disturbing sound that made Sawyer uncomfortable. Still, he closed the gap between them and put his fingers on her shoulder. As she dropped her hand from her face, she let out a wail of laughter. She laughed and laughed until tears streamed down her cheeks and she eventually stopped making any sound at all.

"I don't get it." Sawyer moved his hand from her shoulder to the top of his head. Women confused him more than just about anything else.

"This was my mother's pin." She shuddered with laughter aftershocks. "My parents left it to me in their will but no one could ever find it. And . . . and—" She started another series of silent laughs and slapped her leg. "They call you Sawyer the Magician, and you just made it appear!" She doubled over again and he started to laugh, too.

"So it's been in the desk the whole time?"

"Yes! This has been in my garage for a year and in my parents' house before that. I don't even think my dad knew it was in here. My mom must have moved it. For God's sake, I almost threw away a twenty-thousand-dollar pin!"

Sawyer gagged. "Are you shitting me?"

"I shit you not!"

Now they were both laughing again. He was probably laughing at her for swearing but she didn't care.

"The pin belonged to my mom's aunt who worked as a maid for a family on Beacon Hill for, God, nearly forty years. They gave her the pin when she retired and she didn't have any kids so she gave it to my mom on her deathbed."

"May I?" Sawyer asked, reaching for it.

"Sure." She plucked it carefully out of its nest and placed it in the palm of his callused, outstretched hand. He whistled his admiration.

"My dad told me that once, when they first got the pin, my parents took it to a jeweler to have it appraised. They got paged over the intercom at the mall and were asked to return to the store. The jeweler said he didn't feel comfortable with it in his possession because the diamonds were of such high quality. I guess my mother died before she had a chance to let my dad know she moved the pin."

"Wow. That's. Wow."

Coco didn't have any sentimental attachment to the pin. She'd only seen it one other time before, when she was snooping in her mother's china cabinet as a child. She'd never seen her mom wear it and, frankly, it probably made her as nervous as the jeweler to own it. The mystery of the pin had been solved, and she couldn't wait to tell her sisters. It was crazy to think it almost ended up in a landfill.

She tucked it into her coat pocket.

"Never a dull moment at The Mission of Hope," Sawyer said as they returned to the job of picking up the debris and tossing it into the dumpster.

46

When Ernie arrived an hour later, Coco was sitting on the edge of his desk.

"Morning, kiddo," he said as the little bell tinkled.

"Morning."

"What are you smiling about?"

"Nothing." Her ear-to-ear grin made his eyes narrow with suspicion. "How did we make out yesterday, Ernie?"

"Not as well as I thought."

"Really?" she asked but kept smiling.

He regarded her cautiously like one would a raccoon in the middle of the day. "I mean, we made some good toaster money, but the downside is that we have no inventory left for the clients. I think I got so distracted by the Louie situation that I didn't think it all the way through. I was up all night. I don't know what to do about getting more furniture and mattresses. I might have to shut down for a few weeks. We've never had to do that before." He squeezed his bottom lip together with a forefinger and thumb. "Or maybe I can take out a loan." Then he shook his head to dislodge the negativity. "It's okay, kid. I'll figure something out. It always works out." He shrugged off his coat and went to hang it on the back of his chair. As he passed by her he said, "Why are you still smiling?"

She pivoted on the edge of the desk to face him. Without breaking eye contact, she reached into her coat pocket and withdrew the blue box.

"You know how you keep bugging me about finding the shine?" she asked. She held the box suspended on her palm in front of him.

"Yeah." Confusion was written all over his face.

"Well, I found it." She smiled. "And I want you to have it."

ACKNOWLEDGMENTS

This novel, while a work of fiction, was inspired by an organization in Massachusetts where my father loved to volunteer after
he retired. It is much larger than the charity portrayed in this
story and the staff and its volunteers work tirelessly to provide
mattresses, toasters, linens and furniture to those in dire need. If
you would like to learn more about how you can help them,
please visit www.missionofdeeds.org

I want to express my heartfelt gratitude to my early readers,
especially my sister Jan who read the generations of manuscripts
more than I did. Her kind and insightful comments and smiley
faces in the margins kept me going through a succession of
versions. My other readers—Maddie, Bill, Rose, Sue, Allison,
Carolyn, Donna, and Jimmy—helped me believe that people
might actually enjoy the story I wanted to tell. Emma came up
with a brilliant idea that helped me feel like the story was finally
complete. And my good friend Katie blazed the trail ahead of me
and sent me sweet words of encouragement.

Thank you to my editor Carolyn Haley who lit the fuse that
helped me push the story into publication. Without her laser
focus, attention to detail, wisdom, and kind help, this book

would have stayed in the drawer to be read only by my future grandchildren on a snow day.

My family was very supportive throughout the process. Much love to my children Maddie and Jack and my three sisters for believing.

Finally, thank you to my husband Billy. When I came home from work one day last year and casually told him that I was going to write a novel, he said "I think that's a *great* idea, babe!" I would have tried it even if he hadn't said that, but it mattered a lot.

DISCUSSION QUESTION

1. There were many "missions" throughout the story. Besides the charity itself, discuss the other missions Coco, Ernie, Piper, and Daisy were on throughout the course of the novel.

2. Nicknames played a role in the story. Explain a few examples and why it was important to the story that those characters were known by two different names.

3. It is common for women in their forties and fifties, who left the workplace to become stay-at-home mothers in their twenties or thirties, to find it difficult to go back to work for a variety of reasons. Do you think women who made this choice are undervalued in society? Do you believe in the theory of "one then the other" or "one or the other" as it pertains to women who choose full-time mothering or full time work? Discuss Coco's experience as it might compare to your own or your mother's.

4. There were a lot of lost things and people in the novel--the diamond pin, the photo of Coco's parents,

Houdini, the snow globes, friendships, Chewy, a sense of purpose, etc. Discuss some of these.

5. Value can still be found in giving pre-owned things a place, such as the furniture and linens at The Mission and even Ducky the dog. The older generations tend to value repairing over replacing and those who reside in affluent communities are often more likely to dispose of things because it is more convenient. What is the message in the story about re-using those things that might otherwise be discarded? In your opinion, does this vary according to socioeconomic status, or is it a reflection of the declining quality of these things compared to decades ago?

6. Often we find a close connections with someone who reminds us of a lost loved one. Some people seem to channel or project a sense of how that lost loved one made us feel (protected, special, loved unconditionally, etc.). These platonic relationships/connections can often help to patch the loss of a loved one. Have you even found a person who reminded you of a lost parent, friend, sibling, etc. and how did this person help to keep your loved one alive in your mind?

7. We find that one of the missions of the Mission (of Hope) is to treat all of their clients with dignity and respect. Surely these clients are surprised that they are not being treated as a number but instead as a fellow human deserving of such compassion. Pride is a very strong sentiment especially in circumstances where you rely so heavily on others for basic human needs. Discuss this approach placing yourself in a situation where you're invited in to an intimate setting such as the "meeting room" at The Mission and treated as if you had all the money in the world and were simply

shopping for what you needed instead of it being handed to you.

8. In our society there is no hiding from the myriad of smartphone pictures circulating on social media and on the internet. Photos on unwitting subjects or very personal situations go viral every day. Ernie and his team seek to provide their clients with a framed photo of families starting the next chapter in their lives but do so only with consent and in with a Polaroid photo assuring that the photo is not for public viewing but as a private reminder of the value of a bed, a home and a roof over one's head. Discuss a time where you've been uncomfortable with a picture of you or your family being shared without your consent. Why do we feel its ok to post a picture (perhaps unflattering or providing information which could put them in harm's way) without the subject's approval just because technology allows us to do so.

9. We've all found ourselves thinking we know how someone would behave or respond to a situation knowing where they live, where they come from or how they look. Describe a situation where you had assumed something negative about someone only to be surprised by their reaction or behavior. How did you feel when you acknowledged you judged someone unfairly? How can we break this behavior and instead let people's actions speak for themselves?

10. Coco felt that she needed to be validated outside of the home by getting a "real" job (i.e. a job with a salary) but found that the larger reward was in contributing to a need greater than her need to have a real job. Many of us find validation in making small or behind the scenes contributions every day. In your life do you feel

validation only by the things you do that are visible to others or are you satisfied yourself in the quiet, behind-the-scenes contributions that you make which have huge impact on others?

ABOUT THE AUTHOR

Maureen Eustis was an average water-
color artist who decided to be a writer
instead because the medium was easier to
work with and she could cut and paste.
Her writing style is to picture every
chapter as a movie scene and try to put
the reader on the set, because she is also a
frustrated movie extra. She has a bachelor's degree in Sociology and never used it
because how can you?

After being in a neighborhood book
club for many years she started to chew
on the idea that she would secretly write her own novel, get an
agent, get it published, order a dozen copies, autograph them,
and announce that she selected her own book when it was her
turn to host. But the momentary surprise that would generate
wasn't worth all the trouble and waiting so she told them about it
before she started to write the first chapter. This same impul-
sivity led her to buy a Newfoundland puppy and now she's tied
down and works on her next book whenever he takes a break
from demolishing the house.

Maureen lives in Rhode Island with her husband and two
children.

She can be contacted at:
TheMissionByMaureenEustis@gmail.com

Made in the USA
Middletown, DE
18 February 2019